BARBER | CHEF | RIPPER

By

Jason Mayer

Happy Duck Publishing
PO Box 607
Belle, MO 65013

Genre: Fiction, General
ISBN: 978-1-7369596-1-9
First Edition.

For Ed
The Original Magnificent Bastard

Journey to a New World

"Once you have traveled, the voyage never ends, but is played out over and over again in the quietest chambers. The mind can never break off from the journey."

– **Pat Conroy**

The SS *Frisia* was a German steamship built in 1872 by Caird & Company for the Hamburg America Line. For a short time, the company could legitimately claim that the ship was the "best and fastest of the fleet." The three hundred fifty by forty foot vessel sailed its maiden voyage in late August 1872, starting a long string of round-trip voyages from Hamburg, Germany to New York City. The SS *Frisia* was a mix of old and new world technology featuring two large masts rigged for sailing along with a string of coal-fired steam engines that powered a single propeller. The ship's massive engines could create enough steam energy to produce seven hundred fifty horse power, which mixed with sail power to create a top speed of just over thirteen knots.

It took a crew of more than one hundred thirty-five to service the iron-hulled ship, including a captain, four officers, four engineers, and at least one hundred twenty-five crewmembers. Depending on the cabin configuration, the steamship could accommodate more than eight hundred passengers, including one hundred first-class, one hundred thirty second-class, and over six hundred steerage passengers.

During the average fourteen day journey from Hamburg to New York City, most upper class passengers lived in eight by ten staterooms that were well furnished and nicely adorned. The ship boasted saloons, conversation rooms, smoking rooms, sitting rooms, and other conveniences. The ship's upper deck was laid in teak, while the cabins and convenience rooms were made of mostly mahogany and featured maple panels with gilded trim.

Victoria Jackson looked up at the huge vessel in awe. Not much impressed her, but the sight of the hulking immigrant ship was breathtaking. The ship had already been in service for four years, but it still looked like a shining gem in the Hamburg port.

She signaled for her fourteen-year-old son Octavius to follow her. He picked up his suitcase and satchel and walked up to her side.

Victoria looked back at their traveling companion, Augustus, and pointed to a gangway extending from the vessel's large iron hull holding a sign that read "Zweite Kajüte" signifying the boarding area for second-class passengers.

Augustus, or Augie as he preferred to be called, was a tall, bulky German. He had a round face framed with dark bushy eyebrows and a neatly trimmed beard. He always wore a felt bowler hat, three-piece suit, black bow tie, and nicely polished leather work boots. Everything he wore was slightly weathered, but he always made an effort to look as professional as possible.

Augie had lost his ability to speak in the Franco-German War, where he served as a captain of infantry in the German Army. He could make guttural sounds and mumble a few noises when absolutely necessary, but even then he only communicated with Octavius.

Augie easily lifted two large suitcases and fell in line behind Victoria and Octavius. The three of them walked over and joined the long line of other second-class passengers waiting to board the ship.

The line moved painfully slow. Victoria stood silently looking over the crowd of passengers. She focused most of her attention on the gangway located directly across from them. This entrance was reserved for the first-class passengers who were boarding at a much faster rate. She watched as group after group climbed aboard and was pleased to see that the majority of the boarders were men. She estimated there was at least a three to one ratio of families and couples to single men, which was exactly what she had hoped to see.

She looked down to see a roped area holding the steerage passengers waiting to board. She could see that this group was made up of an even larger ratio of single men. She was surprised to see that the majority of these passengers were well dressed and decently groomed. She hadn't known what to expect from steerage passengers on an immigrant ship, but she could tell that there was a decent amount of money to be made from even the lower ranks.

Lastly, she focused on her own gangway. The second-class passengers were not as agreeable to her needs. This group was made up of a large ratio of families. There were a few single men among the crowd, but most of them had their noses in newspapers or could be seen carrying briefcases, both signs of working-class business men. Men like these were tight with their money and cautious with their reputations. She grunted her disapproval and decided she would need to concentrate primarily on the first-class clients and use the steerage men to fill in the blanks.

Finishing her analysis, she looked down at Octavius. Her little Otto was a quiet and serious young man. Most days he could get by with saying less than fifty words, which suited her just fine. His quietness was not a symptom of sadness or depression; he simply preferred to keep his words and thoughts to himself. He was tall for his age, but rail thin, and he shared his mother's dark black hair and hazel eyes. His daily wardrobe consisted of black wool trousers, a light gray dress shirt, and a wool pea coat that hung loose on his skinny frame.

Otto kept himself occupied by whittling on a four-inch block of cherry wood. The image of a lion's mane had started to form on the small piece of wood. He carved with amazing speed and accuracy over the course of thirty minutes as they shuffled along in line. After finishing the initial carving, he pulled out a small piece of sandpaper from his pocket and began smoothing out the rough spots and creating more detail in the head, mane, and bulbous tail.

"That is a magnificent figurine you have created young man," said a well-dressed lady standing in front of Otto. "Is that something you made as a gift or do you plan to sell your little lion?"

Otto looked up at the woman and studied her for a second before answering. He forced a smile and made eye contact. "I would normally ask a half a pound, but you look like a very nice lady. How does ten shillings sound, ma'am?"

The lady showed a wide toothy grin as she lifted her coin purse and pulled out a few coins. "Aren't you the salesman? Here, I'll pay the half pound."

The transaction was made, and Otto slipped the coins into his coat pocket. Victoria looked down at her son and gave him a smirk. She knew he had been eyeing the passengers as diligently as she had been, and she was impressed that the cunning little bastard had made such a quick sale.

It took them nearly an hour to reach the end of the gangway. Victoria handed the man three tickets and he compared them to his ledger. His face shown a curious look as he found their cabin numbers and grabbed two keys from his box. "Here you are, my lady. You will find your accommodations on the far side of the ship. It looks like you have been assigned adjoining cabins."

Victoria quickly grabbed the keys and started walking across the ships teak wood deck before anyone could ask questions about why a "family" of three would need two second class cabins for such an expensive voyage.

Augie entered Victoria's cabin holding two large pails of water. He quickly placed them on floor next to a small vanity table that featured a large ornate gold-framed mirror. The table was already filled with multiple bottles of perfume, brushes, combs, jars of powder, makeup containers, and other assorted instruments of beauty.

Victoria was standing near the bed unpacking one of her large suitcases. The room held a decent size wardrobe, which she began filling with an assortment of dresses. She started by hanging three casual daywear dresses. Next, she hung up two fancier dresses that were suitable for first-class dining. Then she gently pulled out an elaborate evening gown and held it up for closer inspection. She made sure to smooth out any wrinkles and carefully hung the gown in the wardrobe.

She closed the suitcase and Augie secured the latches and removed it from the bed. He grabbed the second suitcase and sat it on the bed. He quickly opened the latches on the new case, before carrying the empty one out of the room to be stored in the cabin next door.

Victoria began pulling out a large selection of bustier tops, corsets, garter belts, silk stockings, and other undergarments. She stored these items more discretely in the wardrobe drawers. She pulled out a jewelry box and placed it on the vanity table. Opening the top, she could see that her collection of costume jewelry was still in place. Next she opened a small flap in the suitcase revealing a double-barrel Derringer and two stiletto daggers each boasting three-inch blades.

She checked the chamber to make sure the weapon was loaded and placed the small pistol on the top shelf of the wardrobe and covered it with a silk scarf. She took one dagger and found a place to hide it between the headboard and wall. The second knife she sat on the vanity where she planned to conceal it in her garter belt before heading out for the evening.

Otto entered the room carrying an extra set of bedding and a stack of towels. He placed the spare bedding and half the towels under the bed. He then placed the remaining towels next to the water buckets. Reaching into the suitcase, he pulled out two glasses and a crystal decanter. He set them all on a small table positioned next to the bed. He reached back into the suitcase and found a wax sealed bottle of brandy.

He used his pocket knife to cut through the wax and uncapped the bottle. He smelled the cork and gave it a quick lick to be certain that the liqueur hadn't turned. Satisfied, he poured two fingers into a glass and handed it to his mother. The rest he poured into the crystal decanter and inserted the topper. He grabbed the empty brandy bottle and scurried out of the room.

Augie re-entered the room and Victoria motioned for him to remove the second suitcase. He quickly complied by closing the lid, securing the latches, and carrying the case to the adjoining the room.

Now that everything was set, Victoria stepped back and assessed the scene. She was not impressed with the room's small size, but it would have to do. The lighting was horrible and the cabin smelled of over-lacquered wood. At least the bed was sturdy enough, and the full length mirror would be helpful.

Otto and Augie filed back into the room and stood behind Victoria as she conducted her inspection. The small team had gone through the process of setting up shop dozens of times over the past year, and there had been no need for words as everyone completed their assigned tasks.

After a few seconds Victoria nodded her approval and turned around. "Augie, why don't you go get us some food, while I finish getting ready. Otto, you can start setting up shop in your room."

Augie headed out of the cabin as instructed while Otto entered the adjoining room and shut the door. He opened the suitcase he had been carrying and took out a large bundle of canvas secured tightly with rope. He undid the knots and unrolled the canvas on his bed revealing four polished straight razors and two pairs of scissors. He pulled them out and set them neatly on the small table.

He went back to the case and pulled out three sharpening stones and two long strops, one made of canvas and the other made of leather. He placed the stones on the table next to the razors. Then he found a hook on the wall where he could hang the strops.

He then reached into his second case and pulled out a box. He opened it to check the contents, which consisted of two tooth keys and a pair of pliers. He shuddered at the sight of the dental tools and shut the cover.

The only seating available in the small room were two wooden chairs, but at least they were well-built, and had high backs. He sat one chair in the middle of the room. The other, he positioned to the side of the cabin with its back facing the wall. He then pulled out two blocks of wood from his case that had been cut at forty-five degree angles. He wedged the blocks under the front legs which canted the chair back to a reclined position.

He was pleased to see that they had a small coal burning pot stove in the room. That would make shaving much easier and greatly increase the opportunity for tips.

Satisfied with the setup in the room, he headed out to fetch a couple buckets of clean water and some extra towels.

Victoria pulled the brush through her dark hair one last time before standing up to take a look in the mirror. The stuffy cabin was already causing her to sweat, and she didn't like the way it made her forehead and face shine. She used a handkerchief to wipe away the moisture and dabbed on a little powder. She didn't bother wiping down her cleavage. Men seemed to like a bit of dampness on a woman's chest.

She took a second look in the mirror and was happier this time. At twenty nine, she still retained most of her youthful beauty. She was a tall lady, with a slender waist and large breasts that she always kept pushed up using a bustier. The blue dress she was wearing made her dark hair appear even more black than usual. A strand of blue ribbons had also been woven through the back of her hair, which matched the silk fabric of her dress.

She detested bustles and refused to wear them even though they were still in fashion with many of the aristocrats. Instead, she had tailored her dress as tight as decorum would allow.

She opened the cabin door and looked down the long hallway to see other passengers heading out for the evening meal. She looked back the other way to see Otto standing in front of his cabin affixing a sign that read "Barber Shop."

"I'm heading to dinner. Since it's the first night, I'm sure the rich men will be more cautious with their reputations. Still, I'm confident that there will be enough libations for me to bring back at least one decent paying customer tonight. Tell Augie to stay close in case he is needed."

With that Victoria left for the dining hall. Otto went back into his room and nodded to Augie and laid down in his bed. Augie looked up for a moment, then leaned back in the chair and pulled his bowler hat down over his eyes.

A few hours later, they could hear the door open next door. It was clear that Victoria had delivered on her promise to find a customer. Otto closed his eyes and rolled over in the bed doing his best to block out the sounds. He had heard them nearly every night for as long as he could remember, but it never got easier to stomach.

Eventually the pounding and moaning stopped, followed by a few moments of silence. Then the sound of scraping caused Augie to sit up in the chair. Otto turned to look at him and pressed his ear against the wall using a cup to amplify the sound. He could hear arguing and looked back at Augie with widened eyes. Then two clear knocks could be heard on the wall.

This signal sent Augie into motion. He quickly walked out of the front door and stepped in front of the adjoining cabin door. He opened the hatch with authority and stood ominously in the doorway.

A tall skinny man in fancy evening wear startled at the sight of the hulking German. He quickly finished putting on his jacket and looked at Victoria with an indignant gaze. She did not bother addressing him, so he looked back at the man in the doorway not sure what to do.

"Augustus, this man seems to have lost his coin sack. Could you accompany him to his room and help him find it. I am sure he would be happy to pay you three pounds for your assistance."

"THREE POUNDS, but we had agreed on two..." The man's voice trailed off as he realized the foolishness of the situation.

"You are correct, sir. We did have an agreement, but you decided to change the terms of that agreement. Now that my valet is involved, the price has changed."

"Fine then." He straightened his coat and headed for the door. Augie did not move until the man looked up at him.

"Right this way Mister Augustus." He said waving his hand.

Victoria hung her dress and other articles in the wardrobe and started brushing out her hair in preparation for bed. Augie returned a couple minutes later and placed the coins on the table.

"Thank you, Augie. I had a feeling he was going to be trouble. Hopefully, it will go smoother the rest of the trip, but you should stay alert just in case."

The man nodded and backed out of the room. He retired to his cabin and saw that Otto was already sleeping. He took off his hat and sat back in the chair. He was not used to sleeping in beds. He preferred staying in the ready position in case he was ever needed.

A soft knocking next door woke Augie from his slumber. He sat up in the chair and listened to the voices he heard talking.

Otto already had his ear and cup pressed against the wall. "It's the captain. He is checking in on her. Looks like they are talking business now. It might be a while."

Otto got up and started preparing the cabin for the work of the day. He placed a couple small pieces of coal in the stove and lit the flame. He then soaked two towels in a pail and placed them on top of the stove to begin steaming.

He started sharpening his favorite straight razor using the wet stones. It was a wonderful blade made by Böker in Solingen, Germany. It was one of the many fine German blades Augie had introduced him to over the years.

He had just started pulling long strokes on the stropping leather when a knock on the door signaled their first customer. He was an older man with a scruffy face and shoulder length hair. He told them he needed both a haircut and a shave.

Augie nodded to the man and pointed to the chair in the center of the room. Otto asked him how he would like his hair styled, as the German grabbed the scissors and started cutting.

Once the cut was finished, Augie held up a mirror to make sure he was happy with the work.

Otto then led the man over to the slanted chair and had him lie back. He grabbed a steaming towel from the stove and tested it on his arm to make sure it wasn't too hot before wrapping it around his face. He grabbed the bowl with the shaving butter and a damp brush and mixed it into a lather. Once ready, he pulled the towel off the man's face and slathered on the shaving cream.

Otto then stood on a small crate to get the proper angle and shaved the man with amazing speed and a precise, steady hand. He was finished in less than two minutes and handed the man the mirror so that he could inspect the handiwork.

"That is the quickest shave I have ever gotten. You didn't miss a hair. And not a drop of blood. That is an impressive feat young man."

"Thank you, sir. That will be a pound for the haircut and a half pound for the shave."

"Here is two pounds. And I will make sure to come back before I leave the ship for a freshening up. Have a fine day, gentlemen."

A few minutes later another customer arrived saying he heard that a man could get a quality cut and a shave at this end of the boat. The two went to work and sent him on his way in less than fifteen minutes.

Word quickly spread around the first and second class sections, and the pair stayed busy throughout the day serving thirty-five passengers. Most men only wanted shaves, which kept Otto in constant motion throughout the day as Augie washed out the towels and kept the stove hot.

Victoria only entered the room twice during the day. Once to bring them food at midday and once in the afternoon to tell them she was going to start preparing to leave for the dining room for an early supper.

They closed up shop at six in the afternoon, and Otto laid down on the bed exhausted. His calves ached from standing on the narrow box and his left forearm was numb from gripping the razor for so many hours.

His mother entered the room at six thirty and told them she was heading for the dining room. Before leaving she told Otto to replace the water in her bowls and to change her sheets and towels.

She returned within the hour with a customer and entered her room. Augie sat at his post and leaned against the wall. Less than fifteen minutes later, they heard the door open and close.

Victoria opened the door adjoined to their cabin and nodded to Otto who sprang into action. He entered her room carrying two buckets. He poured the dirty liquid in the bowl into an empty bucket and replaced it with clean water from the other pail. He then pulled out a set of clean sheets and made the bed.

"It is still early, so with any luck I may be able to turn three tonight. I'll see what steerage has to offer." She checked herself in the mirror and headed down the hallway.

She returned an hour later with another gentlemen, who took even less time to finish. The process repeated itself, and she headed to the smoking room to see if she could find another mark.

She did not return until nearly midnight this time. Otto pressed his ear and cup against the wall. "She is pretending to be drunk. He is definitely drunk. I have a feeling you will be needed shortly."

The ruckus continued in the room for quite a while followed by a long period of silence. Then there was the sound of three solid knocks on the wall. This was the signal for them to enter the room, but it was not an emergency.

They entered the room to see that she was fully dressed. The customer however, was passed out on the bed with his pants around his ankles. The pair pulled his pants up and laid him out flat. Augie grabbed his shoulders and Otto grabbed his feet as Victoria opened the door.

As they passed her, she reached into his pocket and pulled out his coin pouch. She pulled out a few coins and closed it back up. The two men carried him to the end of the hallway and down the stairwell. They left him at the landing just inside the steerage section.

They returned to their cabin to find that Victoria had already settled down for the night.

The next seven days followed the same routine. Otto continued to shave thirty to forty men a day, while Augie gave half as many haircuts. Victoria found two customers a night in first class, then visited the raucous steerage section to bring back another man. Without fail, the third mark always fell asleep at the end of their time together. The soft beds in second class were more inviting than the hard wooden benches in steerage.

Throughout the week, Augie rarely left the confines of the cabin, even eating his meals in the room. His only ventures outside were to get supplies, use the bathroom, carry out drunkards, or when he had to escort someone back to their room to help them find a few coins.

Otto also stayed in the cabin during the day. He would rush to the bathroom between customers and became very familiar with the laundry room as he changed out towels and bed sheets quite often.

It wasn't until after six in the evening that Otto had a short window where he could explore the ship, after his mother left for her first hunt. He would stroll along the deck of the large vessel staring up at the huge sails billowing in the wind. He would watch people and try to pick up on the conversations. Most everyone spoke about the opportunities that awaited them when they reached New York.

He was also excited about the idea of America. His mother's sister had travelled to the New World two years ago to open a brothel in Portland, Oregon. She wrote frequently about how much better life was for her there. She encouraged her sister to come out at once, but Victoria had resisted not wanting to fall under her older sister's shadow.

The tipping point came a few months ago, when her sister

wrote about a new logging town up north called Seattle that was growing rapidly. She described it as the greenest place in the world with cedar trees reaching well over a hundred feet tall. The area was still fairly remote and there were not enough businesses or saloons to support the burgeoning population or the hundreds of people who passed through the town every week. The area was in serious need of another brothel to support the loggers and miners, who earned more money than they could spend.

On the morning of the ninth day of sailing a storm rolled into the Atlantic. It brought torrential rain and heavy gusts of wind. No one could go on deck for fear of being blown overboard. Even the dining rooms were closed down. The kitchen passed out bread and dried meats to the few people who dared to try and eat anything.

Most everyone in first and second class stayed in their cabins and braced themselves as the ship bucked back and forth during the storm. This meant that there were no customers for the barber shop. The rocking of the ship would have made it impossible to shave or cut hair, and Augie was in no condition to work anyway. The swaying had brought on a horrible case of seasickness, and the German kept his head buried in a bucket.

Otto found the whole experience exhilarating. He rather enjoyed the chaotic atmosphere. He also liked that he was able to spend some time with his mother. He sat in her room as she worked on mending one of her dresses. He tried not to laugh as she poked herself a few times with the needle as the waves knocked against the vessel.

She finally got frustrated and gave up the attempt. "Well, this is going to be a wasted day, isn't it? There must be something we can do."

"Why don't we go down to steerage and see if there is anything to do down there?" Otto offered.

Victoria shrugged her shoulders and pulled on her boots. They looked in on Augie, who was in no shape to be walking around the ship.

The hallway was vacant and so were the stairs leading down to the steerage section. As soon as they got to the entrance, they could hear music playing. It was a lively Irish song that was accompanied by people playing a variety of instruments.

The steerage area was a mostly open with wooden benches and stacked sleeping planks along the sides. A few tables sat in the middle along with a smattering of chairs and crates. People sat in groups all over the large area. Many were suffering the same fate as Augie as they sat on benches trying to keep from vomiting into buckets. Others were holding on to railings and posts trying to steady themselves as they rested.

A large, loud group gathered in the center enjoying the volatility of the ocean and turned it into a party. They were singing, dancing, and drinking from large jugs. The whole scene played out in stark contrast to the vacant hallways of the first and second class decks above.

Victoria and Otto took a seat on an open bench and watched as a group of ladies stood up and performed an Irish jig. A jug was passed around and Victoria took a swig of the harsh liquor. She passed the jug to Otto who took a sip before making a strange face. She laughed at him. It was the first genuine smile Otto had seen from his mother in a very long time.

The pair stayed in steerage for several hours listening to the singing. At one point they even joined in on the dancing. The song they played as they danced was called *A Violet I Plucked from Mother's Grave When I was a Boy*. He watched as his mother's long black hair flowed as she circled around him. She had those beautiful blue ribbons weaved into her braids and they swayed as she twirled about.

He watched as she danced with others in the group, both men and women without pretense. She understood there was no money to be made that night, and it freed them both to enjoy the festivities.

It was one of the best nights of Otto's young life. He could not remember a time when just he and his mother had been together doing something other than work. It was a night he would remember forever.

After a few hours, one of the ship's officers came through the area signaling that it was time for lights out. The groaning passengers dispersed, and Victoria and Otto went back to their cabins to retire for the night. Checking in on Augie, Otto saw that the man was fast asleep in his chair. He took his bucket to the water closet and cleaned it for him before going to bed himself.

He lay in his bed for a while staring up at the ceiling. He knew it was a rare day, and one that would likely never come again. He wished life could be simpler for him and his mother. But those were just the wishes of a foolish boy, and he would not be a boy for much longer.

By the next morning, the storm had passed. The cloudless blue skies opened and the sun shined warmly overhead. Everyone had been ordered to come above deck so that the lower areas could be cleaned and serviced.

It was odd to see the different classes of passengers all gathered in the same place. Below deck, the ship had strong barriers between the classes, but on the top deck everyone was free to walk around as they pleased.

No one who could afford passage on an immigrant ship was destitute, but there were still very visible differences in wealth between the groups.

The first-class passengers remained huddled together and had their servants to shield them from the riff-raff. Even though it was hot on the deck, they continued to dress in their finest clothes in order to showcase their stations. The second-class passengers consisted mainly of families, and they also sat in tight groups, but they at least had the sense to wear more comfortable clothing.

The steerage passengers were a hodgepodge of different styles and subclasses. It was clear by the way they dressed that many of the men in steerage could afford better tickets, but chose to save their money.

Most of the men from the lower decks were tradesmen hired by companies to sail to America to bolster one business or another. There were also a number of small families who had cobbled up enough money to try their luck in the New World.

Standing above deck proved to be uncomfortable for Victoria. She was nicely dressed, so she could fit in with first class. However, her profession was now well known among the other women in those ranks, and their cold looks let her know that she was not welcome. She had been through this scenario enough times to know that she had fully worn out all the easy business in first class.

Steerage still had plenty of opportunity, but there were a number of other prostitutes working the boat who were willing to render their services for a third of what she charged. Now that they had learned the best hiding spots in steerage to conduct business, the men were not as willing to pay for privacy.

This left mainly second class for the final three days of the voyage. She walked a few slow laps around the deck concentrating on her new target market. The numbers were not in her favor. She would not be able to work the small group the same as she had before. Instead of looking for three or even two marks, she would need to concentrate on milking one man for as much money as possible.

She told Otto about her plan and sent him searching throughout the deck for candidates. He had a knack for reading people, and he would be able to scout the area without drawing attention. After nearly an hour of searching he returned to her with a report.

"There is a man on the bow who is alone and decently dressed. But he is overweight and reading a book."

"No readers. Not this time. They spend too much time in fantasy land and don't have much use for the real world."

"I saw another man by the engine room. He had a scar on his

face, but he looks like he has money. He might be a bit gruff though."

"I saw him too. He is a possibility, but I would like to find someone a little more... pliable."

That is when Otto noticed a man standing on the other side of the boat. He was wearing an amazing stovepipe top hat. It was deep black and was one of the finest pieces of clothing he had ever seen. How had he missed him before today? Maybe he had never worn the hat below deck.

The man was medium height and build and looked to be in his forties. He held his chin high like he came from a formal background. He was too far away from first class to be in that group, but he also looked overdressed for second class. He stood by the railing smoking a pipe.

Victoria noticed that her son was distracted by something so she followed his gaze to the man. She nodded her head. "He definitely looks promising."

Otto watched as his mother walked over to the man and engaged him in conversation. No matter how many times he saw her in action, he was always impressed with how easily she could manipulate a man. She would stand close enough for her perfume to catch his attention. Then she would find a reason to touch his arm. She would turn her head at just the right moment to give him ample opportunity to sneak a peek at her cleavage.

But her true talent was knowing when to walk away. She would allow her target to gain just enough interest, then walk away slowly. This would give the man an illusion of control, and he would give chase.

This scene unfolded in just a few minutes with the man in the top hat. She walked away and the man took a few long strides in her direction. He tapped her shoulder and she turned slowly feigning surprise. They spoke for a moment longer, then she headed back across the deck.

She sat down on a bench next to Otto. "He is the ship engineer. I will be accompanying him to dinner tonight. He certainly has means, so hopefully there is money to be made."

It was late morning before the whistle sounded allowing the

passengers to return to their quarters. Otto and Augie wasted no time setting up shop, and it didn't take long before men started showing up looking for shaves. The pair stayed busy throughout the day and didn't get through the last customer in line until early evening.

Victoria stopped by the barber shop as the last man sat in the shaving chair. She was wearing her fanciest dress, and her hair was set in a French braid that was doubled over and tied with a blue ribbon. She told the boys she was leaving for the evening and directed Otto to take care of her room when he was finished with his work.

After she left, they finished with the last customer and cleaned up the cabin. Otto then changed the water and sheets in his mother's room and headed to the kitchen to pick up dinner. He took the opportunity to walk out on the deck of the ship and stare out at the dark ocean for a while. It was well over an hour before he returned to the room where he could hear loud mumbling coming from his cabin.

Otto hurried into the room where he saw a short stocky man holding his jaw. He was pale and sweaty and mumbling something to Augie who couldn't understand what he was trying to say. Otto grabbed the man's arm to get his attention, and he looked at the boy and started babbling incoherently at him.

Otto led the man to the reclined chair and pushed him back. He stood on his crate and told the man to open his mouth. He shook his head no, so Otto grabbed his chin and pushed his jaw open.

"Grab the lantern, Augie."

It didn't take long to spot the problem. The man had an ugly black molar on his bottom right side that was cracked and oozing puss. The bad tooth was located far to the back. It was going to be hard to reach.

Otto stepped off the crate and privately told Augie what he had discovered. In his experience it was best not to let patients know what was about to happen. It would only make the situation more precarious. He then stuck a pair of pliers into his back pocket, grabbed the right angled tooth key, and jumped back on the crate. Augie stood on the man's left and put his large hand over the patient's forehead while still holding the lantern.

Otto told the man to close his eyes and that he might feel quite a bit of pressure. Before the man could protest, he wrenched the key onto his tooth and rocked it back and forth. The man wriggled wildly and kicked his legs out trying to get away from the demon child. Tears filled his eyes and he moaned loudly. Once the tooth was properly loosened, he removed the key and exchanged it for the pliers in his back pocket.

Augie pushed even harder on the man's forehead and waited until Otto had fitted the pliers on the tooth. He then sat the lantern down and put his other hand on the man's jaw, holding tight. He nodded at Otto to let him know he was ready. They both knew the next part was going to be hard for everyone involved.

Otto squeezed tightly on the tooth and pulled as hard as he could. The man groaned loudly and tried uselessly to get away from the large German man's grip. The stubborn tooth did not want to let go, so Otto worked it back and forth a bit more before he felt the root give way. He pulled out the large tooth and tossed it into a bowl on the table. He then grabbed a piece of cloth and soaked it in a glass of brandy before sticking it in the gaping hole in the man's mouth where the tooth used to be.

Augie let the patient loose from his grip and watched as he sat up sharply. Sweat covered the man's forehead, but his color was already starting to return. He slumped forward and shook his head back and forth trying to get his bearings. Otto sat down on the bed and rubbed his forearm. He was already sore from a full week of shaving, and he had strained it even more when he bore down on the tooth.

The man stood up slowly still holding onto the chair for support. He pulled a few coins out of his pocket, then nodded to the two barbers and gave them each three coins before leaving.

Augie waited until he was gone, then sat down to start eating his supper. Otto laid back in his bed still rubbing on his arm. He knew that he should clean up the mess from the dental work, but he needed to rest a while first.

He was just about to drift off to sleep when he heard the door open next door. He sat up and pressed his ear against the wall. He could hear his mother and the engineer speaking. The conversation sounded as expected so he gave a quick nod to Augie and laid back down.

Otto stayed awake for a while thinking that he might be needed to turn his mother's bed. After a long while, he drifted off to sleep. He was awoken later in the evening to a loud continuous knocking on the wall. That was the signal for real trouble.

Augie was already in motion, headed for the door to the adjoining room. He threw the door open to see the engineer standing over Victoria. She was lying face up in the bed with a dagger in her right hand. Blood dripped from the corner of her mouth.

The German quickly grabbed the man by the back of his coat and spun him away from his victim. He then turned to Victoria to make sure she wasn't badly hurt. The tall man was still wearing his suit and held a walking cane in his right hand, which he used to smash Augie on the top of the head.

The German stumbled backward through the adjoining room door. He tripped over the chair in the middle of the room and crashed into the slanted barber chair breaking it into pieces. The man gave chase, swinging his cane in wide arcs. Now that Augie was on the ground, he made for an easy target. The engineer continued to deliver strong blows to his arms and shoulders.

Otto froze at the start of the tussle, but he could now see that Augie was in trouble. He jumped up from the bed and grabbed the man by the waist. The much larger engineer kicked at him, then delivered a hard blow to the side of Otto's face causing him to crash into the wall.

The man went back to hitting Augie with his cane, and Otto could see that his companion was in serious danger at this point. The young man pulled himself up and grabbed the nearest weapon he could find, which was the tooth key laying on the table. He jabbed the pointed end of the key into the man's side, causing him to yelp. The engineer swung the cane back in a looping angle and caught Otto below the knee. He crashed down in a heap hitting his head on the floor.

Seeing his young friend injured spurred Augie to roll to his knees. He tried to lunge forward, but the man kicked him solidly in the chest. He fell backwards landing in a precarious position. He was now facing the man, with one arm pinned beneath him, and his front exposed.

The man took advantage of the open target and started swinging the cane, delivering devastating blows. Augie could only crane his neck and turn away, trying in futility to block the cane with his free arm.

Otto had recovered quickly and this time he chose a better weapon. He grabbed his favorite straight razor from table and backed against the wall. The tall engineer was now stooped over Augie trying to get at his head. Otto saw the crate at the man's side and used it to launch himself onto the man's back. He wrapped his arm around the man's forehead and dug his heels into his side holding on with all his strength.

He drug the straight razor across the man's neck in one deep cut. An arc of blood shot out from the wound spraying the wall. The man stood up sharply and dropped his cane. There was a moment of stillness before the man fell backward, crashing down on Otto who was still on the man's back.

It took a moment for Augie to pull himself up, and he rolled the now dead engineer off Otto. The young man was holding his left arm, which had taken the brunt of the man's fall. His favorite razor had also been snapped in half.

Victoria stood in the doorway looking at the scene. She looked concerned, but Otto knew her concern was not about Augie or his wellbeing. A knock at the door caused her to hurry in her assessment. She grabbed a towel off the table and cleaned the blood off her face. She kicked the man's foot over the threshold to her room and motioned for Augie to close the door after her.

A few seconds later another knock sounded, followed by Victoria opening the door. They could only hear mumbled voices, which eventually subsided. They heard the door close, then Victoria returned to the room.

She knelt down to take a closer look at her son's arm. "It does not appear to be broken, but it will take a while to heal properly."

She walked over to Augie who was bleeding from a gash on his head. He also had welts forming on his arms, and she was sure he had several other bruises and injuries under his clothes.

"Damn you." She kicked the dead engineer in frustration. "I should have assessed the situation better. He actually thought he was wooing me. Talking about taking me with him to places in New York. When it came time to talk business, he became indignant. I tried a few negotiating tactics, but those just made him angrier. When I told him to leave, he felt honor bound to have his way with me to cure me of my dubious behavior, as he called it."

The three of them sat in silence for a few minutes. They were in a tight spot, and only had a few hours before daylight to work out a plan. It was clear that they were not going to be able to carry the man out of the room in his current state. He was covered in blood and his throat was open wide.

Augie slowly climbed to his feet. He was still woozy, but he appeared to have a handle on all his faculties. He reached into his bag and pulled out a small hatchet. Victoria went into her room and pulled the sheets off her bed and laid them out by the dead man.

Otto stood up and used his good arm to help arrange the man's arms and a leg onto one of the sheets. He used the scissors to cut the other sheets into large squares.

Augie went to work dissecting the cadaver into manageable sizes. They packed the larger pieces in the sheets and filled up the two buckets with the soupier bits.

Cleaning up the blood took even longer. Otto and Augie did all the scrubbing as their clothes were already ruined. Otto changed into his only spare shirt and trousers, which were older and did not fit very well. Augie had to toss both his shirt and jacket. He had one spare shirt, but he would have to go without a jacket until they reached the city.

It was early morning before they were ready to start carrying items out of the room. One by one, they left the cabin carrying as many packages as they could without drawing too much attention. This proved fairly easy, as there were not many people up at such an early hour. The few passengers they did encounter did not seem to notice anything out of the ordinary. It was common to see people carrying buckets and other trash to throw overboard.

It took them several trips to get everything out, and the sun had begun to peek over the horizon when Otto returned from cleaning out the buckets. Victoria walked around the room inspecting the area to make sure they hadn't missed anything. There were still pale stains of blood on the wooden floors and back wall, but there wasn't much that could be done about that.

The linen closet had been left unlocked, so they were able to grab new sets of sheets and fresh towels without drawing attention. By mid-morning, they felt comfortable enough with the situation that they could lay down to rest. It took only a minute for Augie to fall fast asleep in his chair. Even Victoria decided to forego brushing her hair and laid down fully dressed on top of her sheets.

Otto was the only one who could not sleep. The images of the gruesome task filled his mind. Plus, his arm continued to throb, especially after carrying several large pails out of the room.

He finally drifted off to sleep as one last image filled his mind. It was the image of his hand holding the straight razor, pushing it deeply into the man's throat and dragging it across his neck in one fluid motion.

It was late evening before Otto awoke. He got up to find his mother and Augie sitting at the table. She was sorting through a pile of coins, while the German rewrapped the wounds on his arm.

"You boys did really good on this trip. You collected nearly two hundred pounds. I only collected two fifty, but the engineer had nearly a hundred on him. That is not a bad haul."

Augie pushed a plate of food over to Otto, who started eating slowly. He felt awkward holding the fork with his right hand, but his left arm was useless at this point.

"When we get to the city, we will need to get you both some proper clothes. We should also see about getting some new dental tools. One of the tines broke off that key thing you use. Plus, all those tools are at least ten years old now and could use replacing anyway."

Victoria stood up and straightened her dress in the mirror. "I am going to the dining room. I want to make sure that I am seen tonight in case any inquiries come about due to the missing engineer. I don't believe anyone saw us walk to my room last night, but you can never be too careful."

She looked back at Otto who was staring at his plate of food. She could see that his arm was swollen and bruised as was the side of his face. "You both rest up tonight. I will not be bringing any customers back. We are done with business this trip. Go ahead and pack everything. The ship will arrive at the dock tomorrow afternoon, and we will get you both checked out by a doctor."

Otto finished eating and went back to his cabin. He pulled out his suitcase and started packing. He took his time putting everything in its place. He then helped Augie secure most of the items in his mother's room, before laying back in his bed. He was still sore from the fight, and after only two hours of work he found himself ready for sleep again. Augie also looked haggard and slumped back in the chair.

The next morning Victoria let them both sleep until mid-afternoon when the ship's whistle sounded as it floated into the harbor in New York City. Augie was the first up, and he pulled out the large suitcase so that Victoria could finish packing up her dresses. Otto stowed away the rest of his things, and they were all packed and ready within a few minutes.

The debarkation process was slow but steady. All the

passengers were released from their cabins by class and funneled through a single gangway. As they disembarked, they were divided into smaller groups and processed through the Emigrant Landing Depot at Castle Garden in Manhattan.

The lines at the depot moved at a steady pace as passengers gave their names and countries of origin. They were then given a quick physical by a nurse who mainly checked for signs of disease.

Victoria was relieved that Augie's bandaged head and Otto's busted up arm did not draw any attention during the medical examination. Once they made it through the custom's process, they walked several blocks into the city until they were certain they were clear of all the other passengers. They found lodging at a hotel and Otto was sent out to find some food.

They spent the next three days in the city collecting the supplies they needed. Both Otto and Augie were fitted with new American style suits along with extra shirts and a spare pair of trousers. Victoria bought a couple of new dresses and a bonnet, which seemed to be the current fashion. A new dental set was purchased, along with a pair of scissors. Augie also found Otto a new German straight razor to replace the one that had been broken during the fight.

Victoria took Otto to a doctor who determined that he had indeed fractured his arm. He fitted him with a splint and told him he would need to wear a sling for the next three weeks. Augie refused to see a doctor but did allow Victoria to put medicine on his head wound and wrap it with a clean bandage. His other wounds seemed to be healing nicely.

On the morning of the fourth day, the group left for the train station to continue their journey westward.

The Transcontinental Express was considered one of the world's greatest technological marvels. The first train had completed the initial journey in July 1876, traveling from New

York to San Francisco in just over eighty-three hours.

Before the Express opened, the original Transcontinental Railroad would have taken even the richest of travelers a minimum of two weeks to travel from coast to coast, and those with less means had to hop a multitude of trains over the course of several weeks.

The Transcontinental Express was primarily a passenger train that carried both passengers and packages and did not stop at every station along the way. This allowed the train to average nearly forty miles an hour over the course of more than three thousand miles.

For around sixty-five dollars, passengers could purchase a third-class ticket, which left them sitting shoulder-to-shoulder with other travelers on narrow wooden benches. The trip for these travelers was not all that comfortable and took longer to complete. Since third-class cars were normally attached to freight cars and redirected to make way for priority express cars, the trip normally took around ten days to complete.

First-class passengers rode in luxurious Victorian-style Pullman cars, sitting in plush velvet seats that could be converted into compact beds. They also enjoyed heated cars, porter service, nicely appointed restrooms, and other luxuries. These passengers could also upgrade to the Pacific Hotel Express, which allowed access to dining and smoking cars as well as a number of curtained booths for private encounters.

Victoria walked out of the train terminal and got her first look at the large train they would be riding. She was only mildly impressed with the red and green Pullman passenger cars. They looked much the same as many of the trains she had ridden throughout Europe over the past few years, only a little larger. However, she did have to admit the giant steam engine was a sight to behold. It towered above the small European engines she was used to seeing.

She hated spending so much money for three first-class tickets, but the exchange rate had made the transaction more palatable. The pound was outperforming the dollar two to one, which gave them more traveling money than expected.

Victoria handed the tickets to the conductor as the three of them boarded the train. He looked at the tickets and pointed them to the front of the car. They found their seats and stowed the luggage in the racks located overhead.

Otto laid his head on the window and shut his eyes. Victoria started her routine of assessing the crowd. She watched as several passengers boarded the train. After a while she decided it wasn't worth the time. The ratio of men to women in first class was at least ten to one. She would be on the train for less than four days, and she was sure she could get all the business she wanted by the looks of things.

The first leg of the trip went quickly. The train sped along making only a few stops until hitting Kansas City. Otto and Augie kept mainly to their bench seats, which had been folded down into a bed. Victoria had upgraded her ticket to Pacific Hotel Express, which allowed her access to the dining car and smoking rooms. She had already spent a few hours in those areas getting a lay of the land and meeting a few of the passengers.

The train pulled out of Kansas City at two in the afternoon, which meant there was plenty of time left in the day to see what money could be made. She left the boys to their sleep and made her way to the dining car.

She was gone for several hours until the sun started to set, and it was clear that Augie was uncomfortable with the situation. He did not like the idea of Victoria being left alone while conducting business. Otto did his best to calm the man.

At a little past ten Augie started to show signs of real concern. Otto feared the man was about to jump out of his seat and run up the stairs, so he volunteered to go check on things. He walked to the end of his car and through another first-class car before getting to the dining car.

He was not allowed to climb the stairs to the seating area but could order food at the counter. He placed an order and waited for the attendant to take it to the kitchen before climbing up a couple of steps and looking in the dining car. He could see his mother sitting at the bar speaking with a well-dressed man. She looked over to see Otto's head peeking up from the stairs. She waved for him to go back down, and he ducked out of sight.

Satisfied that she was fine, he took the food back to his seat and gave Augie the update. The German calmed a bit, and even took his hat off to rest. Otto took the opportunity to change the man's bandage before lying down to sleep.

Victoria did not return until after midnight. Augie was still sitting at attention and his shoulders finally relaxed when he saw her push her way into the booth and lie down next to Otto. She held up her coin purse and gave it a jingle.

"I think I am going to like this new country, Augie. The men here really like their women."

After less than four days, the train pulled into the station in San Francisco. The three travelers had to switch trains that afternoon to a smaller passenger train headed to Portland. The ride through Oregon continued through the night, and they arrived early the next morning at the depot.

In 1876, Portland was an expansive city that wound around the Columbia River. The population had crested fifteen thousand making it by far the largest city north of San Francisco.

The three of them walked from the train station to the edge of downtown Portland where they found the brothel that Victoria's sister owned. They entered the establishment, which looked like a large two story house. It had a large open foyer and a long bar along the back wall. There was an open staircase leading to the second level. At least eight small rooms could be seen on the second level, and possibly more behind the staircase on the first level.

Victoria's sister approached them wearing a yellow dress with white flowers. Her dress and smile were in direct contrast with Victoria's more traditional attire and stern demeanor. "Victoria, you look like you are ready to go to the ball."

"And you, Amanda, look like you are ready to pick berries in the field." Not missing a beat, Amanda spun around letting the sides of her dress lift up showing her knickers.

"The boys just love it when I do that. And how are you Otto?" She patted him on the head and looked down at his arm. "Did your mean old mommy do that to your arm?"

He just shook his head and tugged on his sling a bit.

"Come on now, let's get you boys into a room so you can relax. Your mother and I need to talk business."

The next two days were comfortable for Otto. He had no responsibilities and just spent his time walking around the brothel learning about American life. He found the people to be entirely undisciplined, but that was not necessarily a bad thing. Their undisciplined nature came from a sense of freedom and opportunity. They seemed to enjoy life more than the people he had met in London, and they were certainly more entertaining. They were also much looser with their money and willing to spend every penny they had on liquor, gambling, and women.

Victoria spent her time studying the men as well. She learned the nuances of entertaining American men, which she had already discovered were much quicker on the draw. Plus, they did not quibble much about price, as long as they felt it was reasonable and they had the means to pay.

Americans also liked to drink whiskey during every activity and were prone to passing out in their seats and in the rooms. This meant that all payments had to be collected up front, including room fees for overnighters.

Augie was not as happy about the new setting. Every man he saw come through the door carried a gun around his hip. To make matters worse, Americans had short fuses and liked to fight as a matter of pride, principle, and just for fun. And the more they drank, the more they liked to shout at one another.

Before their arrival, Amanda had struck a business deal with a man in Seattle named Carl Coats who owned a house similar in size to hers. He was willing to sell it to Victoria for eight hundred dollars. He would also take ten percent of the house earnings in exchange for making sure the brothel stayed in good graces with the city government.

Amanda had also selected four prostitutes from her house to travel to Seattle. They agreed that Victoria would send four ladies back in the future as an exchange. Men always liked to see fresh faces, so having two fully staffed houses of prostitutes to swap back and forth was always good for business.

Victoria was thankful for the arrangement but nervous about spending nearly every penny she had on a new building in an untested location. She knew this was probably her best opportunity to own her own brothel , so there was really not much to decide.

On the morning of the fourth day, the stagecoach arrived to take Victoria, Otto, Augie, and the group of prostitutes to Seattle. After the goodbyes were said, the driver whipped the horses into motion.

The Birth of a New City

"I was told that the world would be harsh, and I was informed that life would be hard and painful. But I was not warned that it would be the ones I loved most who would cause the majority of that pain.

– Author Unknown

The first settlers arrived in the Puget Sound area in November 1851. They had traveled from the Midwest through Oregon and finally stopped in Alki Point with the intent of founding a town. They built a number of small houses and buildings, but many of the settlers determined that the land was poorly protected from the ocean and decided to relocate to Elliot Bay near what eventually became downtown Seattle.

The first official plats for Seattle were filed in 1853, but it wasn't until 1855 that the legal land settlement was established in the area encompassing Pioneer Square and the International District.

The settlement grew very slowly during the first decade. Most of this growth was realized by family members joining the original settlers who had built businesses centered around the logging trade.

The settlement was originally founded by Methodists, but the area quickly developed a reputation for being wide-open to all vices including liquor, gambling, and especially prostitution. The first brothel opened in 1861 and quickly became one of the most profitable businesses in the area.

By 1865 the population had reached approximately three hundred fifty and the settlement was incorporated. The town experienced several periods of unrest and lost its charter in 1867. Eventually, it was officially re-incorporated as a city in 1869 with a population of just over one thousand.

By 1870, the city was beginning to see an explosion in growth, with the population nearly doubling every year. The logging industry was proving to be a lucrative industry, supplying lumber for the growing city as well as cities to the south including Tacoma, Portland, and San Francisco.

Octavius was now twenty-four and it had been eight years since he first arrived in Seattle. He was living in a small apartment and was much happier having a place of his own outside the brothel.

He still worked at his mother's house at night, serving as a cook. He and Augie had given up on the idea of running a barber shop out of the brothel shortly after their arrival. It took his arm longer than expected to heal, and Augie's security services were in much higher demand at a busy American brothel than they had been in London.

His mother had found success almost immediately upon her arrival to the fledgling city. Her arrangement with Carl Coats proved to be mutually beneficial. He stayed true to his word in selling her the house, and even gave her good terms. He also helped to smooth things over with the city government and continued to work on her behalf whenever new leadership came into power.

In turn, his mother accompanied Mister Coats to social gatherings and even kept his bed warm on occasion. He also enjoyed the fact that he had his pick of the other girls anytime he wanted. Mister Coats was a modernist who believed that women should neither be kept nor limited in their business dealings.

In less than eight years, the city had grown from just over one thousand to a population that now exceeded thirty-five hundred. But even that growth did not capture the true opportunity that abounded in the city. Hundreds of travelers passed through every day looking for supplies. Even more visited the city looking to spend their hard earned money from logging and building railroads. In recent months, a new influx of men started passing through the city on their way to some new gold claim that had just been discovered up north.

Otto was more comfortable now that the city had grown larger. He missed the bustle of London and the anonymity that a large city provided. When he first arrived in town, everyone quickly knew his name. He couldn't travel around town without seeing nearly everyone he knew.

Now that the streets were more crowded, he could find more time to himself. He loved to watch people, and that was hard to do when everyone recognized you.

He had spent his first few years working in the brothel cleaning sheets and changing out water bowls. When he turned seventeen, he told his mother that he was going to find a job out in town but agreed to help out at the brothel at night.

He also told everyone that he now wanted to be called by his full name, Octavius. It took a while, but it finally caught on with everyone; everyone but his mother of course.

He got a job sharpening edges with a local bladesmith named Seamus. Nearly every profession in the area needed tools to be sharpened on a regular basis. Trappers needed blades for skinning. Loggers carried a number of different axes and hatchets. Butchers needed chopping and deboning knives. Even barbers and cooks started bringing their knives to the small shop.

Seamus was a burly but kind man that had an appreciation for fine knives and pretty much any tool used for cutting. Octavius was already a seasoned knife sharpener, so it did not take the bladesmith long to teach him how to apply his skills to sharpening other edges.

Before long, Octavius had built up a reputation as the finest blade sharpener in the area. He would sharpen most blades on a stone grinding wheel before wet sanding them to a fine edge. He would then spend extra time stropping the blades, a step that was often overlooked by novice bladesmiths.

He enjoyed the solitary nature of sharpening. The sound of the grinding stone was soothing and loud enough that no one bothered trying to strike up conversations with him while he worked. But it was not work that he truly loved doing. He would rather be using blades than sharpening them.

He got that opportunity in the afternoons when he worked at the brothel kitchen. There he served as the assistant to Tumas Edwards, a Prussian who had served as a chef for Napoleon Bonaparte until leaving the country in 1870 when France declared war on his homeland.

Tumas was a master of the culinary arts. He had cooked for kings and queens and had created banquet feasts for hundreds of guests. But as a seventy year old exile with arthritis and bad knees, working as a night cook at a brothel in Seattle was at least a job.

Tumas was very demanding and had little patience for mistakes or incompetence. He spoke harshly to his assistants, all of which quit within a few days. Octavius had been thrust into the position at the age of eighteen when one assistant left in the middle of preparing a large dinner service. Octavius felt like a fish out of water the whole night, but he did his best to follow instructions. The harsh criticism from the chef did not affect him much as he had heard much worse his entire life from his mother.

Tumas ended the night by saying he should come back the next day with two sharp knives. Octavius showed up the next day ready to work. He was certain he would be replaced at any point by a more qualified assistant. After a month passed, even Tumas' constant criticisms started to wane. After six months, he stopped the tantrums altogether and started training Octavius on more complex cooking techniques.

The two had now worked together for six years, and Octavius had developed into a fine cook. Tumas had taught him everything he could in the small kitchen that served less than a hundred meals a day. They had even started to get businessmen and a few women coming into the brothel just to eat meals. This did not sit well with Victoria, but she would not openly spurn any paying customers.

Tumas knew that the only way for Octavius to grow into a proper chef would be for him to leave Seattle. He needed to go somewhere he could receive training in a large kitchen with proper ingredients and discerning palates. This was a sentiment that he shared with Octavius often. He even wrote to some of his friends in Europe about potential opportunities for the young man.

Octavius relished the idea of going back to Europe to train as a chef. He missed London and longed to see what it would be like to visit there as a man instead of only knowing of life there as a boy. But he could not leave the brothel.

He had little concern for his mother. She could take care of herself, and she had grown even more independent and colder since purchasing the establishment. She managed the business with an iron hand and was known to fire prostitutes for the smallest of infractions. Octavius had done what he could to temper her moods, but even he couldn't get through to her most days. They never had a true mother-son relationship and had continued to grow further apart each passing year.

His concern was for Augie. The German was now in his mid-sixties and had developed a severe cough. He was still strong and could beat anyone in a fight, but he appeared to be in constant pain. His mother was willing to pay for the doctor visits, but she had little time or willingness to care for the man when he became truly ill.

Augie would sit in his chair perched at the top of the stairs on the second floor every night. His presence alone kept the ruffians at bay most of the time. At the end of the night before heading to his apartment, Octavius would check in on him and make sure he had taken his medicines. He would try to convince him to go to bed early but that rarely worked.

The past few days had been especially hard for Augie. The old German was starting to have problems catching his breath after climbing the stairs. This was an embarrassment for the man who had always been able to best anyone at feats of strength and endurance.

Things came to head one Saturday evening when a group of loggers came in from the north country. There were four men in the group and they were obviously looking to spend handfuls of cash on liquor and women.

The first hour they plowed through three bottles while

visiting with some of the ladies. Then the largest of the bunch, a long haired behemoth of a man, started to get rough with one of the girls. Augie stood up from his chair, descended the stairs, and approached the man. He grunted forcefully at the patron. The man ignored him but took his hands off the girl who quickly walked away to diffuse the situation.

After another hour, two of the men went upstairs with partners. The big man and another stayed behind and continued drinking. A few minutes later the smaller logger slapped one of the girls on the behind hard enough to make her scream and start to cry.

Augie had seen enough and stood up to confront the man. As he approached, the behemoth grabbed a girl and pulled her onto his lap. She tried her best to pull away from the man, but he grabbed her arms and pinned them to her side, kissing her on the neck. Augie stood over the man and grunted again.

The logger laughed and told him to go away. Augie slapped the man in the back of the head with his meaty paw, knocking the man forward. The logger released the girl from his grip and stood up to face the German. He cocked his fist back ready to swing, but Augie was already in motion. He sent an elbow into the side of the man's head causing him to fall back over his chair.

The man's smaller companion took a swing at Augie from the side, but he ducked forward just in time. Unfortunately, the man's momentum continued forward and his fist landed between the eyes of one of the prostitutes who had rushed in to help. Her nose exploded in a spray of blood as she held her hand to her face.

The large man was now back on his feet and approaching Augie, who was concentrating on the injured woman. He turned around just in time to see an enormous fist crunch into his temple knocking him out cold and sending him crashing into a table.

The other ladies started grabbing trays, candle sticks, and other makeshift weapons and swung them wildly at the loggers. Chaos erupted in the room, and the men yelled for their friends and ran out of the brothel.

Hearing the commotion, Victoria ran into the room just in time to see the two men scurry out of the brothel. She watched as two other half-naked men ran out after them. She also saw one of her top earners holding a broken nose and bleeding all over her expensive rug. She looked down to see Augie lying stretched out in a heap over a shattered table.

Octavius came rushing in from the kitchen and looked at his mom with knowing eyes. He shook his head and pushed his way through the circle of people to get to her. Before he could get to her side Augie started to moan and opened his eyes.

"You're fired, you old sick bastard! If you can't protect my girls, then you are just dead weight to me. Get out of my sight!" She spun around and stormed out of the room.

Octavius finally reached his friend and helped him to sit up. "Don't worry about mother. She is just reacting to the moment. Here are the keys to my apartment. Go there and wait for me. I will calm her down, and we will get this all sorted out in the morning."

Augie stood up not fully understanding what had happened. He looked around in confusion as Octavius led him toward the door. He told him again to wait for him at his apartment, which was just around the corner.

Once back inside, he helped the girls clean up the mess and told one of the ladies to fetch a doctor. He led the injured women to the kitchen, sat her down in a chair, and handed her a towel. Tumas knelt down in front of her and made sure she kept her head up with the towel in place.

Once everything was under control, Octavius headed out in search of his mother. He found her sitting at the desk in her office and steadied himself before going inside. She was writing something and did not bother to look up, so he just stood in front of her desk staring at her.

"Don't give me that look, Otto. You knew this was coming. I have never been one to stand for incompetence."

"Even you can't be that cruel. Augie is family. He has been with us since the beginning. He has saved your life and mine dozens of times. He has done everything you have ever asked of him and more."

"Well, he didn't do anything tonight did he? He has been sitting in that chair every day, dying. Just sitting there dying in front of me. In front of the girls. In front of customers. I should have thrown him out a long time ago."

"You can't do this mother. He deserves…"

"Don't tell me what I can and cannot do in my house. This is my business, and I will not let anyone, especially a man-child tell me how to run my business." She was standing now, punching her fist into the table to accentuate her point.

"I am not telling you how to run your business. I am talking about what is right. About how a decent person should act. How a person should treat family."

"Augie is not family. I have always paid him more than his fair share. Here take this. It is everything I owe him and more." She grabbed a stack of bills and shoved it into his hand.

Octavius stood there slack jawed trying to think of something to say. He wanted to be angry, but all he could feel was pity. Pity for his mother's lack of empathy and love. Pity for the man who had been like an older brother to him his entire life. Pity for himself and the fact that he had supported this foul woman for so long.

There was nothing more that could be said, so he turned to walk away. "Otto, I don't want to speak of this matter again. My mind is made up. He is not to return to this house unless he is here to spend his money on hookers."

Octavius looked at her with disgust as he exited out of the office. He passed through the kitchen and saw that the doctor was attending to the injured woman. Tumas looked at him, but Octavius turned his head quickly so that he couldn't see the tears that had started welling up in his eyes.

It was nearly midnight when Octavius left the brothel. The moon was full and lit the roads well. He needed to walk for a while to calm his nerves.

He had no idea what to tell Augie. The man was already devastated by his ailing health. Now that he was unemployed, he would be even more lost.

Octavius didn't care about any of that. He had room enough in his apartment for the both of them, and the large German could still find plenty of work in the busy city.

He walked the deserted streets for over an hour before heading back to his apartment. He wasn't ready to speak to the man, but he knew that he should be there for him in his time of need. He grabbed the doorknob and took a deep breath before entering the room.

As soon as the door opened he could see Augie swinging from a rope in front of him. The moonlight shining through the window drowned out his features. All that could be seen was a silhouette of his oldest friend.

The police had taken less than five minutes to determine the matter a suicide and asked if Octavius needed any assistance with the body. He understood they would just carry Augie away to be used as a medical cadaver, so he refused their help. Instead, he borrowed a wagon from the brothel and used it to load up the body and wheel it to the undertaker.

The next morning, he returned to the undertaker's house and secured a coffin and a plot in the local cemetery. He paid the undertaker to dig the grave and told him he would be back before dawn for the service.

He knew his friend would not want a church funeral or even a preacher to attend the service. He never had much use for such social conventions. Instead, he told Tumas about the service and asked him to invite anyone at the brothel who wished to attend.

He stood at the gravesite a few hours before dawn and waited for the others to arrive before starting the service. It had begun to rain a little, but not enough to delay things.

Most of the girls from the brothel, as well as other staff and even a few customers, attended the burial. Octavius thanked everyone for coming then opened it up to the others to talk. A few of the girls told sweet stories about how Augie had helped them over the years. Tumas added a story of his own. Then it was left to Octavius to say the final words.

"Augie was my oldest and best friend. He was a brother to me and a protector. There was nothing that he would not do for my mother or for me or anyone else who asked. He was a devoted man. And a kind man, unless you hurt someone he cared about. Then he became a devastating force. I hope someday, I can match his devotion and his devastation; that I can learn to impose my force on those who deserve it. I am a better man because of his influence, and I will continue to grow from that influence. We will miss you Augustus. I will miss you Augie."

Octavius picked up a shovel and started throwing dirt into the hole. Tumas grabbed another shovel and helped. Some of the girls threw flowers, ribbons, and other keepsakes into the grave as it began to fill with dirt.

Once the service was over everyone started to walk away. Octavius asked Tumas if he could meet him at their favorite breakfast restaurant the next morning, then he started the walk to his apartment. As he got a few yards from the gravesite he saw his mother standing at the edge of the cemetery wearing a black dress and holding an umbrella. It had started to rain harder now, and he had to get close to her before they could talk. She stared at him with dry eyes and pursed lips.

"It was a nice ceremony. He would have liked that it was short and simple." Her voice grated in his head and he did his best to keep a blank face. "I guess I should pay for the burial since you no doubt feel I am responsible for all of this."

"It has been taken care of, Mother. He has no need of you any longer and neither do I."

"You have become an ungrateful little bastard haven't you?"

For some reason her snideness made him smile. Lashing out in anger meant that her guilt was betraying her. "I am leaving for Europe tomorrow, Mother. So you will have one less ungrateful bastard to worry about."

"It's about time you stopped suckling at my breast. Don't you come crawling back to me looking for a hot meal when life bites you in the ass. The milk has all dried up for you, boy."

"Goodbye, Mother." He walked past her still wearing a blank expression. He felt the weight lift from him the further he got from her. He was free now.

The next morning he met with Tumas for breakfast. He felt sorry for leaving the kitchen without a trained assistant but there was no way he could ever work at the brothel again.

Tumas, on the other hand, was ecstatic about the news. He had been waiting for the day that Octavius was ready to move on to bigger opportunities. The old chef handed him a note and told him that he should go to Paris and search out his old protégé Henri-Paul Pellaprat at the Gilded House. Once there, he should hand the note to Henri, who would know what to do.

He also handed him a wooden box. Octavius opened it to reveal a beautiful eight inch chef's knife. It had a lightly stained wooden handle with pins made of metal. The blade was lightly polished to a brushed finished. He looked at the maker's mark which read Zwilling J.A. Henckels. Even though it was not ornate, it was still the finest blade he had ever seen. The balance was magnificent, and it fit perfectly in his hand. It instantly became his most precious blade.

The two men hugged goodbye, and Octavius returned to his apartment to pack his suitcase, satchel, and knife roll. He headed to the train station and booked a third-class ticket to New York City.

His possessions were meager, but he did have some money thanks to his savings and Augie's final payment. It wouldn't buy much, but it would get him to Paris.

The Publisher and the Chef

"Writing is turning life's worst moments into money."

– **J.P. Donleavy**

Thaddeus Harper took off his glasses and rubbed his eyes. He had been staring at his ledger for an hour now trying to make sense of the numbers. Even though it was only April, the year 1888 had not started out well for the man.

He knew he was in debt; everyone knew he was in debt. He just didn't realize how drastic the situation was until tonight.

He pulled a bottle of whiskey from his desk drawer and poured himself a quarter of a glass. Stiff drinks had helped get him into this mess, and his Irish mind told him that a few more stiff drinks might help him think of a way out of the deep hole he was sinking in.

He had taken over as the publisher of the *East London Observer* nearly a year ago after the death of his father-in-law. Johan was a stalwart in the newspaper industry and a first rate business man. Thaddeus, on the other hand, was a decent journalist, good storyteller, and great print operator, but he knew nothing about running a business. He had only been promoted to managing editor by virtue of marriage, a position he held for only six months before Johan passed.

Throughout that period Thaddeus split his time between chasing political stories and running the company's steam powered rotary printing press. He had not spent much time learning to deal with payrolls, vendors, advertisers, and even less time learning to balance the damn ledger.

Now he was left with a mountain of bills, angry vendors, dwindling circulation, and a long list of disgruntled advertisers. It was a miracle that he continued to somehow squeeze three editions out every Sunday, Wednesday, and Friday; for the time being at least.

He closed the ledger and gulped down the drink while

looking out the window of his upstairs office. The sun was starting to set on a long Sunday, and he would be missed at home soon. He wasn't looking forward to facing his lovely wife. Sarah was well meaning, but each innocent question just reminded him of his failure and inevitable doom.

He poured himself another drink, a half glass this time. Maybe, the larger helping would produce better results. He swallowed it and left the office to check on the typesetting room before heading home.

Octavius finished sharpening his prized eight inch chef's knife and slipped it into its pouch with the other finely tuned cutlery. He closed up the knife roll and tied the string tight.

He looked in the mirror one last time checking the fit of his white chef's coat. Satisfied that he looked the part, he headed out the door to start the mile long walk to the Langham Hotel.

He was surprised to feel a twinge of excitement, or maybe it was nerves. Either way, any hint of an emotion was a surprise to the young man who was not accustomed to such feelings. This was his first day at his new job, and his first time working as a head chef.

The upscale hotel had recently decided to open a small bistro to accompany it's more traditional main dining room, and he had been picked for the job. It was to be a small restaurant with only a bar and seven tables, but it was still a tremendous opportunity for such a young chef who only had a couple years of professional training and no experience running his own kitchen.

Octavius had spent the past two years in Paris working at the Maison Dore'e, also known as the Gilded House by the English speaking patrons. It was the nicest restaurant in all of France and possibly all of Europe. While there he worked under the tutelage of Henri-Paul Pellaprat, a man whose passion for cooking was only matched by his desire to teach others the art of cuisine.

Octavius had only gotten a coveted position at the restaurant after handing him a letter from Tumas. Henri read the letter and immediately told him to pick up his knives and get to the kitchen. He had a rough start to the job, as others in the kitchen were disgusted by his lack of experience and openly showed disdain for the unrefined "American."

Sous Chef Marthe Distel was especially bitter about his lack in knowledge of even basic cooking techniques and could not imagine why Henri would hire a man who could not properly make even one of the five mother sauces.

It wasn't until Octavius began breaking down protein that she saw a glimmer of raw talent in the young man. He had a very impressive collection of chef's knives, and he could wield the blades with speed and precision. He did not know the correct techniques for separating hens, dissecting slabs of beef, or slicing lamb quarters. However, he only needed to be shown once before becoming surprisingly proficient.

After the first month, the young man could out knife any cook in the kitchen. Even Henri couldn't match his speed and precision. Octavius' meticulous nature also helped him to quickly master the basics of the mother sauces and gain a general knowledge of advanced cooking techniques.

Marthe was always amazed by the young man's vault-like memory regarding ingredients and recipes. What he lacked in intuition and imagination, he made up for with perfect execution.

Henri would laugh every time Octavius became frustrated by the head chef's constant changing of recipes and cooking times. "You have to let the ingredients speak to you. You cook with all head and no heart."

Octavius would just shake his head and make a note of the adjustments to the recipe in his mental vault – use Roma tomatoes instead of Beefsteak tomatoes when in season.

After working at the Gilded House for only six months, Octavius was promoted to sous chef after Marthe was hired as the head chef at La Tour d'Argent, another famous Paris restaurant.

The kitchen staff was resistant to his leadership at first, but his diligence eventually won them over and he excelled in his new role. As Henri put it, "Octavius runs the most efficient, clean, and professional line I have ever seen. If I could get him to open up his heart, he could one day become the best chef in all of Europe."

Octavius continued to learn and grow as a chef, and Henri put increasing pressure on him to excel. He pushed him to create new dishes and develop his own flavor palate. Every day became a new experience for the young man.

Working on the line and even leading as sous chef were comfortable roles. He had always had an independent mind, but he had spent too many years pressed under his mother's control.

She had driven nearly every decision he made as boy and young man. Becoming a barber was by her direction. Becoming a cook was done at her instruction. Even leaving America to come to Europe had been driven by her, or at least his need to get away from her.

His new role as a sous chef had opened his eyes to a world of possibilities. There were days and sometimes weeks where he was fully in charge of the kitchen while Henri was away on business. During these times, he was encouraged to change the menu, try out new recipes, and even hire new staff members.

This new freedom was intoxicating for Octavius, and he decided to embrace it. He never had much use for sleeping and would stay at the restaurant after it closed working on dishes. He had access to the finest meats and seasonal vegetables. He personally tended to the herbs in a small garden in the courtyard. He learned to make an assortment of cheeses and worked at creating his own sauces.

Just after his second year at the Gilded House, Henri asked Octavius to accompany him on a trip to London to consult with a friend who was thinking of starting a new restaurant. This was the first time that both Henri and Octavius had been away from the kitchen at the same time. Even though they would only be gone during the slower weekdays, the trip would still keep them out for at least three days.

During the day-long journey to London, Henri outlined all the best restaurants and described which parts of the city to visit and which parts to avoid. He made it obvious that he wanted Octavius not to only listen to his stories but to also take notes. It was clear after a few short hours that there was more to this visit than a simple consultation.

Upon arrival in London, the men wasted no time in heading to the Langham Hotel. While there they met with Gustavo, the managing owner of the hotel. They had lunch in the hotel's main restaurant, where Gustavo described his plan to open a bistro at the hotel.

Gustavo immediately dove into a rant about the overabundance of fancy hotel restaurants throughout the city, how costly these monstrous restaurants were to run, and how none of them were able to gain the profits they needed at the bar.

His plan was to add a bistro to compliment the hotel's main restaurant. The bistro would be a place where traveling businessmen would be far more interested in eating a good meal and spending money at the bar. Nothing too fancy, but upscale enough to filter out the ruffians and justify higher prices.

Octavius was not very familiar with bistros. Marthe had once described them as obnoxious, boutique eateries designed around only one or two dishes. That description appealed to Octavius' meticulous nature. A restaurant with a simple menu and controllable line would be just fine by him.

Once the men finished lunch, they headed to the back of the hotel where a nice wooden sign hung above a stairway leading downstairs. The sign read "Café Langham" in large red letters with an arrow pointing down the stairs.

At the bottom of the stairway sat a small but nicely appointed eatery. It featured a medium-size kitchen with an ornate stove and all the conveniences you would expect from a much larger establishment. The dining area was narrow but open with a long wooden bar along the left side with seating for ten. Seven rectangular tables that could each comfortably sit four lined the right side. There was also a second entrance at the far end of the bistro that led out to the side street.

Octavius could immediately visualize the café full of people. A bustling bar, full tables, two bartenders, one server, and a kitchen staff of three running at full speed. The image was spinning like a Swiss watch in his mind as he continued to look around the room.

Henri knew exactly what was going through the young man's mind and asked him the defining question… "So what are you serving?"

"Cassoulet," The word was immediate and almost subliminal. The traditional French dish was perfect for a fancy new bistro. A rich, slow cooked medley of meats, pork sausage, duck confit, mutton, or whatever was easily available and fresh. Add in some white beans and seasonal vegetables and cook it all in large pots. The smell would permeate through the hotel and draw in people looking for a hearty meal and a stiff drink.

The dish would need to be simplified for the unrefined tastes of London, but that would be simple enough. Reduce the richness of the sauce. Replace the duck confit with simple roasted duck or even chicken. Mix in some duck fat to replicate the taste. Add in carrots and other more familiar vegetables.

"Yes, an English-style cassoulet stew." He said again with more confidence. "Cooked in metal pots instead of clay. It could be served in clay pots with French bread to make it feel more authentic. Marthe would hate it because it goes against French tradition, but it would be haute cuisine in London."

Gustavo's eyes lit up. "That's it! That's it! I will purchase the necessary pots. Along with sturdy clay bowls with large spoons." He took out pencil and paper and started writing and mumbling to himself. "What do you think? Five staff members, maybe six? Oh who cares, I will hire seven and you can fire the ones you don't want. What about the stoves? We may need to modify the burners for the pots, I'll get Packo on that…"

He continued asking and answering his own questions as Octavius shot Henri a confused look. "It looks like he has found his new chef for Café Langham."

Gustavo didn't even look up as he waved at the two men. "I'll need you back here in three weeks Octavius. I will have everything ready. That will give you a few days to train the staff, buy the ingredients, and be ready to open the first week in April."

Thaddeus walked into the typesetting room at the *East End Observer* and looked over the table to see that everything was being prepared for the next run. He hung his head as he saw that the print rollers were already being setup for another blasted catalog.

"Don't knock it, boss," came a familiar voice from behind him. He turned to see Walter sitting at the typesetting table wearing his thick glasses as a he leaned in to look at the line he had just punched out. "These ugly catalogs are what pay the bills around here. We could add a couple more paying jobs if you ever decide to let go of that silly old newspaper."

Walter looked up and smiled. He knew that wasn't about to happen anytime soon if Thaddeus had anything to say about it. The old technician stood up, hiked his pants around his skinny frame, and walked the lines of text over to one of the rollers.

"I know, Walter. And it just might come to that if I can't find a way to turn things around soon."

"We could always go to a weekly. There is no shame in that."

"There is plenty of shame in that, Walter. We already went from a daily to three times a week. Weeklies aren't even seen as real newspapers. We can barely keep advertisers on the hook now, if we go to a weekly, we might as well start putting nails in the coffin."

Walter just nodded his head in agreement and continued his work.

"How long will it take to finish the run on this dry goods catalog?"

"It is a big run, so it won't be finished until Tuesday afternoon at this point. That is unless we run into problems, which you know is bound to happen."

Thaddeus turned sharply. "That is going to make things tight for the next edition."

"Settle down, boss. We will make the Wednesday afternoon deadline. We always do. I will have the rollers typeset and ready that morning. I can get the presses fitted in a couple hours, and we can start the engines by noon."

"I should have never let you talk me into adding such a large catalog run before the Wednesday paper." Thaddeus stomped out of the room and headed upstairs to his office.

He knew Walter was right. They had no choice but to take on as many catalogs and outside printing jobs as they could fit into the schedule. He could not let his love for the newspaper cloud his decisions about what was right for the future of the company. He would hang on as long as possible, but he just might need to let the paper go if things didn't turn around soon.

It was a crisp, cool Sunday morning as Octavius looked up at the towering building. When the Langham Hotel was first built in 1865, it was the first Grand Hotel in all of Europe. Eighteen years later, it was still an impressive hotel, standing ten stories high with over four hundred rooms and a grand ballroom. It featured all the conveniences of a modern high-end hotel including hydraulic lifts, water closets, and a world-renowned lobby.

He still could not believe that he was going to be running a restaurant in such an impressive establishment, even if it was only a small bistro.

He pulled on the edges of his chef coat, tucked his knife roll under his arm, and headed for the main entrance. He nodded at the bellhop who was running to meet an approaching carriage and walked through the large entranceway.

It took him a moment to get his bearings in the ornate lobby, but he soon figured out where he needed to go. He started heading toward the back of the hotel when he spotted Gustavo hustling his way.

"Well, there he is. And don't you look just the part," Gustavo said with a smile.

"Good morning, sir."

"Come on boy, or I guess I should say chef. Let me show you to the new Café Langham."

As they walked, Gustavo spoke quickly rattling off a few of the things that had been done. Octavius couldn't catch all that was said. "Didn't have much time… Hired some staff… Don't care… Fire them if you want… Pulled a maître d' from the main restaurant… Release him if you want… He is a bit stuffy…. Used décor is from the main restaurant… Trash it if you want… Same thing with the uniforms."

Reaching the staircase Gustavo turned to look at Octavius. "Look, Henri said you are the man for this job. I trust Henri, so I trust you. This is your bistro now, run it as you see fit. But if it doesn't turn a profit by the end of June, I will send your sorry ass back to Henri."

He let out a toothy grin and slapped the young chef in the back. "Come on let's see what you have to work with."

At the bottom of the stairwell Octavius could already see that changes had been made. The tables were covered with white linen table clothes and glass candle centerpieces were placed in the middle with bright flowers. A female server stood in the back wearing a formal white blouse and long black skirt. The man behind the bar also wore a server uniform. Octavius recognized these uniforms from the main hotel restaurant. In fact the whole bistro had been turned into a mini version of the upstairs restaurant.

An older man wearing a very formal suit stepped out from behind the bar and straightened his jacket. He held his head high and waited for instructions.

Octavius' face scrunched up like he smelled a rotten egg. He looked back at Gustavo who just smiled at him and waved his hand as he headed back to the stairs. "I know. But it's your problem now."

Before speaking, Octavius turned into the kitchen. He was

much happier with this area. The stove had been fitted to hold four large pots along with a decent size griddle. Six large metal pots and two frying pans hung from hooks on the ceiling along with a row of spoons and ladles. Everything was cleaned and polished. There were two large prep tables in the middle and a storage area in the back with some shelving and a row of water pails and baskets. In the corner sat a grinding wheel and leather strop for sharpening and honing knives.

Two young line cooks stood in the back polishing on more large pots. He nodded at them as they stood up sharply and greeted him, "Good day, chef."

He returned to the dining area and walked up to the maître d'. "Good day, sir."

"Please, refer to me as chef."

"Good day, chef. My name is Jean Paul. Excuse the mess. We have just started setting up the café. I took the liberty of setting the tables and centerpieces. I hope they meet your satisfaction."

"They do not." The young chef walked past him and looked at the bar. A sparse amount of liquor bottles lined the shelves. Everything was top shelf. Fancy vases and bobbles were situated between the bottles of booze. It was an elegant design that clashed a bit with the bar's wooden features.

He looked to the lone bartender. "Take down all those fancy decorations. Replace them with more bottles. Add in some more variety. Nothing rot-gut, but something in the middling range. Every open spot should hold a bottle. And tomorrow come in wearing traditional bartender attire. You know, slacks, vest, white shirt. Just something less formal."

He turned to the waitress who was standing in the corner with her head bowed. "Madam, would you please remove those linens and centerpieces and put away all that fancy cutlery. We won't be needing it. And tomorrow can you wear a black skirt with a red blouse, something that matches the red in our sign. Just stop by a store tomorrow morning and pick up a few pair of each. Bring me the bill and I will take care of it."

"But, sir, I mean chef, this is the Langham. We have a standard to uphold." Jean Paul looked shocked.

"Thank you, Jean Paul. Your services are no longer needed here. I am sure you have been missed upstairs. Give my regards to Chef Simon."

The old maître d' stiffened his neck and whispered something about a petulant young man as he pushed his way to the staircase.

Octavius felt a twinge in his stomach as the man left. He could only hope that he was making the right decisions. The smiles on the bartender and waitress' faces gave him all the reassurance he needed that he was on the right track.

It was early Monday as three reporters gathered around a table typing out stories while Walter measured out potential headlines for the stories that were finished.

Thaddeus entered the room and hung his bowler hat and coat on a hook. He grabbed a piece of chalk and turned to the story board. "So men, what do we have?"

"Not much from Scotland Yard," said Sam, a gray haired man and the oldest of the group at nearly sixty. "Just an update on the Calvin murder. That rich lady in the fancy mansion. They are circling in on the husband, but nothing damning yet. He doesn't have much of an alibi, so I'm sure he will be arrested soon."

"That isn't going to cut it for much longer. This is London my good man, there has to be more crime than that on the streets. How about you Frank? What's new on the political side?"

Frank, a tall fit man in his early 30's was chomping at the bit. "Well everything, sir. The general election continues. We are a couple weeks out, but it is looking more and more like the Liberals might finally unseat the Conservatives. The Marquess of Harington is already making speeches like he has been sworn in as the next Prime Minister."

"Where is Prime Minister Disreali in all this?"

"Silent as usual. Rumors of his failing health continue to

spread throughout the city. Even if the Liberals were to win the election, I doubt that he would stay for another term."

"So we have stories from the Liberal and Conservative sides?"

"Yes, we have both covered. Plus, Peter has one on Disreali's health and another one on the proposed new Bill of Rights."

Peter was Frank's younger and skinnier brother. He nodded his head and continued to type.

"That should work. Not very exciting, but at least it's real news."

"Well then O'Conner, it's up to you. What does the city beat have to offer?"

"I've got a story on the ringer prostitutes," bellowed O'Conner, a short stocky man wearing a scruffy beard. "They are making noise that more independent girls are leaving the brothels and are starting to overrun the streets and driving down earnings. They say the registration fees are too high for respectable girls to make a living."

"Leave it to O'Conner to find a prostitution story." Frank chimed in while doing ballerina twirl. The other men joined in on the laughter.

"Okay, okay. You've had your fun. But sex sells, gentlemen, and everyone loves a good story about disgruntled whores."

"Agreed," said Thaddeus as he updated his story board. "Punch up the prostitution story. See if you can get a quote from a house madam or possibly a politician. We'll stick that above the fold."

"Get everything to Walter by noon tomorrow and he'll get started on the typesetting. I'm headed out to collect a couple checks and wrestle up more advertisers. Walter, I'll see you tomorrow afternoon to help finalize the headlines."

Marcus was a fit twenty year old but even he was struggling to keep up with Octavius as they wound their way through

London's largest meat market. Even for a Monday, the market was crowded.

It was Marcus' second day as sous chef, and he wasn't sure he was cut out for the new title. He had been given the position simply because he was a year older than Stephane. It didn't help that the young man was carrying a metal pail in each hand filled with assorted packages of meats and fats.

For his part, Octavius was carrying a large basket filled to overflowing with a mix of vegetables and spices. "That should be enough for today. Remember where we got that duck fat and the fresh basil. Those were the only two vendors that had those vital ingredients."

Marcus nodded as he dropped the buckets and wiped the sweat from his brow.

"Let's get back to the Langham and see if Stephane had any luck finding good beans outside the city."

The two men walked the mile and a half back to the hotel. As they reached the back entrance to the bistro they saw Stephane unloading sacks of dried white beans from the cart.

Octavius walked up to an open bag and grabbed a handful of beans. Looking them over, he smiled. "These will do nicely. Let's get them into the kitchen, then we will see if either of you knows how to boil water."

A few hours later the aroma of cassoulet wafted throughout the small eatery. Octavius stood watch over two quarter-full pots adding a variety of seasonings into each at random intervals. Each pinch of herbs was accompanied by a notation in his notebook.

The young helpers sat back on the sacks of beans, exhausted from the day's work. They had been impressed by the head chef's amazing knife skills and overwhelmed by his extensive culinary knowledge. Neither man had considered a career as a cook before, but they knew they would never get a chance to learn under such a talent again.

"Okay, boys. Watch the pots. They should stay at a slow bubble for a while longer. And don't add anything else!" Octavius wiped his hands with a towel, straitened his jacket, and headed out to the dining area.

Natasha was a pretty girl in her late twenties with light blond hair and pleasant demeanor. She was very different than Octavius' mother, which provided him comfort for some reason. She was not intimidating or authoritarian, and she always stood tall when he entered the room and greeted him as chef. He found this fascinating, but not in a sexual way. He found it more empowering than anything else.

She was currently on her knees scrubbing the floor with a sponge. She stood up as Octavius walked into the room, gave him a curtsy, and said "Greetings, chef."

"You must stop doing that, Natasha. This is not a formal restaurant, and it will make the patrons uncomfortable. For that matter, it makes me uncomfortable."

Natasha nodded and went back to scrubbing the floor.

"I apologize for the mess. I will tell the boys to be more tidy with their boots and packages next time they do a shopping run."

"No problem, chef," she replied. "This floor is easy enough to clean."

Octavius turned his attention to the two bartenders, both of whom were in their early thirties.

Victor was a serious looking chap. A lot of that came from his handlebar mustache, slicked back hair, and svelte black vest. Still he was approachable enough and had good knowledge of fine cocktails and quality liquor. Victor had introduced Octavius to Tom after Jean Paul was let go.

Tom was a happy man and natural bartender, who counteracted Victor's seriousness. He smiled a lot, sometimes for no apparent reason, and he always had a story to tell. What he lacked in barista skills he made up for in being able to keep people jolly and drinking.

"Victor, I am appointing you maître d'," Octavius said as he handed him a pin in the shape of an "L" signifying the position.

Victor looked shocked at first, then concerned.

"Don't worry, you can still stand behind the bar. I just need someone to watch over things out here while I'm working the kitchen. I can't leave those two boys alone back there for long without worrying about the hotel burning down."

"I appreciate the title, chef, but I don't even know what a maître d' does."

"You are already filling the role as far as I'm concerned. Just make sure the place stays clean, that people show up on time, and order extra booze and equipment when it's needed. Otherwise, come and get me when something goes wrong that you can't handle. Plus, it pays an extra three pounds a week."

Seeing his hesitation, Tom jumped in. "Hell, if he doesn't want the job, I'll take it."

"Shut up, Tom and clean those glasses," barked Victor as he slipped on the pin. "Sounds good to me, chef. Dealing with Tom every day probably does warrant another three pounds."

Octavius smiled and turned toward the kitchen. "Alright then, grab a bottle of that wine and let's all head to the kitchen and see which one of these recipes we want to serve as our signature dish."

Two hours later and the matter was settled. The entire staff was sitting back nursing full bellies.

"That might be the best thing I've ever eaten," belched Tom as he rubbed his belly.

"There is no might about it. That is the best thing I've ever tasted," agreed Natasha.

Octavius looked around the room to nods of agreement. "So it's settled then? This is the one. The official Café Langham cassoulet."

"Now go home and get some rest. Be back here tomorrow morning at eight. We are hosting a soft opening for the main restaurant kitchen staff at noon. Trust me, they will not be easy to please."

Through the window, Thaddeus could see that Walter's brow was scrunched up into a torrent of wrinkles. He knew that look.

It was the look of an old man trying to find exciting headlines for mundane stories.

"Is it really that bad?" He said as he entered the typesetting room.

"Well they're not all bad, but how do you write a gripping headline about the third update to a murder that happened a week ago."

"Let me try a couple. How many characters?"

"Less than forty."

"'Killer Thwarts Police for Second Week' or 'Socialite's Murderer Still at Large' or how about this, 'Boring Story Wastes More Expensive Ink.'"

"Funny, but I think I will go with the second one."

Thaddeus read through the stories on the rollers. It took talent to read type that had been set on rollers. All the letters were backwards, upside down, and the lines curved around. For the experienced publisher, he was accustomed to reading stories this way. It felt like the natural way to edit. He pointed out a couple mistakes before slumping back in a chair.

"We are printing lipstick on pig stories, Walter. Where are the good articles? We haven't had a proper scandal in weeks. This election drama has sucked all the life out of the city."

"Don't worry, sir, something horrible is bound to happen soon."

"Well, it better, Walter, or we are going to be adding a couple more of your ugly catalogs to the print run next month. Let's get out of here and finish this thing in the morning."

"Right, sir, I'll lock up behind you."

By Tuesday at noon, the staff at the Café Langham were running at full steam. Four pots of cassoulet were bubbling on the stove, and fresh bread was being baked in the oven.

The tables were set with slightly oversized spoons wrapped in simple black linen napkins. The bartenders were busy preparing a unique cocktail that Victor had selected to accompany the upcoming meal.

Octavius walked back and forth from the kitchen to the dining room checking over every detail. The staff was surprised by how calm he was. He was being thorough, but there was no sign of nerves. No sweating, no fussing with things, and no biting comments. In fact, he was in a rather pleasant mood.

At two o'clock in the afternoon footsteps could be heard on the stairwell and everyone took their places. Gustavo was the first to appear followed by Chef Simon. "Octavius, you can smell all the wonderful food from the top of the stairs. I can't wait to see what you have for us today."

"Chef Simon, thank you for taking the time to visit us," said Octavius. "Henri speaks so fondly of you."

"The pleasure is mine, chef. Is that cassoulet I smell?"

"Yes, chef. I took a lot of liberties, but it is still a cassoulet at heart."

"What a bold choice for a bistro. The smell alone should fill Gustavo's pockets. I wish I could cook such vibrant dishes in the main hall, but I'm afraid it would overpower all the expensive foie gras and filet mignons that make Gustavo so rich."

"Gentlemen, please have a seat and let me get you a drink."

He headed to Victor who poured out two drinks from a mixer. He took them to the table and watched as the men tasted the brown liquid.

"Good heavens, what is this? It is wondrous!" Exclaimed Gustavo.

Octavius waved at Victor. "Gentlemen, it is an American drink called a Manhattan. It is made with rye whiskey, sweet vermouth, a dash of bitters, and topped with a cherry."

"After you have a good run of things Octavius, I will have to send my bar manager down to learn how to make one of these." Chef Simon took another strong pull and motioned for a second drink.

As the men worked on their cocktails, Natasha appeared from the kitchen holding a tray of food. She presented the men with two large clay bowls filled with steaming cassoulet. She then placed plates containing small loaves of crusty bread next to each bowl.

Chef Simon politely examined the dish dissecting the ingredients as a show of respect. He was looking over a nice piece of pork shoulder when Gustavo interrupted his train of thought. "By corker! This soup is wonderful. You've got to try this."

Chef Simon resisted the urge to correct him about the dish not being a soup and sipped a bit of the broth. Finding it to his liking, he pulled a proper spoonful filled with a mix of meats, fats, and vegetables. He ate it slowly without expression. He then sat the spoon down and wiped his mouth with the napkin.

He turned his attention to Natasha. "Ma'am, could you do me a favor. At the top of the stairs should be a group of fifteen members of my kitchen staff. Could you please ask them to come down here? I want them to experience this meal, so they know why they are all getting fired for being inadequate cooks."

A broad smile appeared on his face. "Chef Octavius, you have truly outdone yourself. I am going to have a hard time keeping people in my restaurant after they try your food. This is really something special."

Gustavo clapped his hands together and let out a loud laugh. "Good man. I think we are going to make a lot of money with this place. Let's feed some people now."

The rest of the kitchen staff poured into the bistro and Octavius helped Natasha serve up steaming bowls and plates of bread. The bartenders rattled out one drink after another. More hotel staff were invited into the restaurant throughout the afternoon and evening, and everyone agreed that the Café Langham was a huge hit.

It wasn't until after midnight before Octavius was ready to leave the hotel. He was too excited to sleep, so he took off his chef's jacket and headed out for a walk.

He walked airlessly throughout the city for about a half an hour going over the events of the day. By all accounts, it was a perfect beginning to his new life as a head chef. It had been weeks since he had thought about his mother or the life he had left behind in Seattle. He had found a new home in London, and he had no intention of ever returning to America. This was his home now.

Walter had just finished typesetting the last story when Thaddeus entered the room. It was ten o'clock Wednesday morning and they were running about an hour ahead of schedule. With any luck they would have the newspaper printing before noon and ready for distribution by four, just in time for the first work shifts to be released in the city.

"Everything looking good, Walter?" Thaddeus hung up his hat and coat and started looking over the stories on the rollers.

"I was just getting ready to start carrying the rollers to the printer. Did you want to take a second look at everything? We have a little time."

"No, that's fine. Not much has changed from yesterday. Just let me check the headlines and we can get this thing ready to go."

Frank entered the room wearing his overalls and carrying a pipe wrench. "Well, I think I've fixed that leaking steam pipe. We should be able to turn up the speed for the next run."

"Thanks, Frank," said Walter with a smile. "I think we are about ready to start fitting the rollers."

Just then O'Conner came barreling through the doorway. He crashed into one of the tables, nearly knocking over two of the rollers.

"Careful, man! We don't have time to reset an entire drum this morning!" Yelled Walter.

"Sorry, sorry," wheezed O'Conner. "We've got a late story. Is there time to fit in something new above the fold?"

Thaddeus' eyes widened as he helped O'Conner to a seat. It was clear the man had been running for a while.

"There has been a murder in the Whitechapel District. A prostitute named Emma Smith. She was attacked by thugs last night. She died first thing this morning in the hospital."

Thaddeus looked at Walter, then at the clock, then back to Walter.

"We can do it," said the typesetter. "We will need to write it to fit where the current prostitution story is set, but I think we can get it done in an hour or so."

Thaddeus handed a pencil and paper to O'Conner and instructed him to start writing. He told Frank he would help him start fitting the other rollers on the printer so they could have it ready to go by noon as planned.

"We are going to need to pull another roll of paper. I want to double the circulation. We are the only paper in town with a Wednesday afternoon delivery, so this is our chance to scoop all the big guys."

Everyone jumped into action, and the new story started to appear on the typesetter. By noon the last of the headline was ready for placement.

TRAGEDY IN OLD WHITECHAPEL DISTRICT
PROSTITUTE ROBBED, BEATEN, MURDERED

Octavius arrived at the hotel at nine in the morning still buzzing from the success of the bistro's soft opening. He was surprised to see both cooks already working in the kitchen. Marcus had tears running down his cheeks from working on a batch of onions. Stephane was on the meat table cutting the excess fat off a large hunk of pork shoulder.

Grabbing a towel, the chef pulled three trays of cooked bread out of the oven and inserted three trays filled with dough. He then loaded the cooked loaves onto a cooling rack.

Before leaving the kitchen, he tore off a piece of dry bread and stuck it in Marcus' mouth. "Don't chew on it. Just let it sit in your mouth. It will keep you from crying like a baby."

He headed to the bar where Victor was setting out clean

glasses. "Good morning, chef. Everyone is still talking about yesterday."

"That was a captive audience, Victor. Now we have to prove our worth to the masses. People may not be so inclined to order an expensive bowl of stew or one of your fancy Manhattans when they have never heard of such things."

Tom came in through the back door carrying two boxes of whiskey followed by Natasha. "Am I late?" asked the waitress.

"Not at all. Everyone else just came in early out of excitement. You are still a half hour early," Victor said while grabbing one of the boxes from Tom.

"Natasha, why don't you look around for a nice wooden crate or a basket. We can pre-wrap the spoons in the napkins to get a head start. I don't know how many customers we are going to get today, but we should be ready just in case." Octavius looked around the restaurant to make sure it was clean and ready.

"Alright everyone, we have about two hours before we should start seeing our first guests."

At ten forty-five a couple of businessmen came down the stairs asking if the dining room was open. Natasha showed the men to the bar and Victor poured them a couple of whiskeys. A few minutes later another group of four came down the stairs. By eleven thirty all the tables and half the bar was full.

"Marcus, it looks like it is going to be a four pot day. Two pots for serving and two for cooking. No pot is to be served until I have tasted it. Keep the rotations going until I tell you to reduce down to two pots." Marcus acknowledged the order and started pouring water into another large metal pot.

"Stephane, get another pot off the wall and fill it half full with beans, then pour in enough water to cover them. That will reduce our cooking times in case we get another rush. When you are done with that, get back to chopping vegetables."

Octavius tasted the food in both pots and deemed them ready to serve. He started filling bowls and placing them on a serving tray along with chunks of bread. He brought the tray out to the dining room and handed it to Natasha. "Serve these, and I will have another tray ready for you when you are done."

The bistro stayed full for the rest of the day and into the night. Word had quickly spread about the new hotel restaurant and its tasty "soup." It wasn't until after seven that Octavius reduced the stove to two pots. At nine he stopped adding new batches, and by ten they started ushering people out of the café.

The chef was fairly satisfied with how the opening day turned out. He needed to tighten up things in the kitchen a bit, and it was clear that they were going to need another waitress. Natasha was overrun with orders within the first hour. Tom spent more than half his time cleaning tables and helping with the washing. The bar had also gotten overwhelmed at times, but that would be solved by keeping Tom at his post.

Octavius decided that these were all good problems to have as he felt the heft of the moneybag. He carried it up to Gustavo's office where the gregarious owner was sitting behind his desk.

"My good man, what a wonderful haul for your first day. If we can keep up even half this pace, I would call it a rousing success."

A smile broke across Thaddeus' face; probably the first one to ever appear while sitting in his office looking at his ledger. The ledger was even, down to the last penny it was even. Not making a profit, but at least they were finally out of debt.

It had been a historic week for the *East End Observer*. When the newspaper hit the street Wednesday, the *Observer* was the only paper in London to report on the grisly murder in Whitechapel that day. The larger papers didn't come out until Thursday morning, and by then the news was all over the city. Thaddeus had ordered a double printing in anticipation of selling more copies, and they sold out in two hours. They even had time left in the day to fire the presses back up and print an extra run of five thousand copies.

They got a second break for the Friday edition when

O'Conner caught the lead inspector on the case having lunch at some new hotel restaurant. Inspector Edmund Reid granted O'Conner a full interview and all it cost was a couple drinks and a bowl of soup.

Thaddeus took a risk with the Friday paper and printed a triple run of fifteen thousand copies. The paper expense alone ate up half the profits from the Wednesday edition, but the gamble paid off. Every copy sold out, and the interview cemented the *Observer* as the leading source for news on the investigation.

By the time the Sunday edition was ready, O'Conner had uncovered more details on the investigation while Frank talked to politicians about the murder. Normally, politicians wouldn't care much about one murdered prostitute, but the story was taking headlines away from the election. They became desperate to attach their names to anything that was getting press. The *Observer* added four pages to fit the extra copy and new advertisers who had jumped on board for the Sunday edition. Thaddeus pushed the print run to eighteen thousand copies, which was the largest run they had ever pushed out of the steam powered press.

Emma Smith's murder continued to enthrall the public, who were tired of reading stories about stuffy politicians, election woes, and squabbles within the royal family.

The forty-five year old widow was an independent prostitute that worked Brick Lane in the Whitechapel District. At around twelve fifteen on Tuesday, April 3rd, Miss Smith was seen accompanying a man in dark clothes and a white neckerchief into a dark alley on Burdett Road. This area was known for its rough clientele, but it was one of the only areas where independents could find regular customers.

It is estimated that Emma Smith stayed in the area sitting in front of Taylor's Cocoa Factory after finishing with a customer. That is when she was attacked by at least two assailants. She made it back to her lodging at 18 George Street, where the lodging house deputy Mary Russell became immediately concerned by her condition. Miss Smith had obviously been beaten. Her face was bleeding and she had a badly cut ear. She was also holding her stomach and was doubled over in pain.

Emma Smith could not describe her attackers, but said that they were all young men. The one she could see clearest was possibly around nineteen years old. The men had beaten her, robbed her of all her money, and ran away quickly.

Mary, and other fellow lodgers Margaret Hayes and Annie Lee, eventually convinced Miss Smith to go with them to the hospital. While at the London Hospital she was seen by house surgeon Doctor George Haslip. He told investigators that Miss Smith had been drinking, but was not drunk and stated that "she knew what she was about."

Doctor Haslip confirmed that her injuries were truly horrific. Her ear had nearly been dislodged and her face was bloody and bruised. He also stated that at one point a blunt instrument had been rammed into her with great force. This act had pierced her peritoneum and ruptured many of her internal organs.

Emma Smith's injuries caused her to slip into a coma shortly after her examination, and she died at nine o'clock the morning of Wednesday, April 4th.

Inspector Edmund Reid, head of the Criminal Investigation Department of the Metropolitan Police's H Division, was assigned to the high-profile case. He spent many days on the case confirming witness accounts and speaking with the doctor and coroner. The investigation continued, but no suspects had been named.

It had been a solid week for Café Langham, and Octavius was ready for a day off. He had worked from eight in the morning until midnight every day until Saturday, when he wasn't able to leave the bistro until after two.

Sundays were the only day that the restaurant would be closed, thank goodness for religion. Octavius was wide awake at seven. He had never been comfortable sleeping in and rarely slept for more than four hours at a stretch. On the hardest days, he could usually get by on a couple of catnaps and continue unfazed.

He decided to hit the market that morning and see what new seasonal ingredients he might be able to add to his now infamous cassoulet. He spent most of the day filling a basket with exotic spices and a few new herbs.

He also tried out a restaurant on the edge of the East End that Henri had recommended. The food was only slightly above average, but the experience was pleasant. The chef recognized him immediately upon his arrival and gave glowing reviews on his cassoulet. They spent the afternoon exchanging stories about Henri and his sous chef Marthe "with the giant stick up her rear end."

At the end of the day, he returned to his apartment building. While passing through the small lobby he saw a stack of old newspapers sitting on a table. One of the headlines caught his attention.

TRAGEDY IN OLD WHITECHAPEL DISTRICT
PROSTITUTE ROBBED, BEATEN, MURDERED

He grabbed the paper, along with the two older editions of the *East End Observer* that were lying on the table and headed up to his room.

It had been three months since the murder of Emma Smith, and things had pretty much returned to normal for the *East End Observer*. Thaddeus had wisely reduced the print runs to ten thousand a month after the incident and now they were back to printing five thousand a run.

The extra money had helped get the publisher out of debt. He was also able to use the surplus to make repairs to the overworked old steam press and purchase a second set of rollers.

This allowed them to setup more than one print run at a time and increased their overall capacity for outside jobs.

Still Thaddeus was not satisfied with the progress. He was happy to be making money, of course, but his real dream was for the newspaper to grow in its success and influence. If the newspaper could have continued with the higher circulation and increased advertisements, he would have been able to move it back to a daily.

For now, he would just have to be thankful that the bills were being paid and that he had figured out how to balance the ledger. Maybe his luck would turn and something tragic would ignite another fuse in the city. At least the damn election was over and having the Liberals in power was providing enough fireworks to keep the news cycles churning.

The crowds at the Café Langham had relented a bit, but the profits were still strong enough to keep Gustavo happy. Octavius had changed the recipe of the cassoulet a couple of times to match the fall harvest and added a beef pot-pie to the menu.

The staff at the bistro had noticed a marked change in the head chef's demeanor over the past few weeks. He was always professional, but he was rarely interested in engaging in idle conversation, and he would not provide details about his personal life. He wasn't unpleasant to be around, just rather boring.

For most, boring was just fine. Victor enjoyed the quiet even pace, and Natasha was also happy that things had settled down a bit. Her sister Margaret had joined the staff just after the opening, which had helped. But even with an extra hand to clear tables and wash dishes they were barely able to keep up when things got busy. Now, that things were slower, they were able to take a few short breaks during the day. Natasha had even started to spend a few minutes each day speaking with Victor, who she found to be quite charming.

Marcus and Stephane were learning a lot in the kitchen. It had been a challenge to learn the new dishes, but now they were able to complete most services on their own. The chef still insisted on tasting a lot that went out, but they could tell he was trusting them more every day. Marcus had even considered recommending a few new dishes of his own in the near future.

Tom was the only one who was not entirely happy with his position. He felt like he deserved more money, at least as much as Victor. Tom knew he was not as good a bartender as Victor, but he was much better with the customers and in convincing them to buy more drinks. He just needed to work up the courage to speak with Octavius.

Most days Octavius split his time between the kitchen and sitting at an open table writing in his notebook. Sometimes he would leave after the lunch rush to walk the markets in search of new ingredients. He would always leave on his own, and he never seemed to speak to anyone other than the staff, Gustavo, or the occasional chef that would stop by to say hello.

It was now nine in the evening on a slower than usual Monday, and Octavius was sitting at the table furthest from the staff. He was pretending to write in the notebook as he steadied his trembling hands.

For months now he knew he had not been himself. Something had changed inside him after reading those articles in the newspapers about Emma Smith. Something he did not understand. Something he thought he had left back in Seattle.

Maybe it was that fact that the lady had been murdered in such a brutal manner. Maybe it was that she was a prostitute. Or that she was low-end, independent whore. Or maybe it was that she was nearly the same age as his mother.

He could not shake the images that it conjured or the excitement he felt. He had never been a very sexual man. He hadn't even shared a bed with a women, or even desired such things. Now, he became aroused every time he thought about the event. He kept the papers in his room and read them over and over. He fantasized about being a witness to the event, then about being one of the attackers. He even fantasized about being the doctor that examined the woman and the coroner conducting the autopsy.

These thoughts normally filled his mind after hours when he lay in his bed. But today the images had begun to creep into his daydreams.

Finally, he stood up and tucked his notebook into his pocket. "Victor, I'm not feeling great tonight. Can you make sure the boys clean up the kitchen and lock up for me?"

"Sure, chef. I can do that." Victor looked worried. This was the first time his boss had ever left before the nightly closing. "What should I do with the money pouch?"

"Just take it up to Gustavo after you lock up. He will be waiting in his office." Octavius didn't even look up at Victor as he headed out the door.

For the last few weeks Octavius had been leaving the hotel and walking around the Whitechapel District. He hadn't visited any establishments. No bars or restaurants, and certainly no brothels. He did not talk to anyone. He didn't even make eye contact. He just observed.

He made mental notes of all the prostitutes and watched to see which dark corners were used the most. He made note of the brothels, which he did not find very interesting. They were familiar to him.

He was invigorated and also disgusted by what he saw in the streets. In the dark alleyways. This new environment was foreign to him.

He had spent his childhood and young adult life around ladies of the night. But those circumstances had been structured. There was always a madam or mister in charge of the "house." Everything was contained to a building or at least a room of some sort. Everything was transactional, monitored, and businesslike. There were dangers of course, disagreements and fights, disgruntled customers and upset ladies, but those were dealt with by professionals.

This new scene was something different. It felt chaotic and dirty. The ladies came and went as they pleased. There were no rules. No rules regarding dress or age or decorum. None of the street walkers he saw would even be allowed into his mother's house. They were too filthy, too old, too ugly, or too raw. His mother would not approve of this environment. He did not approve. It disgusted him, but he did not understand why.

He understood that his actions and especially his thoughts were odd and out of character. He couldn't explain to himself why he cared so much about the prostitutes of London. They were not his responsibility. The fact that his mother would not approve of their actions certainly should not have mattered to him. Still he felt compelled to patrol the Whitechapel District every evening.

Octavius had been walking around for at least two hours. He still had his chef's coat on, which made him blend in with the other working class gentlemen that were coming and going on the now dark streets. He continued his surveying of the area. He found himself swaying between spirts of revulsion and excitement.

He turned down the street near the George Yard Arch, which was a particularly ugly part of the district. From his past visits he knew this to be an active area for all sorts of late night activities.

About a block in front of the arch he noticed two couples. Both men in the group were wearing some sort of uniform, and the women were obviously working. All four were clearly drunk.

He took note of the first lady, who was garish in his opinion. She looked particularly masculine and crudely dressed. The other lady was in her late thirties, decently dressed, and far more attractive. This immediately angered him for some reason. He did not understand why she would join company with such a mismatched partner.

After a moment of negotiation, the pairs split off in different directions and headed into dark corners. He decided to follow the attractive prostitute and her male companion as they turned into George Yard. He got as close as he could without being spotted and waited, listening.

He could hear laughing and the rustling of clothes, followed by a slurping sound. Then groans. The sounds made Octavius' vision blur and his stomach lurch. He vomited on a bush near him. He cleaned his mouth on his sleeve and closed his eyes to steady himself. He could feel the sweat beading up on his brow.

About ten minutes later, he saw the uniformed man walk down street in the opposite direction. He waited a few minutes for the girl to appear, but nothing happened. Then he heard her cough a few times. There was more rustling of clothes and more coughing.

Octavius wiped the sweat from his forehead with his sleeve and instinctively tucked his hand into the front pocket of his jacket looking for his towel. That's when he felt them. His eight inch chef's knife and a small paring knife. In his haste to leave the bistro he had forgotten to take them out.

He pulled them both out, gripping the handles tightly. Then an urge started to overtake him. An urge that would not go away.

It was already hot for a Tuesday in August, even at half past noon. In London, the clouds would usually block out the sun until midday. Today, not a cloud could be found, and Thaddeus had to shield his eyes from the bright sun as he looked out the window of his office.

They had wrapped up the assignment meeting about an hour ago. It was looking to be another hum-drum round of stories for the Wednesday edition. The printer was already humming along with another catalog, which would be finished sometime the next morning.

He was about ready to head out for lunch when he caught site of O'Conner running up the street. The man was really in no shape to be running around the city at that speed. Whatever was causing his excitement must be worth the effort.

Thaddeus met the rotund reporter at the door and helped

him to a chair.

"There has been another woman murdered... Whitechapel again... Just down the way from the first one."

"Do we have any details yet?"

"I've got it all, but so does everyone else. It was announced at police headquarters just a few minutes ago."

"Damnit! That means it will be on the street by morning. WALTER!"

Walter came running out of the typesetting room. "What did I do now?"

"When is that blasted catalog going to be done?"

"I don't know, maybe two or three in the morning?"

"What if we turned up the engines?"

"We could probably have it ready by midnight."

"Then do it! Do it now! Thank the heavens we bought that extra set of rollers. Alert the barkers, we are going to get the Wednesday newspaper to them first thing in the morning."

The men set to work writing the new top story.

O'Conner recited the details that he had from the police announcement. "The prostitute's name was Martha Tabram. She was about thirty-nine they think. The only witness so far was her friend Mary Ann Connolly, who is known around the area as Pearly Poll. Miss Tabram was a decent looker from how they described. They had met up with a couple of guardsmen at a bar on Whitechapel Road. Took them to the area near George Yard. That is where they split up to... to... Well, you know what they split up for. Anyway, at around five this morning a man by the name of John Saunders Reeves found the poor woman lying in a pool of blood right in at the bottom of his stairs at the George Yard Buildings."

"My heavens!" Exclaimed Thaddeus. "Anything from the doctor?"

"Yes, yes. That would be Doctor Timothy Robert Killeen. He said the woman had definitely been murdered. Said she had been stabbed thirty-nine times. That would do it I suppose. He said her belly had been pepper-potted from throat to well... well, you know where. Used two knives to do it. A big one and a little one."

"So was this some kind of deviant act?" Asked the publisher as he continued to type out the story.

"The doc didn't think so. He said she hadn't even been raped. Didn't think she had even taken a feller to bed that night."

"That is strange. Makes for quite the mystery. What about the inspector, any suspects?"

"Nothing yet. Inspector Walter Dew was the man doing all the talking. I think he is taking the lead on this one for now at least. He is that new guy who came to H Division about a year ago."

Thaddeus continued typing, and then handed the story to Walter who had just returned from speeding up the printer.

"Get this started, and I'll work on the headline."

The men continued preparing the rollers for an early morning newspaper run. It was nearly midnight before everything was ready. Thaddeus placed the last line of text on the headline for the story.

BLOOD SPILLED IN WHITECHAPEL ONCE AGAIN
ANOTHER PROSTITUTE MUTILATED IN THE OPEN

Octavius was lying in his bed. His hands and arms covered in blood. His chef jacket was also spotted with thick gelatinous red globs. He wasn't sure how long he had been lying there. It had taken hours to get his heart to stop pounding and his head to stop spinning.

In general, he knew what he had done. But the details were gone. He had blacked out as soon as he had felt the knives in his hand. He could remember flashes of the blades moving up and down. He could see a flash of the lady's face. But that is all. He wasn't even sure how he had gotten back to his room. He could only hope that no one had seen him.

He stood up and looked at his hands and arms. They were

stiff and itchy. He needed to clean himself up. He pulled off his chef's jacket, wadded it up and stuffed it into a bean sack he had brought back from the kitchen. He also took off his undershirt, which was also spotted with blood. He dipped it in his water bowl and used it as a rag to wipe his arms. After thirty minutes of washing, he was finally clean.

He looked out the window and saw that the sun was high. He panicked and grabbed his pocket watch. It was already ten fifteen.

Panic stricken, he began rifling through his drawers looking for a clean shirt and trousers. He only had one chef's coat, so he would have to go without for today. He dressed himself in haste and tucked all the soiled clothes in the sack. He stuffed the sack in a drawer and closed it. He looked out his window to see if anyone was around the area. Not seeing anyone, he tossed the red liquid out the window, soaking the red brick building next door.

He looked over his room for any obvious signs of misdeeds. Not seeing any, he closed and locked the door. He rushed downstairs and pushed through the front door. Then he made a mad dash for the hotel.

Octavius arrived at the back door of the café at ten thirty. He could see through the window that a few tables were already seated. He stopped for a moment to catch his breath before walking through the door. Natasha met him as he walked in. "Good day, chef."

He was almost startled by the words. "Good day," he mumbled the words as he walked swiftly past her. He shot Victor a quick look and could see a mix of surprise and concern cross his face. Luckily, the bartender did not ask any questions in front of the customers.

Before even entering the kitchen, his nose told him that the cassoulet was not right. There was a strong aroma of onion in the air and not nearly enough pork.

"Good morning... I mean day, chef," greeted Stephane. The words startled Marcus who was hunched over the pot looking puzzled.

"Damnit Marcus! How many bushels of onions did you put in that pot?"

"Sorry, chef. We did not want to start the broth without you, but it was getting late in the day. I did not think we could get the meat to cook fast enough, so I chopped it into smaller pieces and used more onions as filler."

"You're supposed to be my sous chef. Haven't I taught you anything? Stephane, grab a slab of pork shoulder and start breaking it down. Trim the fat off the top and fillet the meat out flat."

He grabbed a frying pan off a hook, put it on the stove, and cranked the burner to full blast. "We need to sear the meat in the pan to let it catch up."

He then grabbed another large pot off a hook and poured in half the broth from the pot that was already on the stove. He then started the fire under the new pot and grabbed a pail of water. He started ladling in scoops of water to dilute the mixture.

Marcus stood in amazement of how quickly the chef took control of the situation. "Don't just stand there like a stump, Marcus. Why don't you make yourself useful? Go down to the store and buy me a new chef's jacket. Mine got soiled yesterday while I was sick."

Marcus looked ready to protest, but thought better of it. He just nodded his head and backed out of the kitchen.

A moment later, Victor walked into the kitchen. "Good day chef. We have a few customers who have been waiting for a while now." He said it more as a question and in the calmest voice he could muster.

"Understood. We are on track now. We should have cassoulet ready in ten minutes. As for pot-pies..." He looked at Stephane who was now cooking the pork shoulder in the frying pan. He shook his head from side to side. "We won't have pot-pies ready for another thirty minutes. Give everyone a round of drinks on the house, and we will make sure they are all fed one way or the other."

His nose told him there was at least bread baking in the oven.

"We do have bread ready that we can serve with an oil dipping sauce as well. Send in one of the ladies to fetch it in a minute."

Victor shook his head and walked out.

Ten minutes later, the aroma from the kitchen started to smell more familiar. Fifteen minutes later the first bowls went out of the kitchen. A few minutes after that, a tray of pot-pies went into the oven. The chef stood back and surveyed the kitchen. It was a mess. Stephane sensed that a lecture was coming, so he quickly started cleaning.

Octavius stepped into the dining room. He stood back to keep from being seen again without his jacket. He could see thirteen patrons. Most were eating now, and no one seemed to be out of joint. Crisis averted for now.

Marcus came in from the hotel side walking down the stairs. He had a package under his arm and handed it to the chef.

"Thank you, Marcus." Octavius pulled the new jacket out of the package and slipped it on. "Did you charge it to the restaurant account?"

"Yes, chef. To the Cafe Langham account."

"Very good. Help Stephane clean up this pigsty. Then I am going to teach you both how to prepare a proper cassoulet and a couple pot-pies." He said it in an even manner and Marcus couldn't tell if he was saying it out of anger or disappointment. "If I am ever going to get a vacation or be allowed to get sick, then I need to better prepare my sous chef to take charge."

"We just sold the last stack of newspapers," Frank reported as he entered Thaddeus' office. "You were right boss."

The weary publisher was relieved. He had taken another gamble that a new murder in Whitechapel would sell a ton of papers. Even though the big papers were reporting the story at the same time, he decided to print a triple run of fifteen thousand copies. It took them all day to sell out, but that didn't matter, as long as they sold.

"I'm just thankful I let Walter talk me out of doing a fourth run. We would have wasted two rolls of paper."

"Now we just have to get ready to do it again on Sunday. Same routine as before. We should double up on the coverage and see what other angles we can find. Grab O'Conner, and let's see what we can figure out."

The three men sat around for a few hours sharing glasses of whiskey. They were celebrating as much as they were floating story ideas. The *Observer* had continued its reputation as a leading source in reporting on murders on London's East End. Now they just had to figure out a way to keep the story alive for as long as possible.

Frank thought that they should start questioning the police's ability to keep the city safe. O'Conner wasn't so keen on that idea. Not yet anyway. He wasn't a big supporter of law enforcement, but he didn't want to get on their bad side either, at least not until it was really worth the risk.

They eventually settled on keeping the blame and pressure on the politicians who were always a good target for these types of social injustices.

Thaddeus also wanted to make the coroner and doctor's reports a big part of the story. The sensational nature of the medical details helped stoke the public's imagination. He decided he would write a three part exposé on the finer points of the Martha Tabram autopsy and end with a comparison of Miss Tabram's murder with that of Emma Smith. There was no evidence linking the two tragedies, but why not introduce a little speculation into the reporting.

At the end of the night, the men had finished two bottles. They didn't know how much more they could get out of two audacious events, but they were sure going to find out.

The weeks following the chef's tardiness due to a mysterious illness had been chaotic for the staff at the Café Langham. They never knew which chef would be arriving the next morning, or if he would be arriving in the morning at all.

The first week had been wonderful. Octavius had been cheerful and magnanimous. He gave bonuses to all the staff and started training both Marcus and Stephane on how to properly prepare the restaurant's signature dishes.

He publicly praised Marcus for being a fine sous chef, which was very out of character for the stoic leader. He then gave Stephane the title of Head Baker and worked with him to develop new recipes to expand the variety of pot-pies offered by the bistro.

Victor was encouraged to start sampling a few new cocktails to see which one might become a second signature drink. After trying out a few ideas, he settled on a gin and tonic, which was a new drink that had started trending around the British Isles in recent weeks. Tom tried to introduce a couple of new ideas, but his timing always seemed to be off the mark. The chef, while happy, seemed to have a suddenly shortened attention span.

As for the waitresses, nothing much changed for them. Octavius' interactions with them remained sparse and involved even less eye contact than usual. He was always professional, but he rarely smiled in their presence and conversations never lasted more than a couple of sentences.

By the second week, the chef's cheerful mood had worn off and things returned to normal. He was back to being more serious and corrected the staff if they did not properly address him as chef. He stopped accepting recommendations and even had a meeting where he told everyone they needed to tighten the ship and refocus their energy on efficiency and profitability.

By week three, the atmosphere became absolutely tense. The chef derided the young cooks for the smallest infractions. Too much seasoning. Dirty pots not washed immediately after use. Water pails not properly staged. Bread that was too crusty. Bread that was too soft. Nothing was to his liking, and the men started to flinch every time he entered the kitchen.

In the dining area, he would lash out at any perceived criticism from staff or customers. He barked at Tom several times for being too gregarious with the patrons and even threatened to fire him if he didn't "shut his trap and start pouring as he was paid to do."

As maître d', Victor tried to sooth his boss at times by saying he would keep a keener eye on things. This worked at first, but eventually Octavius started directing his ire at the bartender accusing him of allowing the staff to grow lazy and unprofessional.

At the end of the third week a new mood presented itself: depression. Octavius arrived at work on Thursday at nearly ten thirty. The kitchen staff had prepared the meals for the day. The pots were fully stocked and boiling, pot-pies were waiting in the racks, and fresh bread was ready to be served.

He stuck his head into the kitchen briefly and smelled the air for a few seconds. He scrunched up his mouth a bit showing a ho-hum expression then turned away and walked to the dining room. He sat at a table and started writing in his notebook.

Marcus waited a few minutes, then came out to the dining room to check on his boss. "Chef, do you wish to taste the stew before we start serving?"

"Does it taste okay to you?" he asked without looking up.

"Yes, chef, but I just thought…"

"Well, then serve it. And bring me a beef pot-pie when you get a moment."

The chef sat at the table throughout the day. He did not even get up when the other tables were full to make way for other guests. He did not speak with any customers and only sparingly with the staff. When he did speak his voice was soft and low. It was a shock to everyone, especially the waitresses who commented that he looked sad.

The last table was cleared at nine, and Victor told the ladies and Tom they could leave for the night. If anyone came in during the next hour, he could handle it. The group left together wishing the chef a goodnight. He did not look up, but gave a quick wave.

A few minutes later, the chef looked up from his notebook. "Victor, can you bring me a glass of tonic water. Also, can you ask Marcus to bring out three bowls and let's have a talk while we eat"

The request left the bartender stunned. The fact that it had been worded as a request was stunning in itself, but he had never been asked to have a formal dinner with the man. He stood for a moment with his mouth hanging wide. Octavius turned back to his notebook and continued writing.

"Yes, chef." Victor grabbed three glasses and poured a tonic water and two glasses of whiskey. He placed them on the table and headed to the kitchen to fetch Marcus. It took him a couple of minutes to convince the sous chef to come out. He was certain he was going to be fired.

Finally, the men exited the kitchen carrying a couple trays of food. They sat them on the table and waited for the chef to acknowledge them before eating or drinking anything.

The chef wrote for a while longer before looking up. He grabbed a bowl of stew, unwrapped a spoon, and scooped out a large helping. He smelled it first before taking a bite. "Not bad. Make sure you brown the meat a little more next time. And what is your fascination with onions?" He paused for a second then ate another bite. "Still it's better than what I have tasted from nicer restaurants in this town."

Marcus knew that was the best compliment he was going to get from the chef. He tried to hide his smile as he grabbed a bowl and started eating. Victor joined in.

"Do you think you can do it again?"

"Yes, chef."

"Good then. I will need for you to handle the kitchen for the next two days."

Marcus stopped eating and lowered his spoon back into his bowl.

"I have to leave the city for a few days to meet a friend in the countryside. He is a young chef who wishes to learn how to make a few proper French dishes. I owe him a favor, so I will be going. I will be back on Monday."

"You may have to get some more duck fat at the market tomorrow just in case. And watch Stephane on those pies. He used too much salt today, and he loves carrots as much as you love onions," instructed Octavius.

The sous chef looked at Victor for reassurance, then said the only thing that made sense. "Yes, chef."

"Victor, I will need you to take care of things out here, like always. If something goes wrong, get Marcus and the two of you can figure it out. If things get too bad send someone to fetch Gustavo. I will let him know I am leaving tonight when I drop off the money. You will have to handle that as well. You remember where to take the money bag?"

"Yes, chef." Victor took a drink of his whiskey and sat back in his chair.

Octavius ate a few more bites and stood up from the table. He went behind the bar and grabbed the money bag before returning to the table. "Men, do not make a fool of me or this restaurant."

And with that Octavius walked up the stairs to meet with Gustavo. He returned a few minutes later and went to the kitchen and unrolled his knife pouch. He took out the eight inch chef's knife and sat down at the grinding wheel. He continued grinding on the blades as the boys restocked the shelves. He grinded as they cleaned the pots. He grinded as they prepped for the next day's service. He grinded when they wished him goodnight. He grinded as Victor stopped in to say he was locking up.

Once everyone had left the restaurant, he opened his notebook which contained a small clipping from the *East End Observer*. It was an article describing the autopsy from Doctor Thomas Killeen on the murder of Martha Tabram. He had previously described her as having received thirty-nine puncture wounds. He also described her as being well nourished.

Those were old facts that had been known since the day after the killing. What had appeared in the newest paper was the full report of the autopsy.

The brain was healthy; the left lung was penetrated in five places, and the right lung in two places, but the lungs were otherwise perfectly healthy. *The heart was rather fatty, and was penetrated in one place, but there was otherwise nothing in the heart to cause death, although there was some blood in the pericardium.*

The liver was healthy, but was penetrated in five places, the spleen was perfectly healthy, and was penetrated in two places; both the kidneys were perfectly healthy; the stomach was also perfectly healthy, but was penetrated in six places; the intestines were healthy, and so were all the other organs.

The lower portion of the body was penetrated in one place, the wound being three inches in length and one in depth.

From appearances, there was no reason to suspect that recent intimacy had taken place.

I don't think that all the wounds were inflicted with the same instrument, because there was one wound on the breast bone which did not correspond with the other wounds on the body.

The instrument with which the wounds were inflicted would most probably be an ordinary knife, but a knife would not cause such a wound as that on the breast bone. That wound I should think would have been inflicted with some form of a dagger.

I am of the opinion that the wounds were inflicted during life, and from the direction which they took it is my opinion, that although some of them could have been self-inflicted, yet, there were others which could not have been so inflicted.

The wounds generally would have been inflicted by a right-handed person. There was no sign whatever of any struggle having taken place; and there was a deal of blood between the legs, which were separated.

Death was due to hemorrhage and loss of blood.

Octavius did not know what to think of the report. He had read it several times during the day, but a lot of what was stated did not make sense. He was left handed, not right as the doctor had surmised. He also did not remember making so many stabs with the small paring knife.

He read the report again before putting it away. He decided that it did not hold any real answers. He would just have to make sure he stayed more focused next time and remember everything.

The only thing he was certain about was that there would be a next time. He did not understand why he was so driven to return to the whores in Whitechapel, but he had come to terms with the fact that the nagging in his head would not subside until he gave into his compulsions.

He believed that his mother would approve of his actions and that angered him for some reason. But none of that mattered now.

He pulled out his prized eight inch chef's knife and began grinding some more.

Thaddeus was moping in his chair. He had no real reason to mope, but he was doing it all the same. The publishing company was doing great financially. He now had a reputation as a respectable businessman. Something he never thought would happen, certainly not this quickly.

The paper was printing ten thousand copies a run. Advertising revenue had doubled. He had even dropped one catalog to increase capacity for the newspaper. He also stopped printing political broadsides on pure principle and hatred for the vile things.

It had been nearly a month since the last Whitechapel murder and there had been little excitement in the city. Politics were back to ruling the headlines with an occasional royal scandal. The only thing the publisher hated more than political stories were monotonous articles about spoiled rich royals who couldn't keep it in their pants.

They had written ad nauseum about the killing of Martha Tabram and had even done extensive follow ups about Emma Smith. Neither murder had resulted in any real suspects, and the investigations had gone nowhere.

Both murders were being handled by the regular police, which meant his reporters could easily score interviews and draw theories from investigators inside and outside the cases simply by applying a little cash or paying a bar tab.

They still made sure to include a story in every new edition about the murders, but the public had started to wane interest in the past week.

He poured himself a drink and looked over the pages in his ledger for sport. He had a surplus now, but he was weary of spending any of the extra money. They had already made improvements to the press, but Walter wanted to do more. He was convinced they could double their capacity by replacing the worn out steam engine with a larger, more efficient one. It would require replacing half the piping. He also wanted to add an automatic folder, which would allow them to print, fold, and twine up to ten thousand copies an hour. The improvements would also eat up the entire nest egg the company had cobbled together.

He had always been a risk taker, some might even say a gambler, to the point of recklessness. But now he had Sarah. He was a business man. He had a payroll to make. A company to run. A family legacy and a newfound reputation to protect.

The publisher poured himself another glass. This one was a bit fuller. He drank it down in one long gulp. He punched his fist down onto the ledger and yelled out. "WALTER!"

Walter came running up the stairs and into his office.

"Go get Packo. We better have this thing back up and running in time for the Sunday paper."

Walter gritted his teeth and punched his first into the air. Then he ran down the stairs and out the front door.

Octavius rose from his bed at nine in the evening. He really wanted to rest longer, but his mind wouldn't allow it. He knew it wouldn't matter. He was filled with anticipation, and it wasn't going away. Not until he had completed his task.

After lighting a candle, he pulled out his knife pouch and rolled it open on the bed. He studied the blades for a while, then pulled out the eight inch chef's knife. He knew he wanted this one. For his second blade, he selected the thinner and stronger boning knife. He inspected the blades, which had been sharpened and honed to perfection. He had worked on the blades at the bistro throughout the night and into the morning not stopping until the sun had started to shine through the windows.

Having made his picks, he rolled up the other knives and stuffed the pouch under the bed. He opened his wardrobe and took out his black suit. It was a gentleman's suit with vest and long coat. He also had an overcoat but it was too warm this time of year for such a garment. He thought about wearing it anyway because it would provide more concealment, but decided against it.

He laid the suit on the bed, then pulled on his white shirt and fastened the cufflinks. He slipped on the trousers and tied up his black boots. He decided to wear his long tie instead of the bow. He could wear it loose on his neck, and it could easily be slipped off if need be.

He put on the vest and fixed the buttons. Then he grabbed the boning knife and slipped it into a fabric pocket that he had sewn into the left side of the vest specifically designed to hold a blade. Next he grabbed the chef's knife and worked it into the makeshift pocket on the right. He had to be more careful with this blade because it was wider and far sharper.

Next came the jacket, followed by a pair of leather gloves. He could see a bit of his reflection in the window, so he fixed the tuck of his shirt and smoothed down the sides of his jacket.

Satisfied, he reached for a medium-size box he had sitting in the corner. He pulled the lid off revealing a brown, hard leather hat carrier. He removed it from the box and placed it gingerly onto the bed. He undid the four brass latches and pulled back the cover revealing a black top hat.

He had ordered the hat a week ago from a fine haberdasher spending nearly a week's wages on the item. It was a high felt stovepipe design made from stiffened calico and covered in plush silk fabric that had been brushed until smooth and shiny.

A generous amount of mercury had been rubbed into the fabric to deepen the blackness. It was the most expensive item he had ever purchased, and he had only worn it once briefly during the fitting. He had been saving it for this moment.

He lifted the hat out of the carrier and examined it closely. After brushing off a few pieces of fuzz, it looked pristine. He lifted it onto his head and pushed it into place. It was a natural and comfortable fit. The smell of the new materials was intoxicating.

Turning, he looked again at his reflection in the window. This time he did not recognize the man staring back at him. The image was no longer that of a simple chef; no longer that of a man in his twenties. The image he saw was something much greater. The hat allowed him to change into something new. He was free now. Free to become whoever he wanted, whatever he wanted.

Octavius left his room and headed into the street. At first he wondered if anyone else could see the change in him. He quickly realized that he blended in well with the crowd. Without his chef's uniform he looked like any other distinguished gentleman walking the streets of London. Others could not see the change, but that did not matter.

He headed directly toward Whitechapel Street. He walked at a measured pace not wanting to get there until after the crowd had thinned. The street lights would still be on until at least eleven, but his new disguise would allow him to blend in.

Even before he reached his destination his body began to react. His finely tuned sense of smell told him he was near brothels and slaughterhouses. He could taste the familiar scents in the back of his throat. The hairs on the back of his neck stood on end. His hearing became keener, as he started to pick up bits and pieces of conversations as people passed. Even though it was nearly ten-thirty at night, the alleys and shadows seemed to lighten for him as he looked down each crevice. The change was still upon him.

He had spent every day for the past three weeks walking these streets dressed in his chef uniform. He had learned the most popular out of the way dark spots. He recognized the popular girls and the frequent customers. He could easily spot the newcomers. With little study he could discern how hard each girl would have to work to pull money from the men in the area.

All of these women revolted him. Not because they were prostitutes, but because they were whores. "Prostitutes without manners or class are nothing but whores," his mother would say. They needed to be put in their place. Learn to fear the dark corners so that they would leave their whore ways and sign on to registered brothels under the care of proper madams. He pitied them all.

At eleven the gas lamps throughout the slums started to be extinguished. This cast stark shadows across the streets.

Octavius found his favorite bench in a particularly black hidden spot on Bucks Row in the warehouse district. He knew this is where the truly seedy activity happened. He sat for hours not moving or making a sound. He watched as occasional prostitutes and their marks disappeared into alleyways and staircases.

Every time it was the same. Two would go in and only one would come out. The men knew they had debased themselves with shameful women. Then these irresponsible women would let their escorts leave them alone in the dark out of regard for their shame. They all needed to be taught lessens in decorum and decency; how to protect themselves from the evils of the world.

He sat patiently for hours. He knew his intended victim would eventually show up. She always did. Always in the earliest hours of the morning. Always in this spot.

At a little past two thirty she appeared walking with a middle aged man. He was dirty and sweaty, most likely from a hard day of working in a hot warehouse. The pale-skinned whore was drunk, like always. Her black hair was wet and matted against her pudgy face. The man seemed sober enough, but he was drinking from a bottle. They passed within fifteen feet of his spot on the bench. He watched as they stumbled into the gateway at the Board School.

Time slowed to a crawl at that point, and he could hear the pounding in his chest. His vision started to blur. He closed his eyes, clenched his fists, and gritted his teeth. He had to pull himself together. He had to stay focused. He could not allow himself to black out this time. He had to remember the hat. He had to remember who he was becoming. He grabbed the brim of his top hat and pulled it down a smidge. Then he opened his eyes again and focused in the darkness.

That's when he saw it; a shadowy figure appeared in the archway. It was the man, now a bit drunker. He passed through the archway and walked out the same way he had arrived, again passing fifteen feet in front of him.

Octavius waited until he was out of sight, then stood up. He surveyed his surroundings as he crossed the vacant street. He walked straight through the archway where he saw the whore pulling down her inner skirt. Her blouse was still untied and one breast was sticking out.

He approached her without hesitation and stopped no more than four feet away. In her drunken stupor, she had not even noticed that she had company. She stood up from fixing her skirt and started to tuck her exposed breast back into her shirt when she detected the well-healed man standing in front of her.

"Well hello, good sir... Should I put myself back together, or would you rather get right down to business?"

Octavius did not say a word. He just looked at her with disgust.

Thaddeus was covered in grease and wearing only his trousers and a white undershirt. He was pulling hard on a pipe wrench. He gave it one last massive tug, getting another quarter turn out of the coupling.

"That should do it," yelled Packo who was carrying an armful of pipes. Walter trailed him carrying a bucket of couplings and other assorted fittings.

Packo was a giant of a man with a bald head and a booming voice. He was the local machinist, mechanic, pipe fitter, or whatever else he needed to be called. He could work wonders on all manner of engine or mechanical device, but steam engines were his favorite. Today he was in hog heaven getting to replace the heart of the giant printing press.

It had only taken him a few hours to figure out how to retrofit the chain system to drive the new automatic paper folder while still pulling the print rollers. Everything had to work in perfect harmony with no lags between the two systems. Any hesitation in the chain or pulleys would cause a paper jam.

The weary publisher was happy with how fast the upgrades had gone so far. They were at least a half day ahead of schedule. They had started the work on Wednesday afternoon as soon as the newspaper finished printing. It took them until Thursday afternoon to fit the auto folder. Now it was Friday morning, and they were nearly done with attaching all the new pipes. The final step would be to fire up the steam engine, work out all the kinks in the drive train, and make sure everything was calibrated. They had the rest of Friday and all of Saturday to work out those details as the next printing wasn't scheduled until Sunday morning.

The three men continued working on the pipes until about nine that morning. Thaddeus was standing on a ladder trying to get leverage on his wrench when he heard someone yelling his name. He looked down at Frank who was waving at him.

"What's up, Frank? We are kind of busy today trying to put this bucket of bolts back together."

"There has been another Whitechapel murder!"

That was all the publisher needed to hear. He shimmied down the ladder, jumping off the fourth rung. He grabbed a towel and wiped his hands.

"Was it another prostitute?"

"I think so. It was definitely a woman. She was near the warehouse area sometime around four this morning. That's all I know so far."

"For Heaven's Sake, why are we just hearing about this now?

Where is O'Conner?"

"We were both at breakfast together when someone came in with the news. We headed straight to the police station to get the details, but they said they couldn't say anything. O'Conner said that means Scotland Yard is taking over the case. He told me to come here and tell you what was going on. He went to the Yard to see what he can find out. Hopefully, Sam is already there."

Thaddeus was pacing back and forth trying to process the information. He understood that this story would be different than the others. The first murder was done by a band of thugs. The second had been more gruesome and the work of a single assailant so it had caused a bigger stir. But now they were looking at three murders all within a few blocks of each other.

This was now a story that would not go away until people were convicted and punished, which could take weeks even months. They had to find a way to capitalize.

"WALTER!" he shouted.

The round typesetter was standing just three feet away.

"I heard the news, sir."

"Can it be done?"

"I don't know. We have a few pipes left to fit. Then we have to test and calibrate everything. It would take every man we have working throughout the night. We might have to do fewer pages, and we don't have anything from the advertisers yet."

Thaddeus continued pacing. An idea was churning in his head. If they could get out a paper first thing Saturday morning they would become the dominant source for the Whitechapel Murders. It would be a special edition. All the stories would be about the murder.

He knew they could make enough money by just selling the papers, but he was thinking grander. If they could find an advertiser, just one aggressive advertiser who wanted to stand out. If he could find that advertiser, then he could sell just one full page ad on the back cover.

He stopped pacing when it hit him. "Frank. You know the loud, fast talking owner of the Hotel Langham? I think his name is Gustavo. Can you get me a meeting with him?"

"I think so. When do you want to meet with him?"

"This morning. Now. As soon as you can make it happen."

Frank nodded his head and ran toward the door. "Give me two hours and meet me in the hotel lobby."

"Walter, I'm going to go get the other guys to help out in here. Then I'll meet Frank at the Langham. We should be back here in less than three hours," he said as he walked up the stairs to his office to put on his shirt, jacket, and bowler hat.

Thaddeus headed for the door, stopping to bark a few last minute orders. "When O'Conner gets here start typesetting. The entire front page should be about the murder. The inside pages should be about the murder. Hell, every page should be about the murder. You guys can figure it out. Just leave the back cover open."

He didn't wait for a reply as headed out the door.

He popped back in a second later. "And Walter, leave the main headline for me and make it a three liner."

It was late Friday night and Octavius was laying in his bed. He was completely naked with his hands clasped behind his head. His mind and body were completely numb.

In his wardrobe hung his vest and trousers. He had thrown away the jacket along with his shirt, which were both ruined. His knives were safely back in their pockets in the knife roll, which was safely tucked under his bed.

His top hat was sitting on the table. It had taken him a while to get off all the blood droplets. He had used two bowls of clean water and spent hours dabbing each spot. He had even gone to the store to buy a bottle of mercury dye to repair some of the blemishes. It was now pristine again.

He felt at peace as he looked at the hat on the table. It had become more than an object to him. It had become a symbol. A symbol of who he had become. He was still the chef. But when he wore the hat he would become a liberator.

He would liberate the downtrodden prostitutes of Whitechapel and all of London. He would lead them to the safety of the brothels; to the mothering embrace of proper madams. To the safety of clean rooms and comfortable beds; to the dignity that came from registration. To the honor that came with certificates of health.

He understood they would call him a monster. He wanted them to. He needed them to in order to become a liberator. The liberation of these women would come from his notoriety. Their fear of the monster in the top hat would free them from the filthy slums.

He smiled as he looked at the hat. Then he faded off to a peaceful sleep.

The sun had gone down hours ago, but the men at the *East End Observer* were still on the job.

Frank, Peter, and Sam were helping Packo with the printer. They had made two test fires in the past hour with both attempts ending in disaster.

On the first attempt, the belt kept slipping off the drive. Packo made periodic adjustments as the three helpers hoisted the heavy belt back into place every time it fell off.

At one point Frank jammed a finger on a roller and his brother stubbed his toe after kicking one of the support posts in frustration. Luckily, Packo finally found the right setting for the belt guide.

The second run started more promising as they spooled the paper through the rollers. The printer ran for nearly a minute before the tension got too tight and the paper tore off the roll. It took a couple of starts and stops before Sam could get the tensioners calibrated. He had always had a knack for dealing with finicky linen paper rolls.

While the crew worked on the printer, Thaddeus, O'Conner, and Walter finished typesetting the special edition.

Gustavo, who was enthralled by the Whitechapel murders, jumped at the opportunity to advertise his hotel in the special edition. He especially loved that he would be the only advertiser in the newspaper and paid triple the going rate for the opportunity.

O'Conner and Sam had brought back a lot of details about the newest murder, and they were more than sensational enough to fill the front page. The other reporters jumped in with accompanying follow-ups about the other two East End murders and Sam wrote an article on why Scotland Yard had been brought in for this third killing. It was a thin paper, but not so thin that they couldn't charge full price.

Thaddeus read over the lead story making sure they had included all the pertinent details.

Mary Ann Nichols had been found dead at the western end of Buck's Row at the archway leading to the Board School. Mary was a middle-aged prostitute who worked independent of any brothel, the same as the first two victims.

Scotland Yard reported that the first sighting of Miss Nichols had been at three-thirty in the morning. She had initially been discovered by two wagon carters named Charles Cross and Robert Paul. Both men had stopped their wagons and looked at the lady who was lying on the ground with her skirt raised over her waist. Mister Cross had checked her chest and felt a slight movement. The men were late for work, so they pulled the woman's skirt down to her knees to preserve her dignity and left her lying in the street.

The men then went in search of the authorities and found Police Constable Jonas Mizen and told him about the woman they had discovered and informed him that they thought she was either drunk or dead. The officer then left to inspect the area, but before he got to the scene Police Constable John Neil came across Miss Nichols' body while walking his beat.

Constable Neil made a full statement on the matter saying, "There was not a soul about. I had been round there half an hour previously, and saw no one then. I was on the right side, when I noticed a figure lying in the street. It was dark at the time. I examined the body by the aid of my lamp, and noticed blood oozing from a wound to the throat. She was lying on her back, with her clothes disarranged. I felt her arm, which was quite warm from the joints upwards. Her eyes were wide open. Her bonnet was off and lying at her side."

Constable Neil had called for reinforcements and Doctor Llewellyn arrived at the scene. He pronounced Miss Nichols dead due to her throat being cut so deeply that it nearly severed her head from her body.

A large pool of blood surrounded her, indicating that she had been murdered where she was found. It was also clear that her killer would have been covered in blood as well, which would have been obvious to anyone who passed him on the street. However, the area where the body was found was located near several slaughterhouses, so bystanders could have assumed the killer was a local worker.

Scotland Yard had assigned Detective Frederick George Abberline to the case. Detective Abberline was a well-known East Ender, who had only recently been promoted to the Yard. He had spent fourteen years as the lead inspector at H Division in the Whitechapel District. Several leads were being followed, but no suspects had been named as of yet.

Thaddeus was pleased with the amount of details that had already emerged only a day into the investigation. Having Scotland Yard on the case made things better. The case would move faster. More suspects would be named. Public interest would increase. Politicians would have to give statements.

The Whitechapel murders were no longer just an East End story. Now all of London and even Great Britain would be paying attention. The story of the sensational murders would soon reach the entire world.

This was going to be a great month for the publishing company, and their investment in the printer was going to pay off starting on day one. He decided at that moment they were going to print twenty thousand copies.

Now he just needed to write the headline.

WHITECHAPEL MURDER STRIKES ONCE AGAIN
INNOCENT PROSITUTE NEARLY DECAPITATED
SCOTLAND YARD CALLED IN TO LEAD THE CASE

Octavius slept until nearly nine on Saturday. Feeling refreshed and relaxed, he put on his chef's uniform and slipped his knife roll into a bean sack fitted with a string that he could sling over his shoulder. He decided it might be best to take a short trip to the countryside immediately outside of town to stave off any possibility of suspicion and solidify somewhat of an alibi.

He had been meaning to check out a restaurant that Henri had recommended. It was run by a former sous chef of Henri's and was rumored to serve a Coq au vin to rival the best eateries in Paris. The restaurant was located about five miles south of London in the town of Brixton.

Before leaving, he secured the top hat in its case, placed it gently onto the top shelf of the wardrobe, and closed and locked the door.

The street outside his apartment was buzzing with activity. As he headed south, he noticed several people huddled together speaking in excited tones. He continued south on Abingdon Street toward Parliament Square where newspaper barkers were perched on milk crates at every corner yelling out the headlines. He couldn't resist the opportunity to walk around the square listening to the symphony of shouting voices. They were all singing his praises and preaching the sermon set forth by the Liberator.

He purchased a copy of every paper he could find. He quickly scanned the headlines reveling in the way they described his exploits.

He was especially thrilled to see the *East End Observer*, which had dedicated an entire edition to the Whitechapel murders. He spent nearly an hour reading and rereading the information provided by Doctor Llewellyn who was the doctor that investigated the crime scene of Mary Ann Nichols' murder.

Satisfied, he stuffed the papers into his sack and continued south over Lambeth Bridge, then turned down toward Brixton Road.

The walk to Brixton took less than two hours, even with all the stops. He found the small restaurant named Le Champignon, which he knew meant The Mushroom in French. He walked into the restaurant and was greeted by an overly friendly server. He was a small man with a bald head and a bushy mustache that looked four sizes too large for his face. He was wearing a long apron that almost touched the floor. "Bonjour! Welcome to Le Champignon!"

Octavius didn't know quite how to take the bombastic man, so he sat at the first table he came to and looked around. The restaurant was medium in size with a dozen four-chair tables and a large table in the center that could hold at least ten guests. There was a bar in the back corner, but it did not have seating.

The bar was covered by one man, who was also wearing an apron. There were two servers on duty, the man he had met and an older lady wearing a brown dress and yet another apron. Only eight other patrons were seated. This was not the sign of a healthy restaurant given that it was already noon on a Saturday.

The mustache-wielding man walked up to the table. "What can I bring you, monsieur."

"I was wondering if Chef Demar was in the kitchen today."

"But of course, monsieur. I will fetch him for you tout de suite." He shuffled off to the kitchen in a rush.

He appeared a moment later followed by a large, burly man who looked as if he could lift a horse. He had long bushy hair and wore worn slacks and a plain shirt. Instead of a jacket, he wore a large apron like the rest of the staff. The only difference was that his apron was white, while the rest of the staff wore black.

"Greetings chef, how are you today?"

"Good day to you as well chef. Sorry to intrude on your day. My name is Octavius. I just wanted to say hello and offer greetings from Henri. He told me I simply must come and experience your Coq au vin."

"Ah Henri. I do miss him so much. And you? I hear your name as well. You are the chef at the Café Langham, no?"

"Yes, chef. I've been running the bistro there for a few months now."

"Please, call me Demar. We are friends now, no? Any friend of Henri is certainly a friend of mine. Let me get you some Coq au vin and we can talk about the beautiful Henri."

The chef left for the kitchen and returned a few minutes later with a steaming bowl. Octavius took his time examining the dish. He experienced the aroma before filling his spoon with the rich dark broth. He could smell the Burgundy wine and braised chicken, mushrooms, and lardons. He sipped the broth, which was magnificent. He then tasted a full spoonful of the dish as his new friend watched. He didn't even try to hide the pleasure the dish gave him. It was food that warmed the soul, and he liked it very much. His face told Demar all he needed to know.

"I just wish others in this city shared your refined taste. They find my cooking too rich for them. They eat like ravenous dogs, then complain that their stomachs hurt."

Octavius laughed at the statement, while nodding in agreement. He had been forced to change the recipe in his cassoulet a few times at the beginning to accommodate softer British constitutions. He shared this experience with Demar who admitted he had been too stubborn to consider the idea. It was simply not the French way, as Octavius had learned from Marthe and the other French chef's that worked in Henri's kitchen.

The two men spent the next several hours swapping stories about Henri and working at restaurants in Paris. They even spent time in the kitchen, where they shared a few recipes. Demar was impressed by Octavius' amazing knife skills. While Octavius learned a lot from Demar's extensive knowledge of using wines in his broths.

Demar encouraged Octavius to come up with his own version of a British-friendly Coq au vin for his restaurant. Maybe he could get people in the city to open up their palates before sending them out to the countryside to experience a more traditional version.

Once the dinner crowd started to roll in, Octavius decided he should leave and let the chef concentrate on his work. Before departing, Demar embraced him in a large bear hug and promised to visit the Café Langham very soon. As he left the restaurant, the sun was just starting to set and the lamps were being lit.

During the walk back to London, Octavius spent most of the journey thinking about how he could use wine to enhance some of his recipes. He also considered how Chef Demar had set up his prep station in an "L" shape to allow for more efficiency in collaboration between two or more cooks.

He was lost in thought when he arrived at the entrance to Lambeth Bridge. It was very dark by this time, but he could still see that a few people were sitting on the bank of the river drinking. He saw a few others talking around a fire on an outcropping of rocks. Then something caught his attention on the far side of the bridge. It was woman and she was alone.

He drew closer as he crossed the bridge and could see that the woman was looking around at the few people who were walking by on the narrow boardwalk. About halfway across the bridge, he saw a man stop and talk to her. A few seconds later, she took him by the arm and led him into the darkness under the bridge.

A flash of anger coursed throughout his body. It hit him like a short burst of lightning. The feeling quickly left, but it was enough to snap him back into focus. The daytime may belong to the Chef, but the night time belonged to the Liberator. He needed to get back his apartment. Back to his top hat.

Walter was slumped over the typesetting table with his forehead resting on the first row of letters. He was snoring loudly and occasionally moaned as he slept.

Thaddeus was standing in the doorway looking at the poor man as he sipped on his tea. He would have to wake him up soon to finish the Friday paper, but he wanted to let him sleep a few more minutes.

The past week had been rough on the seasoned typesetter. After the success of the Whitechapel Murder special edition last Saturday, they had to immediately start the Sunday edition, which was printed with double the normal amount of pages. Thaddeus then convinced Walter to take advantage of their newfound printing capacity to run their paid jobs in the afternoons to free up availability to move the newspaper back to a daily starting that Monday.

Walter was apprehensive about the aggressive schedule at first, but agreed after Thaddeus promised he would limit the stories and page count and allow the old man to hire a couple assistants. Neither of these promises proved very fruitful.

The publisher did limit the amount of articles slated for each paper, but the page count stayed high due to an influx of advertisers that wanted to capitalize on the paper's growing reputation.

Hiring new assistants proved problematic for the controlling typesetter. Walter was a perfectionist and demanded a higher standard from the new recruits than any could achieve.

He hired and fired two on Monday. Thaddeus tried to help by hiring three more on Tuesday, and Walter had fired two of them by Wednesday. Thursday started promising when a lone candidate returned for a third day. But that assistant only made it to midday before throwing up his arms and walking out the door, firing himself.

Through it all, Walter never missed a deadline. But now the man had been reduced to sleeping at his desk after working through the night. Thaddeus decided it was time to bring out his secret weapon. He only knew one other experienced typesetter, and this was one assistant that Walter could not fire.

"Good morning, gentlemen." The voice of a lady echoed through the room. This startled Walter who bolted up in his chair. The letters "F," "H," and "K" had been formed into his forehead from where he had been laying. He could only see blobs without his thick glasses.

"How is my lovely husband this morning?" Asked the pretty lady in her mid-thirties as she pulled a white apron off a hook and tied it around her waist. "And Walter, you look well rested today." She tried to stifle her laughter.

Walter found his glasses and slipped them on. He stood up when he noticed who it was. "Good morning, Missus Donleavy."

"Now stop that, Walter. You know I prefer for you to call me Sarah, especially if we are going to be working together."

Sarah was a pretty, tall, and slim lady with an air of ease and dignity. She wore her long hair in a neat bun tied with a blue ribbon. She was dressed professionally in a tan shirt and black slacks and looked ready to work.

Walter looked pleadingly at Thaddeus who just shrugged his shoulders as he sipped from his cup. "You're the one who keeps saying we need to find at least one person who knows what the hell they are doing. Well, here you go."

Sarah had already pulled down one of the rollers and started cleaning out the stories from the last run. She restacked letters onto the trays with speed and precision. As a child she had spent many of her free hours in this room helping her father and Walter setup jobs. While home from university as a young lady, she had even taken over for Walter on the few times he had left on short vacations.

"Yes, sir. But I am sure missus, I mean, Sarah, has more important things to do than spending time in this dirty room."

"Now, Walter. You said you needed help, and I am here to help. Once you find someone qualified that can meet your standards, then I can go back to serving tea and crumpets."

"I meant no offense, Sarah. You are as qualified as I am. I just hate that we even need your help."

"Nonsense. I have been a part of this company my whole life. I am happy to do whatever is needed. Now, just tell me what I can do to help."

A sense of relief washed over the old typesetter, and he looked around to get his bearings. "Well, I guess you can shake out the rest of those rollers while I start cleaning off the ink."

Thaddeus smiled as he finished his tea. "Well, I will leave you two to your work. I need to see how the rest of the guys are coming along with today's paper."

It was Monday morning and Marcus and Stephane could smell a new aroma coming from the kitchen as soon as they entered the bistro. They looked at each other quizzically then saw Victor coming from the bar storage room carrying a bottle of red wine. He handed the bottle to Marcus.

"Take this to the chef. He has been in the kitchen all morning. At least before seven when I arrived."

"What's his mood like?" Marcus asked grabbing the bottle.

"He seems energized today. Serious, but energized. He is definitely not moping around like he was last week."

The cooks headed to the kitchen where they found Octavius standing over a boiling pot. He was stirring with a ladle and brought it up to take a sniff. "It needs more onions," he said without looking up. "Marcus, I believe that's your favorite. Make sure to dice them very small. Stephane, there is a slab of bacon over there. Slice it into smaller pieces. Keep them even and about the size of match sticks. Slice up the whole slab."

Marcus sat the bottle next to the stove, then the men jumped into action. They could tell by the smell that one of the pots was not their signature cassoulet.

Sensing their curiosity, the chef pulled out a ladleful and handed it to Marcus. "Give this a try and tell me what you think?"

Marcus lifted the ladle to his lips and tasted the aromatic dish. "I taste poultry, onions, mushrooms, and carrots. And something rich. Is that Sherry?"

"Very good, Marcus." He returned to the pot and grabbed

the bottle of wine. "That is the base. Now I am going to cut it with Burgundy and reduce it down a bit."

"I am not familiar with this flavor. I assume it must be French."

"Definitely French, but adjusted for England. I am thinking we will keep it thin but flavorful. A soup instead of a stew. We will call it Coq au vin soup."

"I have no idea what that is, but I would eat it just for the name," offered Stephane.

"That is the hope." The chef poured the entire bottle of Burgundy wine into the pot. "I am going to talk to Victor for a while about a drink to go with this new dish. Watch this pot. Let it reduce about a third, then add in the onions. Stephane, you will need to cook those bacon pieces for a short while before draining the fat and adding them to the pot. Don't let them get crispy, just cook them until they are clear. And save the fat. I want to see how that might taste in a new pot-pie recipe."

Octavius left the kitchen and headed to the bar where he discussed a new drink with Victor. "You know I don't much care for liquor, so I will leave it up to you. I just want it to feature Sherry and have a decent name. Have it ready by this afternoon. I want Gustavo to try the new features tonight so he doesn't feel like I have been traveling the countryside without reason."

The Café Langham stayed busy throughout the day, and the new soup was a hit. By the early afternoon they had to start a second pot, and it was rivaling the cassoulet in number of orders.

Victor had the audacious idea to name his new cocktail The Langham. It was a variation of a sherry cobbler using dry Sherry, sugar, orange slices, berries, mint, and orange bitters.

Gustavo came down the stairs just before dark and was especially joyful. He sat and visited with Octavius for a few minutes before Victor brought over his new concoction. He took a drink and threw his hands over his head. "Stupendous! What is it called?"

"I call it The Langham, sir," the bartender said with a grin.

"Brilliant. What a perfect name for a perfect drink."

"Wait until you try it with our new soup." Victor nodded to Natasha who headed to the kitchen.

Gustavo ate two bowls of the new Coq au vin soup and drank several glasses of his new favorite cocktail. He could not stop complimenting Octavius, Victor, and the other staff for their fine work. He commented that the chef should take a little more time off to wonder the country if it always inspired him to develop such wonderful creations.

It was only nine when Octavius and Victor had to help the drunk owner up the stairs and into the chaise lounge he kept in his office to accommodate such occasions.

After the restaurant closed, the chef sent the staff home and stayed behind. He sat at his normal table for a while contemplating the events of the day. He knew that many of his actions that day had been an act, manufactured to provide cover for his alter ego.

He understood that he needed to continue the ruse and not become as manic as he had after his first impulsive act. He was more controlled now. He would need to stay that way. He needed to stay patient. Stay careful. Stay in character, both day and night.

Once the lamps had been extinguished outside, he lit a candle in the kitchen, sat at the grinding wheel, and worked on his knives.

The rest of the week at the restaurant went smoothly. The tables stayed full, and the drinks continued to flow. The staff continued to grow more proficient in their roles each day. The cooks had learned to cook the new soup by Wednesday. As maître d', Victor had developed into a strong leader who kept both the staff and unruly customers in line. Octavius had even tasked him with delivering the money pouch to Gustavo at the end of each day, which gave him liberty to leave as early as he wanted.

Octavius worked at controlling his mood as best he could, but he could feel himself start to withdraw a bit by Friday. He wasn't angry or depressed, but rather distracted.

He had spent every night after Monday in the Whitechapel

District watching and learning. He was satisfied at first that his efforts had been fruitful. The newspapers continued to spread fear, which had driven many of the unworthy prostitutes off the streets.

By Thursday, the news had grown stale and the streets started to crowd again. Walking the slums on both Thursday and Friday a particularly nasty whore caught his attention. It became clear that he would need to don the top hat again sooner than he expected in order to force a new lesson upon the city.

With Sarah's help, Walter was able to quickly set the Friday paper and have it running before noon. He was invigorated by her presence, and thankful to have an assistant that could actually help for a change.

In the past, he could recruit some of the reporters to help when he got behind, but they were running as hard as he was now that they had moved to a daily again. Thaddeus was looking to add a couple of reporters as soon as possible, but the publisher was already working twelve hours a day.

At least he would get to spend some time with Sarah during the day now that she was helping in the office. She had not been happy with his absence at home over the past few months, and she had been very vocal about his drinking habits.

By the afternoon on Friday, Walter was already starting to fade. A week's worth of twelve plus hour days had taken their toll on the old man. He could be seen pressing his palms into his temples and rubbing his eyes quite often, and it was obvious that his head was hurting.

Sarah couldn't take it any longer. "Walter, I insist that you go home at once. You have been working too many hours this week, and you are going to cause yourself a serious ailment."

"I am fine, Sarah. Don't worry about me." He stood up as a show of strength, but his legs began to wobble and he was forced to sit back down.

"Go home, Walter. This is just a simple clothing catalog with only a few pages. I can handle it. I will clean out the rollers tonight, and we will be ready for the Saturday run tomorrow morning."

The weary typesetter relented. "Alright, I will go and get some sleep. I will be back before eight tomorrow to get things ready. But send for me if you need anything."

"Stop worrying and go get some sleep. It might also help if you ate something too. If you show up here before eight tomorrow, I will drag you back to bed myself."

Walter left and Sarah continued her work on the catalog. She was able to move quickly now that she only had to worry about the task at hand. She finished setting the catalog in under three hours and stayed until the pressmen had started the run to do a quick print check. It would take them a few hours to print the amount needed, so she was at a standstill for the afternoon until she could breakdown the rollers.

Now that she had a little free time, she decided to see if she could convince Thaddeus to take a break for dinner. The two hadn't spent much time together over the past several weeks, and this was a good opportunity. She started to climb the stairs to his office just as Thaddeus was coming out of his door.

"How are things going my dear?" he said with a smile.

"I sent Walter home so he could get some rest. The catalog is printing now, and I think you should take me out to dinner."

He looked to the clock and did some quick math. "I think that is wonderful idea. I have to be back by eight to review the final stories for tomorrow, but that gives us a couple of hours."

"Perfect. Go get your hat so you can look like a proper gentleman."

Octavius arrived before light on Saturday morning. He was happy to see that the boys had completed even more prep work than usual the night before. This allowed him to start two pots of the cassoulet and complete one pot of the Coq au vin soup. He also made three trays of pot-pies. He worked in a flurry to have as much completed as possible before assistance arrived.

Working at this pace drove out his inner distractions and allowed him to focus on what needed to be done at the bistro. Marcus showed up at shortly after eight and was amazed to see how much had already been readied.

"Good morning, chef. My goodness, how early did you get here today?"

"I decided to go to the market early this morning to get the best mushrooms. I wanted to see if larger ones would hold up better in the soup. That did not take long, so here I am."

Stephane arrived a few minutes later, and the three men had nearly all the food for the day either cooking or prepped within two hours. By late afternoon, there was very little for the chef to do. Stephane was cleaning the prep stations, while Marcus started expediting the orders that were coming in.

Natasha entered the kitchen and told Octavius that Gustavo had requested his presence in the dining room. Octavius walked out to see Victor and Tom working side-by-side on a row of drinks. Victor nodded his head toward the far table where Gustavo was sitting with a couple he did not recognize. There was a man wearing a nice suit topped by an expensive bowler hat. His wife looked very pretty even though she was dressed in professional attire most commonly reserved for office work.

When the owner saw his chef enter the dining room he started motioning for him wildly. "Octavius. Come, come. I want you to meet Thaddeus Donleavy and his wife Sarah. They are good friends of mine. Thaddeus is the publisher of the *East End Observer*, one of the most respected newspapers in all of London. Have you read it?"

Octavius immediately recognized the newspaper from the extensive coverage it had given to the Whitechapel murders. It was by far his favorite. He knew that he could not let his excitement show. "It is very nice to meet you Mister Donleavy. I'm afraid my position here at Café Langham does not allow much time for reading."

"You must forgive my chef, Thaddeus. He doesn't have much use for anything but food. When he gets a day off, you know what he does to relax? He goes to the country to do more cooking. Tomorrow he is heading north to get some special herbs. The man thinks only of food."

"Oh leave the poor man alone, Gustavo," Sarah said as she slapped at his hand. "Not everyone is obsessed with politics and murder. Some people are just a little more cultured than you two heathens. What did you discover in the country Chef Octavius?"

The question from the beautiful woman with a blue ribbon in her hair caught him off guard. He paused for a second before answering. "Umm, well, I met a fellow chef in Brixton and we made Coq au vin. It is what inspired me to create the soup you are eating now."

"Well that sounds like a very good way to relax. And I must say this is a lovely soup. It pairs well with this sherry drink."

"It's called The Langham," Gustavo said proudly. "Victor over there invented it. He makes the most wondrous cocktails. Would you like to try a Manhattan? You must try one. Victor! Make us three Manhattans."

"What about the chef? Wouldn't he like one?" Thaddeus offered looking to Octavius.

"No. Chef Octavius does not drink liquor. Can you imagine? Being around all this wonderful liquor all day. Having two master bartenders at your disposal. And not drinking even one drop of liquor."

"That would be hard on my marriage," admitted the publisher. "Sarah isn't happy when I have a couple glasses at my office at the end of the day. I would certainly be living on the streets if I could claim drinking as part of my job."

Sarah did not laugh at his joke, and instead turned back to the chef. "Tell me Octavius, do you ever go by Otto? I had a professor at university named Octavius and his friends all called him Otto."

The question was jarring to the chef. It instantly reminded him of his mother. He felt like he was a child again standing beside her bed waiting for instructions. It took him a moment to notice that he was staring at his feet. "Not since I was a child, madam."

He said it in such a sheepish voice that Sarah felt guilty for asking the question. "Sorry Chef Octavius, I did not mean to embarrass you. I always thought Otto was such a strong, interesting name."

Pulling himself together, he forced himself to make eye contact. "Not at all, Missus Donleavy. I just haven't heard that nickname since I left America. It made me feel a little homesick for a moment."

Octavius noticed that Victor had just finished the tray of Manhattans and used the opportunity to change the subject. He grabbed the tray, laid it on the table, then handed out the glasses. "This drink is made with rye whiskey and was originally created in New York City. Mister Donleavy, I hope you find that it pairs well with the cassoulet."

Thaddeus took a sip and shook his head in agreement. "That is very good. I definitely don't need any of those at my office. That drink has divorce written all over it."

Octavius forced a smile. "It was very good meeting you both. If there is anything you need, please just let me know. Best of luck with your next paper, Mister Donleavy. I am sure you will find more than enough politics and murder to fill the pages. And Missus Donleavy, I will let Victor know to go light on the Manhattans, so your husband doesn't have to sleep on the streets tonight."

Everyone laughed as the chef gave a slight bow and backed away from the table. He retreated back to the kitchen, where he sat on a stool at the prep table. He was thankful to be released from the social interaction.

A few minutes later, Gustavo stopped by the kitchen to thank the chef for entertaining his guests, bid him good evening, and told him to enjoy his weekend.

Once the owner was gone, Octavius made his rounds in the kitchen and dining room making sure everyone was set for the rest of the evening and tomorrow's service. Satisfied that everything was secure, he excused himself early.

Freed from the restaurant, he headed to his apartment to prepare for his nightly walk. Entering his room, he took his time in making his preparations. He selected the same blades. Put on his shirt, trousers, and vest. Affixed the knives to the vest pockets. Slipped on his new jacket. He'd had to burn the first one along with his shirt after the meeting with Mary Nichols.

He then sat on his bed reading over copies of the *East End Observer* he had collected over the past several weeks. It had remained his favorite of all the London rags, and he was thrilled that it had recently moved to a daily. After meeting Thaddeus and Sarah, he now had an even stronger connection to the newspaper.

He read through every article again soaking up the details. He was surprised to see a few passing mentions of Emma Elizabeth Smith. She had died nearly five months ago in early April. Her murder was still unsolved, but it had clearly been the act of thugs and had nothing to do with the other murders.

Martha Tabram's murder had been more sensational due to the violent nature of the killing. It had been a month since her passing, but she still received a lot of press. Her murder was also unsolved and there had been very little progress to report.

Mary Ann Nichols' murder had raised the stakes on all sides. The public was referring to them collectively as the Whitechapel murders and the papers highlighted the fear gripping the slums. Most importantly Scotland Yard had now been called in to handle the matter.

The deaths of Emma Smith and Martha Tabram had been handled by local inspectors, who had produced little results. They had conducted routine interviews and worked with doctors and coroners to gather facts. However, they had not named any real suspects.

Now that Detective Frederick Abberline was involved in the investigation, things began to progress more robustly in the case of Mary Nichols. In a matter of weeks, several people of interest had been brought in for questioning including Mary's husband, who had not seen his estranged wife in quite some time.

Other people of interest were interviewed including Charles

Cross and Robert Paul, the carters who had found her body. Patrick Mulshaw, a night watchman who had been working that night at the nearby sewer works. And Emily Holland, who had seen Mary an hour before her death and said she had been heavily drinking as she was known to do on a regular basis. Additional witnesses and inquiries were mentioned in the papers, but none appeared to matter much.

Octavius took special notice of Doctor Llewellyn's report. The doctor had conducted Mary Nichols' initial examination, and his full report was now shown verbatim in the *Observer*.

Five of the teeth were missing, and there was a slight laceration of the tongue. There was a bruise running along the lower part of the jaw on the right side of the face. That might have been caused by a blow from a fist or pressure from a thumb. There was a circular bruise on the left side of the face which also might have been inflicted by the pressure of the fingers.

On the left side of the neck, about one inch below the jaw, there was an incision about four inches in length, and ran from a point immediately below the ear. On the same side, but an inch below, and commencing about one inch in front of it, was a circular incision, which terminated at a point about three inches below the right jaw. That incision completely severed all the tissues down to the vertebrae. The large vessels of the neck on both sides were severed. The incision was about eight inches in length. The cuts must have been caused by a long-bladed knife, moderately sharp, and used with great violence.

No blood was found on the breast, either of the body or the clothes. There were no injuries about the body until just about the lower part of the abdomen. Two or three inches from the left side was a wound running in a jagged manner. The wound was a very deep one, and the tissues were cut through. There were several incisions running across the abdomen. There were three or four similar cuts running downwards, on the right side, all of which had been caused by a knife which had been used violently and downwards. The injuries were from left to right and might have been done by a left-handed person. All the injuries had been by the same instrument.

The description of Mary Nichols' death in such detail was fascinating to him. He could remember some of what he had done that night, but it had been dark and the event had only taken a few minutes. With the report he could now relive every cut, every angle of attack, every detail.

He was surprised by the amount of excitement he received from reading the report. Still, it seemed too clinical in his mind. He had killed her quickly by slashing her throat, but the other cuts he made were meant to draw more attention. He wanted the doctors to take notice and be forced to describe them in a way that projected fear. He would have to do better next time.

He finished running through the articles, again soaking up every detail possible. Going over the addresses mentioned, committing the names to memory, and looking for mentions of potential suspects. There were a few outlandish theories proposed, but no real suspects.

This was also disappointing to him. He wanted there to be a name to the killer. Not his name, of course, but any other name. Even a wrong name would help to give the public something more to fear. He knew that would come soon enough. The police had to start producing names soon, even if they proved to be wrong. The public would demand results.

Empowered by what he had read, he stood up and donned his top hat. It was nearly midnight, and he was ready.

Now that he was routinely walking the slums at night, he never started before eleven. That ensured that all the lamps would be extinguished by the time he made it to Whitechapel Street.

Octavius wasted no time in searching out his intended victim. He had first seen her two days ago coming out of Crossingham's Lodging House on Dorset Street. He had never seen her in the district before, and she was far from worthy to call herself a prostitute. She was plump and dirty, which was not uniquely unqualifying. But her health was severely compromised and her face was bruised and battered, which was completely unacceptable.

He turned up Dorset Street and passed by the Lodging House

on the far side of the road, being careful not to be noticed. There were no signs of the woman, so he decided to walk back to Whitechapel and hunt for other opportunities.

His walked the streets all evening and into the early morning. His anticipation never waned, but he soon realized that his night would not end as he had hoped. He decided to walk toward Spitalfields Market, which was an area known to be active at this hour.

It was nearly five in the morning by the time he got to the area. His heart leaped when he caught sight of his original mark walking away from him across Commercial Street and down Hanbury. Noticing that she was unaccompanied, he hastened his pace. If he were to even have a chance he would have to hurry as the glow of the morning sun would start to show within the next half-hour.

Hearing footsteps, the woman turned to see the sharply dressed man approaching. She looked at his top hat and recognized that he must have decent means. She put on her best smile and approached him with an offer of her company. The man did not speak, but nodded his head.

She took his arm and led him between two houses into a backyard area. It wasn't the best place for such activities, but she knew there wasn't any time to waste. Finding a suitable area. She dropped his arm and turned around, ready to begin. As she faced the man she saw that his hand was clutching a handkerchief as he grabbed her by the throat.

She was able to squeeze out two words before the cloth covered her mouth. "No! No!"

Thaddeus sat in a chair in the typesetting room holding his head. His stomach was churning, and he was certain he would be sick soon. He watched his wife as she worked. She was actually whistling as she scurried about the room.

"I told you not to drink those last few Manhattans," she said with a frown. "Now you are going to have a very long Saturday."

The publisher sat up in his chair and belched a bit. He looked like he was ready to say something, but thought better of it and slouched back into his original position.

"It is nearly ten o'clock. Where the hell is Walter?"

"I hope he is still sleeping in his bed. The poor man needs all the rest he can get. I am almost ready to get these rolls on the printer. Stop your whining."

"If you say so, dear. I've just never known the man to be late. Especially not on a Saturday."

"Why don't you make yourself useful and start carrying those rollers back to Frank. He is running the press today."

Reluctantly, Thaddeus got out of his chair and did as he was told. He carried three rollers back to the print room. He was on his way back to the typesetting room when he saw that O'Conner and Sam were already in the room.

"The Whitechapel murderer has struck again." Sam was a bit winded but not nearly as bad as the out-of-shape O'Conner.

"She had her throat cut same as the last girl."

Without saying a word, Sarah started removing the type from the remaining print roller. Thaddeus sat down at the typewriter and inserted a sheet of paper. "Sarah, please set it up for a three liner on the headline, and go ahead and clear the entire front page. I will write enough to fill it."

Sam pulled out his notepad and started reading off the details he had received from the briefing at Scotland Yard, while O'Conner added in the information he had received after speaking with the Divisional Inspector who was the first man to take the report.

Annie Chapman was a forty-seven year old widow with dark hair. She had been in ill health due to a severe lung condition. When money allowed, she resided at Crossingham's Lodging House living there at the daily rate.

She had been found murdered in the backyard of a small house at twenty-nine Hanbury Street at six that morning when the owner, an elderly man named John Davis, stepped outside to use the lavatory.

Mister Davis then alerted three local men and asked them to fetch a policeman, while he left his residence to file a report at the station. The three men came back a few minutes later with Divisional Inspector Joseph Luniss Chandler and led him to the body. Inspector Chandler then called for more officers and sent for a doctor.

Doctor George Bagster Phillips arrived quickly and pronounced Annie Chapman dead at six thirty by way of a cut throat. The doctor also formally established a definitive link between her murder and that of Mary Ann Nichols.

Scotland Yard was immediately notified and Chief Inspector Donald Swanson was dispatched to the scene; however, no one had yet been given command of the investigation.

Thaddeus was able to process the information quickly and completed the article just seconds after the men provided the last details. He pulled the paper out of the typewriter and read it over. After making a few changes in pencil, he handed the page to his wife to start typesetting.

At that moment Walter came crashing into the office knocking over a chair. "Oh my. I am so late. So sorry. I mean I am so sorry I am late. I must have overslept. I never do that. What did I miss? What's wrong? Why are you all in here at this hour?"

"Calm down, Walter. There has been another murder. We are changing out the front page, then we will start the Saturday edition. Sarah is setting it now."

Sarah stood up from her chair. "Here Walter, you are faster than I am. You finish this up, and I will go make sure everything else is ready with the printer."

"Frank, go with her and have the men pull extra rolls of paper. We need to push the run to twenty thousand. Sorry Walter, but the catalog might have to push a day this week."

Walter did not respond. He was moving as fast as he could pushing out lines of type. A few minutes later he had everything finished. "Okay, boss. I just need a headline."

Thaddeus sat down at the table and cleared his mind. Then

he started to arrange the letters.

2ND WHITECHAPEL WOMAN FOUND WITH THROAT CUT
EAST END GRIPPED IN PANIC AS MURDERER RUNS FREE
CAN ANYONE AT SCOTLAND YARD STOP THE MADNESS

Octavius was lying on his bed naked with his hands clasped behind his head. His suit hung back in the wardrobe and the top hat sat on the table. He had managed to keep nearly all the blood off his clothing this time. He had used a neckerchief to shield the spray from her neck. The rest was contained on his gloves, which he threw into the river on his walk back to the apartment.

His heart was still racing. This one had been different than before. He had been rushed. A man next door to where they were standing had come out to use the facilities just as he was reaching for his victim. He was able to shut her mouth by slicing her throat, but then he had to stand there with her until the man went back into his house.

He then rushed through the rest of his work in less than five minutes. He had hoped to have more time to create a dramatic example for the other whores. Nevertheless, he was confident this new murder would have more impact than the others.

He rested for a while longer to be sure his heart rate and breathing had normalized. Then he got up and rechecked his clothing for blood spots or other incriminating evidence. His suit jacket, vest, shirt, and trousers were all clean. He took longer inspecting the top hat. He spotted a couple small droplets of blood so he dabbed them with a wet towel. Then he took out his bottle of mercury dye and brushed over the spots. He also coated the inside of the hat band with the dye to blacken the thin line of sweat stains that had appeared.

He then dressed in his chef's uniform. Reaching into his wardrobe he took out a couple small glass jars and stuck them in his pocket before heading downstairs.

It was afternoon now, so most of the newspapers had already hit the streets. He went to the corner where a boy was selling *The London Gazette*. He bought a paper and looked at the headline.

WHITECHAPEL MURDERER STIKES AGAIN
INVESTIGATION STARTED, DETAILS TO COME

Well, that wasn't very exciting. It was clear that the *Gazette* had to go to press with few details. He knew they would do better for the Sunday edition, but he wanted immediate gratification.

He continued walking down the street to look for more options. He soon found a corner with boys on opposite sides shouting out headlines. One was from the *Gazette*. The other was from the *East End Observer*. He headed that way trying not to rush. Then he heard the barker yelling out the headline. "Second Whitechapel woman with throat cut! East End panics as murderer runs free! Can Scotland Yard stop the madness?"

He could not contain his smile. Now that was a proper headline. He grabbed a paper and paid the boy four times the going rate.

He read the article several times. Each time finding a new line that excited him. He was sure this new story would wake up the prostitutes in London. They would have no choice but to retreat from the streets. Hopefully, soon he would not need to don his top hat anymore. The filthiest of whores would find more fitting work, and the proper prostitutes would sign on to houses with clean beds and professional management.

He tucked the paper under his arm and decided to check on the restaurant. The staff wasn't expecting him, so it would be interesting to see how things were being run in his expected absence.

He arrived at the restaurant at about six. Five of the tables were full, and about half the seats at the bar. Not bad for a Saturday. Natasha met him at the door. "Good day, chef. I didn't think you were working today."

"I'm not, Natasha. Just got back into town and thought I

would stop by to check on things. Think I'll just have a seat at the bar."

He sat down at the bar and waved at Victor. "Hello, chef. Is everything alright?"

"Everything is fine. Can you get me a glass of tonic water?"

"Yes, chef. Right away."

He asked Natasha to fetch him a pot-pie and opened up the newspaper to read the article again. He could hear conversations all over the restaurant. They were all talking about the murder of Annie Chapman. He could only pick out pieces: *poor lady, innocent victim, why aren't there any suspects*, and his favorite, *it's no longer safe on the streets at night.*

Marcus brought out a pot-pie and small bowl of Coq au vin soup out. "Chef, I did not expect to see you today. Here, I brought you some soup so you could taste it."

"I'm sure it's fine, Marcus. I could tell by the smell of this place that things were well in hand." He reached into his pocket and pulled out two bottles of herbs. "Here, I picked this up in the north country. Try a little of this one in the soup, and a little of this one in the stew and let me know what you think on Monday. Not too much now. They are both pretty strong."

Marcus looked at the bottles curiously. "Thank you, chef. I will try them out right away."

With his alibi set, Octavius went back to reading his article.

Thaddeus and Walter shook hands with a tall Romanian man as he left the publisher's office. They waited until he left the building before speaking.

"Now don't be sad, Walter. I know how much you loved printing those ugly catalogs."

Walter scrunched up his face and pushed his glasses up on his nose. "I never said I liked the blasted things. I just said they paid the bills."

"Well now they can be someone else's headache, and we can

get back to the business of printing proper newspapers. Plus, we still own all those accounts and will make a decent bit of money off subcontracting."

"I just hope those Romanians don't screw it up. They have a fancy new printer and all, but that just means they can make mistakes at a faster rate."

The two men walked downstairs and into the typesetting room. "Don't worry; you will still be going over to their office every day to do press checks. I'm sure they are going to LOVE working with such a sweet and easy going old man."

"Sarah, can you do something about your husband? He keeps harassing me."

"Now Thaddeus, you leave Walter alone or he might start letting me write all the headlines."

"Very well. If you both are going to gang up on me, then I will go see if Frank needs any help with the printer."

The publisher walked in to see Frank changing the oil on the steam engine. The old press had performed admirably over the past several days. It had been a week since the last murder and the printer had been put through its paces. They had continued running fifteen thousand copies a day and twenty thousand on Saturdays and Sundays.

Thaddeus was pleased with how things were progressing. They had hired four new reporters, and at least two were decent enough to keep long term. Now that they had subcontracted all their outside jobs, Walter could keep up with the workload on his own with Sarah as a backup. He would try and get the man to hire an assistant, but that was no longer a pressing matter.

The ledger was also doing very well, and he had rebuilt his surplus. He would lose a bit of profits from the reduced catalog revenues, but he felt confident he could make that up by selling more newspapers and adding a few new advertisers.

To make it to the next level, he knew they needed another push. The truly respectable papers weren't just dailies. They also needed to print a respectable circulation. It wasn't likely that they were going to match the circulation of the *Daily Telegraph* or *London Times* or even the *Gazette*. Those papers were running a hundred thousand copies or more a day. They just needed to hit thirty thousand copies a day. Not just on the weekends and special editions, but every day.

To do that, they would need to add more reporters and advertisers. They would also need something more. He just didn't know what the more was yet.

Octavius had found a comfortable rhythm over the next ten days. His staff at the restaurant was able to handle things well on their own. He would move in and out of the kitchen as needed making small changes to the menu while letting the boys handle the majority of the cooking.

He even let Marcus introduce a new menu item of his own, a beef tenderloin with roasted potatoes. It wasn't the fanciest or most original of dishes, but an herb butter added a little distinctiveness to the dish.

Victor let Tom choose the accompanying cocktail, which was an even bigger hit. He mixed sweet gin with lemon juice, sugar syrup, and soda water and poured it into a tall glass filled with ice. The new drink was called a Tom Collins, and it was all the rage in America. However, Tom mostly likely selected the beverage because it shared his name, and he could tell all the ladies that he invented it himself.

Gustavo gushed over the additions, as he seemed to do with all things new, and had to be carried to his office at the end of the night after Tom fed him too many of his namesake beverages.

Octavius even forced himself to engage in small talk with Natasha and Margaret on occasion. He had grown more comfortable around Natasha, especially now that he had known her longer. Margaret was more reserved, which made it was easier for them to both find ways to avoid each other without being socially awkward.

Even his nightly walks in the Whitechapel District had

become almost soothing now that the streets had become nearly devoid of all deviancy after the lamps went out. The independent prostitutes started gathering in groups and hired men for protection. This felt like a passable alternative to Octavius.

He started his nights by reading the papers making sure that the investigation was still making headlines. The *East End Observer* remained his favorite.

They always led with the latest on the investigation and had quotes from all the detectives and inspectors on the case. But where they shined the most was with their contacts in the medical field. After Annie Chapman's murder, they printed Doctor George Bagster Phillips' entire medical report, which caused a stir throughout the city.

The left arm was placed across the left breast. The legs were drawn up, the feet resting on the ground, and the knees turned outwards. The face was swollen and turned on the right side. The tongue protruded between the front teeth, but not beyond the lips. The tongue was evidently much swollen. The front teeth were perfect as far as the first molar, top and bottom and very fine teeth they were.

The body was terribly mutilated. The stiffness of the limbs was not marked, but was evidently commencing. The throat was disseevered deeply; the incisions through the skin were jagged and reached right round the neck. On the wooden paling between the yard in question and the next, smears of blood, corresponding to where the head of the deceased lay, were to be seen. These were about fourteen inches from the ground, and immediately above the part where the blood from the neck lay.

The instrument used at the throat and abdomen was the same. It must have been a very sharp knife with a thin narrow blade, and must have been at least six to eight inches in length, probably longer. He should say that the injuries could not have been inflicted by a bayonet or a sword bayonet. They could have been done by such an instrument as a medical man used for post-mortem purposes, but the ordinary surgical cases might not contain such an instrument. Those used by the slaughtermen, well ground down, might have caused them. He thought the knives used by those in the leather trade would not be long enough in the blade. There were indications of anatomical knowledge.

He should say that the deceased had been dead at least two hours, and probably more, when he first saw her; but it was right to mention that it was a fairly cool morning, and that the body would be more apt to cool rapidly from its having lost a great quantity of blood. There was no evidence of a struggle having taken place. He was positive the deceased entered the yard alive.

A handkerchief was round the throat of the deceased when he saw it early in the morning. He should say it was not tied on after the throat was cut.

Octavius was reasonably satisfied with this description. Like with Mary Nichols, the doctor did not describe all that had been done to Annie Chapman, out of propriety he supposed.

With both victims, he had performed more mutilation to the lower regions. With Annie Chapman he had been especially brutal pulling out some of her insides to make a more gruesome show of things. He did not do this out of entertainment for himself, but to insight more fear among the whores.

He knew it did not matter. The rumors of the mutilations had spread like wildfire through the streets. It was almost better that the doctors and detectives were trying to hide the details. It made people fear them as much as the killer. The fact that no viable suspects had been named and no arrests had been made led to great suspicion among the masses.

He was pleased with the progress, but he had come to a realization that the lessons were not quite over yet. There was fear and maybe a little panic in the air, but more would be needed to finish his goal. He just needed to wait for the right moment to don his top hat again.

It was nearly midnight on Tuesday, seventeen days since the last murder. Thaddeus sat in his office alone sipping from a glass of whiskey. He had been racking his brain trying to figure out how to move his newspaper to the next level. They had been doing fine, but he wanted more.

He had pushed circulation to twenty-five thousand a day, but they were throwing away at least two to three thousand each night after the barkers returned. They were so close, but he needed to find something to keep things moving in a positive direction.

He sat thinking about the investigation. There were plenty of details coming out each day, more than enough to fill the pages of the paper. It wasn't the story that was the problem. It was the headlines. They had gotten mundane. They just weren't scandalous enough.

He knew the biggest problem was the name – Whitechapel Murderer. It was too plain, too boring. It made him sound like a familiar enemy. Whitechapel was a London institution, a landmark. There were businesses, schools, even churches with Whitechapel in the name. No matter what vile moniker you put after it, the people living in the East End would never see Whitechapel as truly evil.

But how could the name be changed now? He could try just calling the killer by another name, but the other newspapers would never follow along. It needed to come from someone else. Maybe a politician or some socialite. Ideally it would come from the killer. But that was never going to happen.

Or would it? An idea started to form in his head. Maybe the killer could name himself after all. He grabbed a sheet of old paper from his desk. It looked too pristine, so he wrinkled it a tad. Then he grabbed a red editing pen he had in his desk. He heated the tip over a candle so that the ink would come out uneven. He wanted to make sure no one recognized his handwriting, then he remembered that the killer was thought to be left handed.

He picked up the pen in his left hand and started to write being sure to use poor grammar. He decided to write in an offbeat style and use strange concepts to make it look more manic.

Dear Boss,

I keep on hearing the police have caught me but they wont fix me just yet. I have laughed when they look so clever and talk about being on the <u>right</u> track. That joke about Leather Apron gave me real fits. I am down on whores and I shant quit ripping them till I do get buckled. Grand work the last job was. I gave the lady no time to squeal. How can they catch me now. I love my work and want to start again. You will soon hear of me with my funny little games. I saved some of the proper <u>red</u> stuff in a ginger beer bottle over the last job to write with but it went thick like glue and I cant use it. Red ink is fit enough I hope <u>ha. ha.</u> The next job I do I shall clip the ladys ears off and send to the police officers just for jolly wouldn't you. Keep this letter back till I do a bit more work, then give it out straight. My knife's so nice and sharp I want to get to work right away if I get a chance. Good Luck.

Yours truly
Jack the Ripper

Dont mind me giving the trade name

Reading it back over he decided it would do the trick. He hesitated when writing the part about sending a lady's ear, but thought it would provide more dramatic impact. If the killer did strike again, he would either play into the letter or dismiss it altogether. Either way, it would still provide more fodder for the papers. In a perfect world the killer would respond with a letter of his own and try to correct the record. This would provide even more to write about.

The real goal was to introduce the world to Jack the Ripper. Now that was a proper title. One that would shine in the headlines and echo on the streets as the barkers shouted the name. Even if the letter was debunked as a fraud, the name would still stand.

He had written the note on both sides of the paper and had room left at the end, so he decided to continue the letter's manic theme. He also wanted to deride one of the prevailing theories that the investigators had about the killer being a doctor. He thought that notion was absurd, so why not have a little fun.

PS Wasnt good enough to post this before I got all the red ink off my hands curse it. No luck yet. They say I'm a doctor now. ha ha

He dated the letter September 25 and addressed it to the Central News Agency, which was a news distribution service that was known, but sparingly used by newspapers throughout London. The agency had a reputation for distributing the most sensational stories, using dubious sources, and not always making facts a high priority. He thought this service would be the most likely to disseminate the letter without too much investigation into its veracity.

He sealed the letter and headed out of the office. He walked a few blocks before finding a mailbox to drop it in. Now all he had to do was wait.

The next morning, Thaddeus decided he needed to make preparations for what came next. He estimated that it would take two days for the letter to reach the Central News Agency. The mail typically arrived in the morning in that area, and it would take a few minutes for the letter to be discovered. It would promptly be taken to Thomas Bulling who was currently managing the daily activities at the agency.

Tom was someone that Thaddeus knew well from their social circles. He was a brash but fairly sensible man. The publisher was certain that Tom would take the letter to Scotland Yard straight away. He was equally certain that he would make a copy first. Lead Detective Abberline would likely not allow the agency to release the letter until they had vetted it properly, but that would not stop Tom from sending out a press release alerting everyone to the letter's existence. He was also certain that press release would introduce the world to the name Jack the Ripper

Before all that came to pass, Thaddeus needed to put a couple of things into motion. First he needed to make sure that he had someone from his office at the Central News Agency as soon as the news broke. Second, he would need to find an excuse to delay the printing of the Thursday paper so that the *Observer* would be the first newspaper to headline the killer's name. And all of this needed to be done in a way that did not draw attention to himself.

The first part was easy. He had recently hired an energetic young reporter named Colton who was eager to please. He asked the young man into his office and told him he was assigning him to start checking the news agencies in town every morning. He told him to start with the Press Association and then Reuters, which were the two more respectable agencies. He was to then stop by the Central News Agency last before coming back to the office to report what he had learned.

As for delaying the printing, he would have to work that out in the heat of the moment. The steam engine was a finicky machine, so he was sure he could turn a couple bolts if necessary.

His plan was set. Now he just needed a bit of luck and some good timing for it to all pay off. He set about the rest of the day as normal. He held the editorial meeting with the team and they set the stories for the Thursday paper. It was a slow news day, so everyone agreed that the Whitechapel murders should continue as the lead story.

By early afternoon, Walter had finished typesetting the rollers for the next day's run. He always left the last set for the morning in case anything exciting happened overnight.

Thaddeus was too anxious to sleep that night. He had taken a huge gamble with his plan and had never really thought through the consequences. He had to start being more careful. If he were to be found out, it would mean the end of the *East End Observer*. The end of the company. Maybe even the end of his marriage. Sarah was a stickler for journalistic ethics and morality in general. She certainly would not approve of his plan.

The next morning Thaddeus got to the office and tried to stay calm. He went through the lead stories with Walter who was as efficient as always. The publisher threw in his first delay by asking the old typesetter to replace the bottom story with a new political article that Frank had brought in that morning about the old Prime Minister's ailing health.

By ten-thirty Walter had finished making the changes and carried the last roller out to the printer. Thaddeus knew that the presses would be ready to run in less than thirty minutes. With no other reason to delay, they would start the engine.

He considered grabbing his wrench, but decided against the idea, remembering his sleepless night and all that he had to lose. They would just have to rush out an early edition tomorrow morning and compete with all the other papers.

He was about to head up to his office when he saw Colton running up to the building. "Mister Donleavy, have they started the printer yet?"

His heart started racing, "I don't think so. Walter is setting the final roller now."

The young man caught his breath and handed him a piece of paper. "The Central News Agency just put this out. They charged five pounds for it, but I thought it was worth the outrageous price."

Thaddeus looked it over and feigned surprise. It was just what he needed and nothing more.

On Thursday Octavius worked at the restaurant all morning and through the lunch hours. It was a calm day with a moderate amount of diners. By early afternoon, he decided to head to the market to see what new fall vegetables were available.

The streets were fairly busy, and the people seemed to be buzzing more than usual. He didn't pay too much attention until he got to the corner near the market where a small group was gathering.

He started to walk over to see what all the fuss was about and noticed two young boys, barely ten years old, untwining stacks of newspapers. One of the boys kicked over a milk crate and stood on top. Then he started shouting out the headlines.

Octavius couldn't hear him at first, so he moved in closer.

Then he heard it. He wasn't certain at first, so he moved in even closer. The boy shouted it again and goosebumps shot up his spine. His eyes widened. At first he felt a wave of shock, not sure whether to be scared or excited. He was both. He was close enough now to see the headline from the *East End Observer*.

WHITECHAPEL MURDERER SENDS LETTER
CALLS HIMSELF JACK THE RIPPER
SCOTLAND YARD TO VERIFY AUTHENTICITY

Octavius purchased a copy of the paper and walked into the market. Finding a bench, he sat down and scanned the article in a flurry. He couldn't believe what he was reading. At first his stomach knotted at seeing the name Jack. Was this a reference to his last name Jackson?

But he quickly dismissed this notion. If someone knew or even suspected him he would have been arrested. The police were now issuing inquests and arrest warrants for even the most mundane of leads. New suspects were named almost daily, even though most were dismissed within hours or at least days. The city had reached a state of panic, and if the authorities could not show results, they at least needed to show activity.

Jack was often used as a stand-in for the common man or any fellow on the street. There was no reason for him to think otherwise in this instance.

Reading the article again, he saw it for what it was – a fraud. A very good, very beneficial fraud, but a fraud nonetheless. He loved the name and the fear it invoked. He could hear people throughout the market repeating the name Jack the Ripper. They spoke it in hushed, almost reverent tones.

He stood up and walked the area pretending to look at the vegetable stands. He stood closer than usual to groups of people listening in on the conversations.

Everyone was repeating the news. Repeating the details of the murders. Repeating the dangers of the streets after dark. Sharing their fears. And now their fear had a name. The

Liberator now had a name. Whenever he wore the top hat, he would now become Jack the Ripper.

That Friday and the Café Langham was packed beyond capacity. The news of Jack the Ripper had spread like lightning throughout London and everyone wanted to gather in public places to talk about the killer's new moniker.

Every member of the staff at the restaurant was rushing as fast as they could. The bartenders were in constant motion mixing, stirring, and pouring drinks. Natasha had to stop taking orders at one point and just started selling bowls of soup and stew one tray at a time. Margaret had been stuck washing bowls, spoons, and glasses nonstop for hours.

Even Gustavo had joined in to help at one point, mainly in collecting coins and throwing them in his bulging money pouch. Of course, he also helped to serve drinks, at least the ones that made it to customers.

By one in the afternoon, Octavius ran to the main hotel restaurant to request help from Chef Simon. Business in the more formal establishment was not nearly as overrun, so he offered up two line cooks and the use of one of his stoves. Octavius sent Stephane to the main kitchen to start boiling four more pots. They had long since abandoned the idea of making pot-pies and only used the ovens for bread.

By early evening, the restaurant had run through every slab of pork, every piece of chicken, and nearly every type of vegetable that could be found in either the bistro or main restaurant. Looking around at his exhausted staff, the chef knew it was time to stop the madness. He made his way through the dining room and found Gustavo clinking glasses with a group of businessmen before swigging a drink. "Sorry, sir, but I'm afraid we are going to have to close the kitchen. We have cooked every morsel left in the building."

Gustavo grabbed his chef by the shoulders and shook him, smiling widely. "Everyone! You have eaten us out of house and home! The kitchen is closed!"

The crowd groaned in unison. "But the BAR IS STILL OPEN!"

The crowd cheered and glasses could be heard clanking. Octavius looked to Victor who looked stoic as always and Tom who was cheerful as ever.

Gustavo sensed his chef's concern. "But it will only stay open as long as you properly tip my bartenders." More cheers went up as a shower of coins were thrown into the metal buckets holding the tips.

It took Octavius and Marcus about an hour to clean up the mess from the meal service. Then Marcus started helping Margaret clean the glasses that kept stacking up from the bar. Stephane came down from finishing his clean up in the main restaurant and joined Natasha in helping to hand out drinks.

Feeling like things were finally under control the weary chef found a seat at the bar near Victor, who poured him a tonic water. He sat in the seat sipping from his drink as he listened to the buzz of the crowd. There was only one thing being discussed. He closed his eyes and soaked it all in. No one there understood they were drinking with the great Liberator. No one knew they were in the presence of Jack the Ripper.

"What a ghastly name." Sarah was looking at copies of Friday and Saturday's newspapers laid out across the table where the journalists were holding an editorial meeting. Both papers prominently showed Jack the Ripper in the headlines.

"It IS a ghastly name. A horrible, wonderfully ghastly name." Thaddeus picked up a paper and held it high. "And we are the newspaper that introduced it to the people of London!"

"To all of Europe!" corrected Frank.

The Thursday paper had been a massive hit for the *East End Observer*. They had started printing at eleven thirty that morning and did not stop until after six.

On regular speed the old steam printer could produce roughly eight thousand copies an hour. On that day, they pushed the printer to its max; printing ten thousand copies an hour, producing more than sixty thousand copies. It was by far the largest run they had ever completed in one day.

They sold out of newspapers even faster than they could print them. Throughout the day newsboys lined up for half a block waiting for new stacks to run to their corners.

It was the most exciting day Thaddeus could ever remember at the company. Every journalist, typesetter, and pressman stayed at the office that day. The reporters didn't even have to leave the office to cover stories because their sources came to the publishing office to give interviews and talk about the news in person.

Advertisers were furious that they had missed out on the opportunity to be in the "special edition." Thaddeus signed up more than a dozen new clients that day and added twice that number on Friday and Saturday.

He had no idea what the next few days or weeks would bring. No idea how long this success would last. But there was one thing he knew for certain – Jack the Ripper was good for business.

Octavius slept in on Saturday morning, thankful to have an extra day off. Normally, he enjoyed the distraction of a busy service, but Friday had been especially taxing. Under normal circumstances he would have been prepared for such an onslaught, but the popularity of Jack the Ripper had affected his focus.

The rush of business had been a good learning experience for his staff. Plus, Gustavo had showered them with praise saying he had never seen so many people served so much food and drink. He even paid everyone double their weekly wages and had given them Saturday off. He did not have much choice about Saturday anyway, as they had run out both food and liquor by the end of the night. They would not be able to restock until Monday, when the vendors reopened.

Now Octavius was ready to switch mindsets. All of London was in a chaotic state. During the daylight hours the city streets were crowded. People rushed to finish work, shopping, and all manner of tasks. Once the sun set, people in the better parts of the city returned to the safety of their homes.

In the slums, a fog of panic had set in, but it did not stop all the unsavory activity. Certainly not enough for Octavius. The whores still came out. They may have changed their tactics, but they still walked the streets.

At first, the independent prostitutes gathered in groups, but this made it tough to attract men looking for comfort. Plus, they would often fight over who had the right of way in accosting potential customers. The need for money outweighed the safety of numbers.

Before the murders, the late morning hours between one and four in the morning were the most active for independent prostitutes. However, these hours were now harder to work. Bars in the slums were now forced to close at midnight and customers did not want to stay out much later. Plus, the streets were patrolled by dozens of more watchmen, especially in the Whitechapel areas where the dark corners were easiest to find.

Scotland Yard had also ordered all street lamps to stay lit until one in the morning throughout the Whitechapel area, which was probably the biggest deterrent to sales. This severely limited the areas where the prostitutes could take their customers without being seen by others. Plus, anyone caught in such rendezvous by the authorities would be arrested on the spot.

Octavius appreciated these restrictions. They were the reason he had donned the top hat in the first place. But they would prove problematic for what he planned to do tonight.

Now that the Liberator had a proper name, he knew that he had to strike quickly in order to seal the legacy of Jack the Ripper. If he could find a victim tonight while the hysteria was high, then the restrictions would stay in place long term and maybe even increase. The fear would stay with every woman who dared walk the streets as an independent whore.

The weather had turned colder that week, which would help his cause. People would be wearing heavier coats, hats, and scarfs. They would also be less likely to stand around on the streets, and would hurry to their destinations. But best of all, it would allow him to wear his overcoat which provided more concealment and larger pockets.

He felt strange starting his dressing routine at only ten that night. First he prepared his blades. He took out the eight inch chef and boning knives. He considered taking others now that he had more room, but decided against it. He put on his shirt, trousers, vest, and jacket. Then he put on his overcoat and slipped his knives into leather scabbards he had sewn into the left and right breast pockets of the coat.

He made sure he was fully ready before grabbing the top hat. He slowly seated it onto his head, then turned to look at his reflection in the window. He looked different this time. More menacing. More imposing. He looked like Jack the Ripper.

He walked down the stairs and quickly made his way onto the street. He turned toward Whitechapel, traveling in large strides. It took him less than an hour to reach the slums. It was nearly midnight, and he stopped at a bench on Whitechapel Street that he had used before to observe the activity in the area.

The light from the street lamps made him feel exposed, so he took a newspaper out of his coat pocket and opened it wide to shield his face from view. After sitting for about thirty minutes a night watchman passed buy and told him that loiterers were not allowed after dark in the area and forced him to move.

Octavius walked about the area looking for another place to situate himself. After twenty minutes of walking he continued to come across policemen at nearly every other corner. At one point he had spotted a whore negotiating with a man. They started to walk together toward an alley, when they were accosted by a night watchman and the pair quickly separated.

After midnight, Octavius was approached by a policeman who asked him where he was headed. He told him he had just finished a meeting with friends and was headed to his room. The officer accepted his answer and bade him goodnight.

It had become clear that the longer he stayed in the area, the more conspicuous he would become. A feeling of anger started boiling in him as a realized he would likely not have an opportunity to achieve his goal that night. He started the walk back to his apartment staying vigilant during the journey.

As he moved away from the slums of Whitechapel he noticed that the streets became darker. There was also more activity in the alleyways. The police had consolidated all their resources into the known problem areas, so other areas of the city were being neglected. As he reached Berner Street he noticed a woman standing near the International Working Men's Educational Club soliciting the men who passed in front of her.

He turned up the street to take a closer look. He was only slightly familiar with the area, but knew it to be a fairly dark street with narrow spaces between the buildings. As he got closer he could tell that the woman was a prostitute. She was middle aged and wore a dress that was ragged and dirty. No not a prostitute, but a whore.

He touched the brim of his top hat and looked around. Not seeing anyone about, he approached the woman. She quickly grabbed his arm and asked him if he "wanted a quick yank."

He nodded and let her lead him into the yard located next to the club. He looked back to make sure no one had seen them enter the dark area.

A banging sound woke Sarah from her slumber. She looked at her husband who was still sleeping next to her and snoring loudly. A second round of banging caused her to start. This time Thaddeus sat up quickly. He looked at his wife who had no answers to give.

A third round of banging sounded as the publisher put on his slippers and headed down stairs to answer the front door. He opened the door to find O'Conner standing there holding his notepad and shivering in the cold.

"Sorry to wake you, boss. There has been another murder."

"Come inside, it's cold out there. What time is it?"

"It's nearly four in the morning, sir."

"This is a little early for murder Mister O'Conner, even for Jack the Ripper."

"I know sir, but it looks definitive."

"Very well then, let me get dressed, and we can head to the office. Does anyone else know yet?"

"Sam is headed to Scotland Yard now, but it might be a couple hours before they say anything. I'm sure the other papers have it as well. I was alerted by an officer friend at H Headquarters. He told me about thirty minutes ago. He wasn't sure when it happened, but it was at least a couple hours ago. The doctor has already left the scene, and Detective Abberline from the Yard is on site."

Sarah came down the stairs wearing her heavy robe.

"Good evening, ma'am," O'Conner said turning his head to shield his eyes.

"Good morning, O'Conner. I will get dressed and come to the office. There is no need to wake Walter at this hour. I can handle the typesetting until he gets there."

"O'Connor, why don't you go wake up Frank and Peter? They can get the printer ready. We have most of the back pages ready, so we can start printing as soon as the details come in."

Thaddeus and Sarah arrived at the publishing building an hour later. O'Conner along with two young journalists that had joined the company less than a month ago were waiting at the table. From the window Thaddeus could see Frank and Peter were working on getting the printer ready.

O'Conner stood up as they entered the building. "Sir, there is rumor that there might be another murder. We are getting reports that there may be another crime scene several blocks away from the first murder, or other murder. We don't know which one was first."

"Any word from Sam?" Thaddeus hung up his hat and coat.

"No, sir. Jimmy here just brought me the information."

"Okay then, Jimmy you go to the area where this new crime

scene is and see what you can find out. Get everything you can by seven. No matter what get back here by seven, understood?"

Jimmy nodded his head and ran out the door.

The publisher turned to the other young man. "You, what's your name again? Never mind, it doesn't matter right now. Get down to Scotland Yard and find Sam. Tell him that we need whatever he can get us by seven. We are going to start setting the front page at seven and get this thing on the printer before eight come hell or high water."

The young man shot out the door.

"O'Conner, see what the Section H Inspectors and beat cops have to say. You know the deadline."

"I'll get back as soon as I can to help start putting together the pieces."

He looked at Sarah to get her reaction. "I'll move as fast as I can. I can get everything else set before seven. The rest will be up to the guys and how fast you can type."

With that everyone jumped into motion. Sarah could be seen running back and forth from the typesetting room to the printer. Frank and Peter knew that they would be running at least fifty thousand copies for such a big event, so they got busy pulling out extra rolls of paper.

Thaddeus sat at his typewriter and contemplated headlines and played around with a few choice phrases. He knew this would be a defining story for him and the *East End Observer*. It didn't matter that every newspaper in town would be covering the same story, people would be buying every newspaper in town today. What mattered was that his story was the best.

At six forty-five O'Conner came back and started reciting what he had found out. Jimmy arrived a few minutes later, followed by Sam and the other young reporter. They were all talking at once.

Thaddeus didn't stop them, instead he let the information wash over him as he typed. He stopped at times to ask a question or to make one of the men repeat themselves. Then he continued typing. The details were immense and very scandalous.

At approximately one in the morning Elizabeth Stride had been discovered murdered in the Dutfield's Yard off Berner Street. Miss Stride, known as Long Liz by her friends, was a forty-four year old long-time resident of London's Whitechapel District. She was a known prostitute who worked the slums like all the other victims.

She had been murdered much the same way as the other ladies by way of a slit throat. However, she had not been mutilated as the other women had been. This was thought to be because the murder was interrupted by the man who first discovered her body, Louis Diemschutz.

Mister Diemschutz found the body when driving his horse and two-wheeled cart into the Dutfield's Yard and his horse suddenly jumped to the left. Seeing a dark object in the way, he prodded it with his whip handle and exited his cart to get a closer look. When he realized it was a body, he ran into the International Working Man's Education Club and reported what he had found. Then he ran down the street to find a policeman.

The police reported that blood was still flowing from her neck and that she was still warm to the touch. The first doctor to arrive was Frederick William Blackwell, who pronounced her dead from a cut throat. Doctor George Phillips, who had also examined previous victim Annie Chapman, arrived a few minutes later to serve as the official examiner for Scotland Yard.

Nearly three miles from where Elizabeth Stride was murdered, the body of Catherine Eddowes was discovered at approximately one forty-five that same morning in the south-west corner of Mitre Square. She was found by beat policeman Edward Watkins, who had walked through the area only fifteen minutes earlier and had not seen another person in the vicinity.

Catherine Eddowes was a middle aged woman who had been booked into custody by Police Constable Louis Robinson Saturday evening at eight-thirty when she was found passed out drunk and lying in the middle of the street. After sobering up at the Bishopsgate Police Station, she was released from custody at around one in the morning, where she was last seen walking toward Frenchchurch Street.

Police Surgeon Doctor Frederick Gordon Brown arrived at the crime scene a little after two and pronounced Catherine Eddowes dead by reason of a slit throat. Unlike Miss Stride, the killer had found the time to severely mutilate her body and had even taken some body parts with him.

Thaddeus was overcome by the audacity of it all. In the span of less than an hour, the Ripper had killed one woman, ran nearly three miles, found another victim, and murdered her in the most heinous way possible. He had also taken body parts, one of which had been an ear.

The ear was especially troubling to the publisher. There was little doubt that detail had come from the suggestion he had added to his letter. He could never have imagined that the killer would take the notion so serious that he would be willing to kill another victim just to make it happen.

He didn't have time to ponder such things at the moment. They needed to get the story typeset as quickly as possible in order to get papers on the street before people started leaving their homes.

He pulled the page from the typewriter and handed it to O'Conner to read. He read it quickly and handed it to Sarah, who ran to the typesetter and punched out the letters.

Thaddeus stood around the table with a piece of paper and pen and started pitching headlines to the group. By the time Sarah was finished with her work, the men had settled on a headline.

JACK THE RIPPER CARRIES OUT DOUBLE MURDER
SLASHES TWO PROSTITUTES IN LESS THAN AN HOUR
KILLING FROM BERNERS STREET TO MITRE SQUARE

Octavius was naked and drenched in sweat. He was lying face down in his bed breathing heavily. He was more exhausted than he had ever been in his life. He could not believe the risks he had taken that morning. It was by the thinnest of margins that he had made it back to his apartment without being caught.

After being nearly discovered at Berners Street, he had been forced to run back toward Whitechapel after seeing policemen approaching from the east. He then headed west along High Holborn, then turned down to Queen Victoria Street and turned again at Cornhill certain he was being chased. Adrenaline had coursed through his body and propelled him at an amazing speed.

Once he reached the end of Cornhill he realized he was alone and no one was in pursuit. He continued walking at a slow pace to catch his breath. That is when he saw another whore speaking to a man at the edge of Mitre Square. He entertained her advances for a while as she tried to convince him to walk with her down the secluded cul-de-sac, but he eventually pulled his arm away from her and hurried away.

Octavius had moved in for a closer look and noticed that her clothes and hair were in shambles and she looked dirtier than any whore he had ever seen. She had now walked deep into the square, and he approached her from behind. As he got closer he could smell the stench of whiskey and vomit. He gagged audibly at the smell causing the lady to turn and look at him.

He could remember the look in her eyes. There was an immediate recognition. She had no doubt that she was in the presence of Jack the Ripper. He had jumped on her in a flash, but that is all he could remember. He had been overcome with anger from her filth. Her smell. Her defilement of the trade.

He knew he had killed her, and in a way much more violent than the others. But he could not remember anything beyond the look in her eyes.

He eventually passed out from exhaustion and woke up sometime in the early afternoon. He sat up in the bed and assessed the situation. During his running, he had removed his overcoat and thrown it into the sewer pit. He had remembered to remove his chef's knife from the pocket, but forgot the boning knife.

After the second murder, he remembered running south to

the River Thames where he tossed his bloody jacket and tore the lining out of his vest before also tossing it into the river. He then wrapped his knife in the silk lining and ran the three and half miles back to his room.

He must have made quite the scene, a tall man in a top hat running through the streets in nothing but a white shirt and fancy trousers.

He looked around the room for other signs of evidence. He saw his white shirt, which was soaked in sweat. There were also blood splatters on it, so it would need to be destroyed. He unwrapped his chef's knife from the silk lining and cleaned it off in his water bowl.

Luckily, the top hat had not been injured during the night. It would need to be aired out for a while to dry the sweat from the band and rim; otherwise, there were no marks on it. He hung it lovingly on a hook in his wardrobe and left the doors open so that it could receive the breeze from his open window.

He spent another hour cleaning his room and making sure that no signs of his activities could be found. He then put on his chef's jacket and headed downstairs. He needed to get to the market to buy supplies for Monday, including a new boning knife. He cringed at the thought of losing such a refined blade. It had taken him years to hone it to his liking, and now he would need to start again.

Once downstairs he turned toward the market. He got to the corner and heard the newsboys barking out the headlines. He realized that he wasn't nearly as excited to hear them as he had been in the past. He still wanted to read the stories, but not for the same reasons as before.

He knew that there would be more panic, more fear, more of everything he had hoped to bring to the city. But he was more interested in reading the papers that would come later. The ones that would contain the doctor's examinations. He needed to remember what he had done to the second girl and understand why he had blacked out.

Still, he couldn't help but be drawn to the corner.

He listened to the newsboys' song as he let the sun warm his face. "Jack the Ripper strikes again… Kills two women this time… Scotland Yard still no closer to an arrest."

Sunday turned out to be a long day for everyone working at the *East End Observer*. The morning stayed exciting well after the presses started running. Walter got to the office at a little after eight and couldn't believe that he had missed all the action. The first bundles of papers had already hit the street before he walked in the door.

The other reporters were already starting to gather facts for the next round of Ripper stories that would appear in the Monday paper. Frank had to leave the office to cover the political angle, so Sarah jumped in to help Peter with running the press.

At mid-morning, Thaddeus pulled away from the excitement and retreated to his office. While there he pulled out a post card and penned a quick note in red ink with his left hand.

I was not codding dear old Boss when I gave you the top, you'll hear about Saucy Jacky's work tomorrow double event this time number one squealed a bit couldn't finish straight off. Ha not the time to get ears for police. Thanks for keeping last letter back till I got to work again.

Jack the Ripper

The ink had smeared on his hand, so he used it to smudge the card a bit for effect. He tucked the postcard into his breast pocket and headed down to the printer. He told Sarah he wanted to see how circulation was doing down by Parliament Square. He grabbed two stacks of papers and headed out.

He stopped about halfway to the square and dropped the postcard in a mailbox. He wasn't sure that the effort was needed, but he thought it might convince investigators that it was from the real killer if it went out so soon after the double murders.

Even if they didn't buy it, the letter would give everyone a little more to write about in the coming days.

News of the second letter went out on Tuesday, but Thaddeus didn't give it much coverage. Instead he concentrated on the sheer number of suspects that Scotland Yard kept calling in for questioning. The legal process appeared to be set aside in all matters relating to the Jack the Ripper murders, which made for very good subject matter.

They had printed fifty thousand papers on Sunday. All the newspapers in the city had increased their runs, and still the public could not get enough. He was forced to cut back to thirty thousand on Monday, Tuesday, and Wednesday, due to paper roll shortages.

For Thursday, he had scrambled to find an extra supply of paper because Frank had used his connections at Scotland Yard to get copies of the full doctor's reports. They were able to print through the night on Wednesday and completed a massive run of seventy thousand papers. Even with the unprecedented amount, they still sold out by early afternoon.

The crowds at the Café Langham stayed busy throughout the week. People were still gathering in public places to converse about the exploits of Jack the Ripper, and the bistro was a perfect location for the upper crust of the city to gather and share opinions.

Luckily for the staff, the authorities had instituted a curfew on the city forcing the restaurant to close at eight each night. This allowed them more time to prep for the next day and restock the liquor shelves.

Octavius stayed focused on his work, making sure they were overstocked on everything that wouldn't spoil. He did not want to run out of food again, no matter how big the crowds got. Victor had also been instructed to double his liquor reserves in the storeroom.

By Thursday, the news had started to settle, and the chef was able to take a mid-afternoon trip to the market. He had stayed up to date on the investigation through the newspapers, including reading the latest letter.

He had to laugh at the poorly written letter, and how trite it was for the author to take credit for something that had already been reported. He was equally amused by the part about how the first victim "squealed a bit" and how it prevented him from cutting off an ear.

He was curious about the timing of the letters and how they appeared to hit the newspapers so quickly after the murders. He had the suspicion that someone in the media must be writing them. But none of that was his concern. Even more letters had come out since the first two, and most of them were even more sensational and entertaining. In the end, they all served his purpose, to keep Jack the Ripper at the front of every whore's mind.

As he reached the last corner before the market, he heard one of the newsboys say something about the doctor's reports. This piqued his interest and he went over to purchase the paper.

He turned a few pages and found the first report from Doctor George Phillips regarding the murder of Elizabeth Stride. It was printed in its entirety.

The body was lying on the near side, with the face turned toward the wall, the head up the yard and the feet toward the street. The left arm was extended and there was a packet of cachous in the left hand.

The right arm was over the belly; the back of the hand and wrist had on it clotted blood. The legs were drawn up with the feet close to the wall. The body and face were warm and the hand cold. The legs were quite warm.

The deceased had a silk handkerchief round her neck, and it appeared to be slightly torn. I have since ascertained it was cut. This corresponded with the right angle of the jaw. The throat was deeply gashed, and there was an abrasion of the skin about one and a quarter inches in diameter, apparently stained with blood, under her right brow.

At three pm on Monday at Saint George's Mortuary, Doctor Blackwell and I made a post-mortem examination. Rigor mortis was still thoroughly marked. There was mud on the left side of the face and it was matted in the head. The body was fairly nourished. Over both shoulders, especially the right, and under the collarbone and in front of the chest there was a blueish discoloration, which I have watched and have seen on two occasions since.

There was a clear-cut incision on the neck. It was six inches in length and commenced two and a half inches in a straight line below the angle of the jaw, three quarters of an inch over an undivided muscle, and then, becoming deeper, dividing the sheath. The cut was very clean and deviated a little downwards. The arteries and other vessels contained in the sheath were all cut through. The cut through the tissues on the right side was more superficial, and tailed off to about two inches below the right angle of the jaw. The deep vessels on that side were uninjured. From this it was evident that the hemorrhage was caused through the partial severance of the left carotid artery and a small bladed knife could have been used.

Decomposition had commenced in the skin. Dark brown spots were on the anterior surface of the left chin. There was a deformity in the bones of the right leg, which was not straight, but bowed forwards. There was no recent external injury save to the neck.

The body being washed more thoroughly, I could see some healing sores. The lobe of the left ear was torn as if from the removal or wearing through of an earring, but it was thoroughly healed. On removing the scalp there was no sign of bruising or extravasation of blood.

The heart was small, the left ventricle firmly contracted, and the right slightly so. There was no clot in the pulmonary artery, but the right ventricle was full of dark clot. The left was firmly contracted as to be absolutely empty. The stomach was large and the mucous membrane only congested. It contained partly digested food, apparently consisting of cheese, potato, and farinaceous powder. All the teeth on the lower left jaw were absent.

Octavius chuckled to himself as he read the report. He felt the doctor used a lot of words to say that a dirty whore in poor health had gotten her throat slit. He laughed out loud when the doctor described her body as being "fairly nourished." What a polite way to say she was a fat whore.

But it was Catherine Eddowes murder that most interested him. He turned to find the report from Doctor Frederick Brown, which was a doctor he did not recognize from the previous investigations.

The body was on its back, the head turned to left shoulder. The arms by the side of the body as if they had fallen there. Both palms upwards, the fingers slightly bent. A thimble was lying off the finger on the right side. The clothes drawn up above the abdomen. The thighs were naked. Left leg extended in a line with the body. The abdomen was exposed. Right leg bent at the thigh and knee.

The bonnet was at the back of the head – a great disfigurement of the face. The throat cut. Across below the throat was a neckerchief.

The intestines were drawn out to a large extent and placed over the right shoulder—they were smeared over with some feculent matter. A piece of about two feet was quite detached from the body and placed between the body and the left arm, apparently by design. The lobe and auricle of the right ear were cut obliquely through. There was a quantity of clotted blood on the pavement on the left side of the neck round the shoulder and upper part of the arm, and fluid blood-colored serum which had flowed under the neck to the right shoulder, the pavement sloping in that direction.

Body was quite warm. No death stiffening had taken place. She must have been dead most likely within the half hour. We looked for superficial bruises and saw none. No blood on the skin of the abdomen or secretion of any kind on the thighs. No spurting of blood on the bricks or pavement around. No marks of blood below the middle of the body. Several buttons were found in the clotted blood after the body was removed. There was no blood on the front of the clothes. There were no traces of recent connection.

Brown conducted a post-mortem upon Eddowes's body that afternoon, noting:

After washing the left hand carefully, a bruise the size of a sixpence, recent and red, was discovered on the back of the left hand between the thumb and first finger. A few small bruises on right shin of older date.

The hands and arms were bronzed. No bruises on the scalp, the back of the body, or the elbows.

The cause of death was hemorrhage from the left common carotid artery. The death was immediate and the mutilations were inflicted after death... There would not be much blood on the murderer. The cut was made by someone on the right side of the body, kneeling below the middle of the body. The peritoneal lining was cut through on the left side and the left kidney carefully taken out and removed.

I believe the perpetrator of the act must have had considerable knowledge of the position of the organs in the abdominal cavity and the way of removing them. The parts removed would be of no use for any professional purpose. It required a great deal of knowledge to have removed the kidney and to know where it was placed. Such a knowledge might be possessed by one in the habit of cutting up animals. I think the perpetrator of this act had sufficient time. It would take at least five minutes. I believe it was the act of one person.

As he read the report, Octavius' memory came alive. He could now recall every detail in vivid color. Every slice with his blade, every sound, every smell, even the taste in the back of his throat.

He read the report multiple times. Each time he found a new phrase that excited him. What a wondrous description. Every detail was outlined perfectly. He went back to the newsboy and bought five more papers. This was now his crowning achievement.

How could the whores of London not fear him now? Before he was just the Whitechapel Murderer, a mere man doing good work. Now he was Jack the Ripper, the ultimate liberator.

Frank raised his glass and the other staff members at the *East End Observer* followed suit. "I want to offer a toast to the best damn newspaper man in London. Boss, you have drug us from a piddly little three day a week rag with two subscribers to one of the largest papers in the city."

"Here! Here!" shouted everyone, as they clinked glasses. Walter was running around with two bottles of whiskey refilling everyone's containers.

It had been two weeks since the "double event," and the exploits of Jack the Ripper had propelled the city into a spiral of terror, fear, and panic. The *East End Observer* had benefited every step of the way.

It had been nearly five months since the first Whitechapel murder, and Thaddeus could not believe how much had changed in that short time. The paper had gone from near bankruptcy to seeing profits ten times higher than they had ever known. Even his legendary father-in-law never achieved such great success.

The publisher stood on a chair and held his glass high. "And we couldn't have gotten here without you fine people. O'Conner has been so on top of the Ripper that Scotland Yard has named him their number one suspect."

"He couldn't be the Ripper, boss," Frank yelled out. "He couldn't run three blocks, let alone three miles."

"And he would never be able to wash all that blood out of his beard!" Sam bellowed as he slapped O'Conner in the back."

"Sam, you, Peter, and all the other new reporters have put in a load of hours over these past weeks. I know it hasn't always been easy, and I haven't always been patient, but I want to thank you for all your hard work and dedication."

The glasses clinked again and another round of drinks were passed around.

"So as with all great businesses, things change. I will unfortunately not be able to man the assignment desk any longer."

A silence fell over the group followed by looks of confusion.

"That's right, I have some sad news to report to all you journalists. As long as O'Conner isn't hauled away by the Yard, I have asked him to take over as the new editorial manager."

Everyone cheered and congratulated the new manager. Once everyone settled down, the publisher started again.

"I have a couple other changes to announce as well. Walter has finally found not just one but two new assistants that he feels might last more than a week, so we will finally be adding a second typesetter."

"About time! My fingers are about ready to fall off with all the pages you keep adding," Walter laughed.

"And last but not least, I have been told by Missus Donleavy that I do actually have a home somewhere in this city. She is insisting that I start visiting that home during the week. So to make sure that I can actually do such a thing, Frank, I am asking if you will sign on as our new managing editor."

Frank was shocked at the announcement and stood there with his mouth open in surprise. He had no idea it was coming. The new managing editor shook Thaddeus' hand and everyone circled around to congratulate him on the promotion.

Everyone continued celebrating for a couple hours before Frank had to call an end to the festivities. They did have a paper to prepare for the next day, and he was now responsible for making sure it got out on time.

Thaddeus thought about staying around for a while longer, but resisted the urge. He knew Frank had it under control, and he wanted to show that he trusted the team to handle things in his absence. Besides, he needed to get home. Sarah had been conspicuously absent from the meeting, which was odd. They had discussed the changes over the past few days, and she knew he would be making the announcements that day after the paper was finished.

He left the office and enjoyed the thirty-minute walk to his house. It was an unseasonably warm day, and he decided to take his time strolling down the street. For the past few months he had always been in a rush traveling to and from work, and his mind was always fixated on stories and headlines. This was the first time in a long while that he could relax during the journey.

When he arrived at his house, he hung his hat on the hook and turned to see Sarah sitting in the parlor. "Good afternoon Missus Donleavy. We missed you at the party. I thought you would want to be there for the announcements."

Sarah did not say anything. She just sat in her chair with her head lowered. She was looking at something on the table, but he could not see what it was from a distance. He walked closer trying to get a read on her expression. As he got closer, he could see that she was upset. She had been crying a little, but it did not look like tears of sadness. She was mad, very mad. He was certain of that, and he started to feel a knot forming in his stomach.

Once he was about ten feet away he could see that she had two open newspapers laid out on the table. They were both copies of the *East End Observer*, and they were both open to copies of the Jack the Ripper letters.

He sat down in the chair across from her not saying a word. He searched his mind for something to say, some sort of explanation or maybe even a lie that could get him out of this situation. He knew that would never work. Sarah was too smart for that. She was certainly smarter than him, and she would see through any sorry excuse he could spout.

They sat there for a long while in silence. Then Sarah picked up the paper containing the first letter. "You know I suspected when the first letter came out. The timing of it all. The way you were so calm and calculated about resetting the cover. But things happened so fast, I just put it out of my mind. Maybe I was just being dull. Or maybe I didn't want to believe it."

"Then the second letter came out. You shouldn't have used Saucy Jacky, Thaddeus. You know that was my father's favorite thing to call unsavory characters. That politician, he's a real Saucy Jacky. Oh Jamison, he's a real Saucy Jacky, should have kept it in his trousers. Did you really not think I would notice?"

Thaddeus continued sitting there in silence. He had written the postcard so quickly that he hadn't thought about all his word choices. He realized now that the phrase was pretty unique. He had heard Johan say it a dozen times, and it must have just stuck with him somehow.

After a long pause he finally spoke, "I know I've messed up Sarah. But you know I did this for us..."

"Don't you dare! Don't you dare say that. You didn't do this for us. You did this for you. The company was doing fine. But fine wasn't good enough for you. It's never been good enough for you."

He sat back in his chair not knowing how to respond.

"You do understand that there is blood on your hands now. He would have killed again, that is certain. But that second girl. That's just as much your fault as his. You taunted him. Told him to take an ear. When he was interrupted with the first one, he had to find another. He had to find her and kill her just to take off her ear."

"Have you read what he did to her? How he mutilated her? Of course you have. Because you wrote about it. You profited from it. Well now Thaddeus, you have to live with it."

She had said all she needed to say. She stood up and folded the papers and handed them to him. "Take your filthy newspapers with you when you leave. I do not want to see them in this house ever again."

It was mid-October and Victor was standing at the bar smiling. The stoic man almost never smiled, but he was smiling now as he wiped down a glass. And he was whistling. Tom had certainly never seen the man whistle, and he had known him since he was five.

"What the hell has gotten into you?" Tom was resting on his elbows just staring at his friend. "You look happy. And you never look happy."

"Well I am happy, Tom. Can't a man just be happy?"

A few seconds later Natasha came in through the back door. She was dressed in her regular waitress outfit, but today she had a bright blue bow in her hair. She wasn't just happy, she was positively glowing. "Good morning, Tom. Good morning, Victor."

She smiled sheepishly as she said hello to Victor. "Okay, what the hell is going on with you two?"

"I asked her to marry me last night."

"Well Bob's your uncle. I take it she said yes by the looks of you both. Congratulations man. She is a right good catch for a stuffy bloke like yourself."

"She is a right good catch indeed. I guess I'll be needing a best man soon. You think Marcus is doing anything in a couple weeks."

Tom punched his friend in the arm, then shook his hand. "Like hell, you need a proper Irishman to be your best man."

Marcus and Stephane walked in together followed immediately by Margaret. They saw the two men speaking in excited tones and walked up to the bar.

"Victor and Natasha are engaged, can you believe that," Tom blurted out.

They were all congratulating the couple when Octavius came walking down the stairs. Victor gave a stern look to everyone and they all scattered to their stations. "Good morning, chef."

"Hello, Victor. Everyone seems more excited than usual."

"Yes, chef. We were just discussing what we did on our free time yesterday." He hesitated for a second but decided now was as good a time as any to tell his boss. Octavius was starting to head back to the kitchen when he spoke up. "Umm Chef. I guess. I mean, I wanted to tell you that I… That Natasha and I… I mean… I wanted to let you know that Natasha and I are engaged to be married. I asked her yesterday and she agreed."

The chef raised his eyebrows then shook his head. "I had no idea you two were even dating. But I am always the last to figure these things out. I am happy for you both. When do you plan to have the ceremony?"

"We were thinking about doing it in a couple of weeks on November third. That's a Saturday, and we were hoping we could take the weekend for the wedding and a short honeymoon. It will just be a small ceremony with a few friends and family. We haven't worked out the details yet, but we would love for you to come."

"Thank you for the invitation. And congratulations again." Octavius started to walk away, but felt like he should say or do something more. He had never been good at navigating these types of social norms. "Where do you plan to hold the ceremony?"

"We haven't decided yet. We are saving all our money to get an apartment together, so we will probably just do something at her father's house."

"Well, you could have the ceremony here at the bistro if you want. You might prefer to do it somewhere other than where you work, but I'm sure Gustavo wouldn't mind."

"That would be wonderful, chef. We just wouldn't want to put anyone out."

"Nonsense, it wouldn't be any trouble. Besides, when have you known for Gustavo to miss out on an opportunity to host a party? Plus, it would give me an excuse to cook something other than stew and soup for a change."

"Thank you, chef, it would be an honor for you to cook for our family and friends."

Octavius nodded and headed to the kitchen. The staff continued to buzz over the news the rest of the day. Gustavo had gushed at the idea of holding the wedding at the Café Langham. He lifted Victor off his feet in a bear hug at the news, then danced Natasha around dining room. He also said they would close the restaurant down that Saturday, and he would pay for everything.

The lunch and afternoon services seemed to fly by. The crowds stayed steady throughout the day, but they were not nearly as large as they had been the past two Saturdays. The evening service was especially slow, mainly because the curfew was still in effect. The only diners that were allowed to come in after seven were hotel guests who would not be leaving the building for the rest of the evening.

At six o'clock Octavius told the cooks to finish cleaning up the kitchen, but leave one pot of stew for anyone that came in later. He then entered the dining room and told Victor that he would soon be sending everyone home early for the day.

By six-thirty, the bistro was empty and the chef was ready to close down for the day. He had just made the announcement when a man and his wife came down the stairs. He recognized the man from somewhere, but he could not place it.

"Are you still open for dinner?" The man asked.

"Yes, sir. But we only have one pot of cassoulet going, and a few loaves of bread."

"That would be wonderful."

Natasha grabbed a couple napkins and spoons and started to walk toward the table before Octavius stopped her. In a hushed tone he turned to the staff who were all gathered near the back door. "Go ahead. Get out of here. I will take care of these two."

"Thank you, chef," Victor nodded as Natasha handed Octavius the napkins and spoons. They all headed out the door, wishing the chef a good night.

Octavius walked to the table where the man and his wife were sitting. They were dressed in formal wear and looked like they had just come from a party. The man had obviously been drinking a bit that night.

"Thank you for seating us, good sir. I see that your staff has left for the day. Are you sure we aren't being a bother?"

"No, sir. Please, feel free to stay as long as you'd like." He was still trying to place the man's face. He was sure that he had seen him recently, but he had looked different somehow.

"Well thank you again. You see, we are starting our honeymoon tonight. We just got married today and are staying at this fine hotel before heading off to Paris tomorrow on a little adventure. We had very little time to eat at our ceremony, so we are famished."

Octavius looked at the bride, who was probably half the age of her husband who was likely in his late fifties. She looked disinterested in the bistro and the chef standing before her. She looked even less interested in her husband.

"Don't mind her. She is just upset because the main hotel restaurant was closed. She is a woman who prefers the finer things life has to offer."

"Can I get you something to drink, ma'am."

"She will take a tonic water. That's all the woman drinks it seems. I myself will take a glass of your finest Scotch. Make it at least three fingers if you don't mind."

"Yes, sir." The chef walked behind the bar, poured a tonic water and grabbed a bottle of Scotch. He could tell by the man's character that three fingers would only be the start of things, so he decided to bring the half-full bottle to the table.

He sat the glass in front of the woman who barely looked at him in response. He then poured the man a full tumbler. "This one is on the house, sir, in honor of your nuptials."

"Well thank you, sir. That is mighty kind of you. And excuse my manners. I forgot to introduce myself. I am Doctor Frederick Brown, and this is my lovely bride Dinah."

Octavius froze when he heard the doctor's name. He recognized him instantly as the man who had completed the autopsy of Catherine Eddowes and described her mutilation in such colorful terms. He hesitated for a moment, then topped off the now half-full glass.

"It is nice to meet you Doctor Brown and Missus Brown. My name is Chef Octavius Jackson. I will head to the kitchen and fetch you both some cassoulet and fresh bread."

He walked to the kitchen and leaned against the table. What were the chances that the doctor would arrive at his bistro at this time of night and with no one else around? He had so many questions he wanted to ask, but he had to contain himself. He could not give off even the slightest clue as to who he was.

The chef returned a few minutes later with a tray of food. He had also brought an extra bowl for himself. He served the couple their food and started to walk to an open table behind them.

"Nonsense, Chef Jackson. You must join us for dinner. We are keeping you here at this late hour, we should at least be hospitable about it."

That was what he was hoping to hear as he moved to their table and sat down. The lady was still showing disinterest, but did perk up a bit when she smelled the stew. They all began eating.

Octavius tried to stay calm and entered the conversation as casually as possible. "Doctor Brown, I believe I have heard your name recently in the newspapers. Do you by chance work with the authorities?"

"Why, yes, I do. I am a police surgeon with H Division in the Whitechapel District. You might have read my name in the newspaper recently regarding the Jack the Ripper murders."

"That's where I recognize your name from. I read your report on Catherine Eddowes. What a horrible tragedy."

"You don't even know the half of it. There was so much more I could have put in that report. Scotland Yard cut out some of it in case they catch the man, and other parts had to be censored for propriety sake."

"That is amazing. I remember thinking the report was so detailed. I can't imagine how much more there could have been."

"Well of course I am not allowed to divulge much more. But let's just say that the killer had a deep understanding of human anatomy. It would have taken considerable skill to do that much mutilation in such a short amount of time. I mean, I have been a surgeon for three decades and I am not so sure I could have removed a kidney so quickly in such a deliberate manner."

"Fascinating." The chef had stopped eating and was hanging on the doctor's every word.

"It is disgusting," said Dinah, dropping her spoon into her bowl. "I am going to need something stronger than this tonic if we are going to talk about mutilated corpses all night. Do you have any honey mead?"

Octavius stood up and walked behind the bar and found a bottle of mead. "What are your thoughts on the killer's profession doctor?"

"Well, I know the prevailing theory is that the Ripper is a doctor or someone in the medical field. I am not so sure about that. It is possible that he could be a doctor or nurse perhaps, but definitely not a surgeon."

"What makes you say that?" The doctor's wife suddenly joined the conversation.

"Well, the killer understands anatomy. There is no doubt about that. But his cuts are all wrong. He does not start his cuts in the correct places and the depths are not that of a learned surgeon. A simple doctor might do something like that, but even an inept doctor should have a better grasp of basic medical techniques. Also, a doctor would likely use a scalpel instead of such a large, wide blade."

"So what is your theory then?" she asked before taking a drink from the tall glass Octavius had just poured for her.

"I am more of the mind that the killer is a veterinarian or someone who works in the slaughterhouses. That would explain his understanding of anatomy. It would also explain the manner of the cuts and the large blade."

"What about a chef?" Dinah asked smirking at Octavius. "They know how to use a knife."

"I seriously doubt it," he said taking another bite. "A chef may be able to use a knife, but removing a kidney without disturbing the other organs is an entirely different thing altogether."

Octavius had so many other questions, but he knew it would be too dangerous for him to lead the conversation. Luckily, the more Scotch the doctor drank, the more he divulged without having to be prodded. Dinah had lost interest after a few minutes and started walking around the restaurant looking for something to catch her eye.

The doctor finished the half-bottle of Scotch rather quickly, and the chef opened a new bottle and poured him another full glass. They continued to talk about the details of Catherine Eddowes murder, then moved on to the doctor's opinions on the other Jack the Ripper murders.

Octavius was impressed with the doctor's ability to recall every detail of each murder. He could describe the angle and depth of the cuts. He made startlingly accurate estimates of the size and widths of the blades used. He stated that he was certain that the man never defiled the victims sexually, even given the sexual natures of the crime.

The most startling claim the doctor made was that the killer was improving. That he was developing his craft to create some sort of sick narrative. That he was sending a message of some sort.

After more than two hours, the doctor started to show signs of the drink. He began slurring his words and repeating things. Octavius knew he was pushing the conversation too far, but he was enjoying the experience immensely. It was also clear that the doctor's wife was ready for the conversation to end. She had tried to convince her husband to retire a couple times but was now showing signs of outright anger.

The situation came to a head when Dinah said that she was ready to spend the first night of her marriage alone. The doctor agreed that it was time to leave and stood up. His first couple of steps were wobbly, then his drunkenness took hold and he had to grab the table for support.

It was clear that the man would need help making it up the stairs and likely all the way to his room. Octavius hooked the doctor's arm over his shoulder and half helped, half carried him up the stairs. Once upstairs, Dinah had to grab his other arm in order to keep the rather large man from toppling over.

Their room was located on the hotel's third floor, and Octavius led them up the back staircase and up the three flights of stairs. He continued to help Dinah support her husband to Room 333 where she unlocked the door.

Once inside, the chef helped maneuver the man into the bed. He immediately slumped over, passed out cold. Octavius removed his shoes and pulled a blanket over his feet. He looked down at the snoring man and considered their conversation that night. He had developed a unique respect for the doctor. He felt that the man understood him in a strange way.

As Octavius looked at the man, he felt a warm hand touch the small of his back. He turned to see Dinah standing uncomfortably close to him. She wasted no time in pressing her body against his. He noticed that she had already removed her blouse and skirt. She was now wearing nothing but a slip and bustier. She stood up on her toes and pressed in harder, kissing the base of his neck.

A whirlwind of thoughts and emotions washed over him. He felt shock at first. Shock at the audacity of the woman. Then arousal, which was something he had never felt comfortable dealing with or fully understood. And finally a wave of anger hit him. He became enraged by the actions of this whore who was trying to violate him right in front of her comatose husband. Her new husband.

"Come on. I need this. This is my wedding night, and he will never be able to satisfy me. He is old and rich. That is the only reason why I married him. But I still have needs. He will never know. He gets blackout drunk almost every night. Come on. You know you want this."

Her words hit him like a sledge hammer. She was right. He did want this. But not in the way she expected. He reached up and wrapped his hands around her neck and pushed her back away from his chest. He looked down and into her hazel eyes. She moaned as she looked up at him. Her eyes narrowed into sultry slits.

Then he began to slowly tighten his large strong hands. She moaned again at first enjoying the game, but soon felt his grip squeeze her throat. Her airway started to collapse and her eyes widened in fear. Reality set in that she was being strangled. He continued to stare into her hazel eyes and squeeze as hard as he could. He stood there holding her by the neck for minutes. Even after the light in her eyes went out, he continued to hold onto her soft limp body. He wanted to burn this feeling into his memory. He wanted to carry it with him forever.

The slamming of a hotel room door down the hallway broke him from his trance. He gently laid his victim on the ground. She looked peaceful and beautiful now. He was surprised to find that he now had a full erection. This was also a new sensation for him.

He sat looking at the woman for a long while. He found her to be lovely. The other women he had killed had all been whores. Old whores with dirty clothes and used faces. But Dinah was something else. She was young, in her mid-twenties. She smelled of expensive perfume and flowery soaps. Her hair was clean and shiny.

He had not been attracted to her before. Living, she was annoying and callous. Now that she was dead, she was gorgeous. Her pale skin glowed in the dimly lit room. Her mouth was fixed open and her hazel eyes were wide with fear. She looked like a goddess to him.

Another slamming door reminded him of where he was. He did not have a desire to mutilate this woman. Instead, he wished he could preserve her and keep a statue of her visage. But he did not have time to contemplate such things. It was very early in the morning, which meant the sun would be coming up in a few hours. He needed to decide a plan of action.

He turned to look at the drunk doctor. He respected this man. He felt a kindship with him. He had not wanted to bring this shame upon him, but it was out of his hands at this point. He would not have reacted if his wife hadn't touched him. If she hadn't acted like a common street whore and shamed her husband.

None of that mattered now. Octavius had no choice but to deflect the blame. He began pulling sheets off the bed and tying them together into tight knots. Once he had gathered enough sheets, he threw one end over a beam on the ceiling. He then sat the doctor up in the bed and tied the end of the last sheet into a noose and slipped it over his head.

The chef then stood back and pulled with all his strength. The doctor was slowly lifted off the bed until he was hanging about a foot off the ground. He then tied the other end of the sheet rope to the bedpost and sat on the bed looking at the hanging doctor.

At first there was no movement as the noose continued to tighten under the man's weight. Then the doctor's eyes shot open and he breathed in a gulp of air. It was the last gasp he could manage as the noose pulled even tighter. He swung in a slow circle until he faced Octavius. He looked at the chef with wide, knowing eyes.

Octavius stood to look the hanging man directly in the eyes. "I am truly sorry, Doctor Brown. I did not mean for any of this to happen. I enjoyed meeting you tonight and our talk meant more to me than you could ever know. I did want to let you know that you were right about almost everything in your report. But sadly, you were incorrect about one important detail. It turns out that a chef does have the skill to remove a human kidney with that level of precision. I am that chef, Doctor Brown. I am Jack the Ripper."

Thaddeus stared at the full bottle of whiskey sitting on his desk. It took all his willpower to resist pulling the stopper and pouring a glass. He wanted a drink more than ever, but pulling that stopper also meant pulling the plug on what was left of his marriage.

He had spent the last several weeks doing all he could to repair the damage he had caused with the letters. The look on Sarah's face when she confronted him was something he would never forget. Until that moment, he had mainly thought about the legal and business ramifications he would face if caught. He had only lightly considered how Sarah would react. He knew she was a moral person, who had grown up with her father's journalistic ethics. He should have let that knowledge be a better guide for his actions rather than his own ego and the desire to sell a few extra newspapers.

He had considered publicly confessing to his sins, but that would have been an end to not only his marriage but also the newspaper and the company. Even Sarah wouldn't want his bad decisions to tarnish her family's legacy.

Sarah still wasn't talking to him, but at least she hadn't thrown him out of the house. He had moved his things into the guest room and made it a point to get home every evening before dark. He had stopped drinking and hadn't brought up work during any of the few one-way conversations they had had lately. He was sure she would come around eventually. The *East End Observer* had always been a part of her life. No matter how angry she stayed at him, she couldn't keep away from the company much longer.

Luckily, work at the paper had been rolling along as strong as ever. The double murder had created an insatiable appetite for news in all corners of the London and around the world. They had continued to print forty thousand papers every day, and he did not see that changing for quite some time. The *Observer* now had a loyal following of readers and had built up its circulation channels and advertising base.

It took little time for Frank to embrace the role of managing editor. He already understood the printing operations better than anyone in the company. His contacts in the business world had also helped him pull in even more advertisers and negotiate the best deals with vendors. He was still struggling a bit in the circulation department. Frank had never been good at working with youngsters, and the majority of the newsboys were under the age of sixteen. Thaddeus kept engaged in that part of the business.

O'Conner had also taken a strong lead as editorial manager. He had developed a dedicated group of steady beat reporters. He also started a stringer program that gave them access to independent journalists and expanded their reach further into the city without increasing payroll too much.

The increased profits had allowed Thaddeus to give everyone pay raises, which always improved morale and helped with hiring a better caliber of employees.

Every part of the business was going strong. But without Sarah to share it with, it didn't matter. The reputation he had built had been shattered in her eyes. His success now felt hollow and selfish.

He looked again at the bottle and what it represented. His desire for a drink had diminished a bit. He knew the comfort it would bring would only be temporary.

To his surprise, he looked up to see Frank standing a few feet from his desk. Frank looked hesitant to approach at first. "Everything alright, boss? You look a little off today."

"No. Nothing to be concerned about. Just a little trouble on the home front is all."

"You'll figure it out, boss. You have to, it's Sarah."

"It will be fine, Frank. What's going on?"

"I know we talked about all these copycat Ripper letters and not running any of them, but one came in today that is different from the others."

Thaddeus looked confused. "What do you mean by different."

"This one was released by Scotland Yard and is much more disturbing that than the others. It was also sent in a box that contained half a human kidney."

The publisher stood up. "That is a very different story."

The two men started downstairs where they could see O'Conner barking out directions to the two young reporters left in the area. When they arrived he updated them both on everything he had so far.

The letter and box had been sent to George Lusk, the head of the Whitechapel Vigilance Committee, and arrived on October fifteenth. He delivered it immediately to Scotland Yard without alerting anyone in the press.

The box contained half of a kidney, which had been preserved in alcohol. Scotland Yard brought in Doctor Thomas Openshaw to examine the organ. He concluded that the kidney had come from a woman in her mid-forties who was prone to heavy drinking.

This all makes it possible that the kidney belonged to Catherine Eddowes who was forty-six at the time of her murder and was known to be a heavy drinker.

Sam walked into the room carrying something that looked like a photo. He laid it on the table where they could all see that it was a copy of the letter.

From hell
Mr Lusk, Sor

I send you half the Kidne I took from one women prasarved it for you tother piece I fried and ate it was very nise. I may send you the bloody knif that took it out if you only wate a whil longer

signed
Catch me when you can Mishter Lusk

"It is obvious to me that this letter was written by a different hand than the first two letters that came out. The handwriting is off. The grammar and spelling are much worse. The ink is different. Even the style of paper is off," O'Conner said scratching his chin.

Sam nodded in agreement. "He doesn't even sign it Jack the Ripper. I would have considered it a fraud like the dozen or so other letters we have seen this week, but that kidney is definitely real. Don't know if belongs to Miss Eddowes or not, but it's a real woman's liver that's for certain."

Frank turned away from the table and headed toward the typesetting room. "O'Conner, get me what you can by the end of the day. I will have Walter start moving things around."

"Wait!" Thaddeus' voice was louder than he intended. "Are we really going to print this? I mean, should we be printing this right now?"

Frank and O'Conner both looked at each other, then to the publisher. Frank walked back toward the table. "Boss, we have to. Every paper in town will be headlining this tomorrow. The letter was sent to us by Scotland Yard. But the letter isn't even the news. The kidney is the news."

"You're right, of course. I guess I'm just getting tired of seeing all the coverage of these copycat letters."

Frank hesitated for a few seconds before heading off to find Walter. O'Conner turned back to the table and sat down next to Sam who was already typing.

"Well, you guys have this under control. I am going to head out for the evening. Something tells me tomorrow is going to be a long day."

Thaddeus quickly climbed the stairs and grabbed his hat and coat. He had to get home to Sarah. He had to tell her about the letter. He had promised her that he would not print anymore letters, but this one was different. He hoped he would be able to explain. He looked over at the bottle before he left. He really wanted that drink.

It was Saturday midday and Octavius was cooking at a feverish pace. The menu for Victor and Natasha's wedding ended up being a mix of English and Scottish food. The bride had requested a simple shepherd's pie, and the chef used a recipe he had made a thousand times back in Seattle.

The smells brought back memories of the hours he had spent in the kitchen with Tumas. Most of the dishes he had learned from the well-trained chef were simple peasant foods meant for the loggers, miners, and railroad men that passed through the area. He wished Tumas could see him now and that they could cook amazing French cuisine together.

The groom had requested Cullen Skink, a hearty soup that was made famous in Victor's home town of Cullen in Northeast Scotland. Octavius had to consult with one of the Scottish cooks in the hotel's main kitchen to get the recipe. The soup was made with smoked haddock, potatoes, and onions. The chef put his own spin on the dish by adding a hearty dose of heavy cream to the pot in order to make the smoked fish more palatable for the British guests.

The chef added in plates of bangers and mash along with some tattie scones to fill out the menu. It certainly wasn't an elegant meal, but it matched the sensibilities of the bride and groom.

Marcus and Stephane had helped in the morning with the prep work, but the chef sent them home later in the day so that they could get cleaned up to help serve at the party. Tom was the best man, so Stephane would have to serve as the bartender. Margaret was Natasha's maid of honor, so Marcus would be helping Octavius serve the food.

The first guests arrived at five, including Victor's mother. She was a large boisterous woman whose demeanor was the opposite of her stoic son. She walked into the kitchen carrying a large basket of French bread and introduced herself as Ruth. She was followed by her husband who was an older even more stoic version of Victor. He was carrying a box, and Octavius could smell right away that it was filled to the brim with balls of haggis.

The chef just smiled and welcomed them to the party. He had them set the food on the prep table and told them he would take care of getting everything ready. Once the pair left, he held his nose and looked at the haggis. It looked well made in all its smelly glory. He was just thankful that he hadn't been asked to make the traditional dish. It would have taken a week to get the smell out of the bistro's walls.

Marcus walked in a few minutes later dressed in a suit. He stopped at the door and crinkled up his nose and looked at the chef.

"The groom's parents brought haggis. Help me figure out how to serve it with the rest of this stuff."

After a few minutes the other guests had arrived and everyone stood around the tables and bar waiting for the ceremony to begin. Octavius and Marcus stepped out of the kitchen and stood in the back. Gustavo came down the stairs and stood next to them. They all watched the short service together.

Victor was wearing standard Scottish formal wear complete with a plaid kilt fitted with a sporran. He also wore a dark jacket and topped it with a traditional floppy bonnet.

Natasha wore a simple white dress. Margaret stood next to her as her maid of honor wearing a green dress. She also had one bridesmaid, who immediately caught the chef's attention. She was a buxom young lady in her mid-twenties. She was tall and slim with fair skin and dark hair. She wore a deep red dress and her long hair was fitted with several small blue ribbons. Throughout the ceremony he could not keep his eyes off her.

Once the ceremony ended, Octavius and Marcus started plating the food and ladling soup into bowls. They started preparing the trays when guests began coming into the kitchen. Neither of the families were used to being served, so they started grabbing trays and taking them out to the dining room.

Ruth rolled into the kitchen and headed to the stove. She tasted the soup and made a curious expression. She tasted it again and decided she liked it. "Not bad. You made it all British and such, but it will pass for a decent Cullen boil. It could use a bit more pepper though." She didn't wait for a response and grabbed the pepper grinder and yanked out a few cranks of the spice.

Octavius just laughed at the whole scene. A more formal chef would have been offended, but he knew this evening had nothing to do with fine dining or proper cooking techniques. This was a family affair and Ruth just wanted to feel like she was contributing.

Family members continued to come in and out of the kitchen until nearly all the food had been taken to the dining room. Ruth turned off the burner on the stove and grabbed the chef by the arm. "Come on young man; let's get out of this hot box."

Octavius walked into the dining room, which was filled to capacity with more than forty guests. People were scattered throughout the area, standing at tables and around the front and back of the bar. He found a seat at the back table closest to the kitchen. Ruth brought him over a plate of food and a bowl of soup and would not leave until he tried her famous haggis. He did his best to choke it down without making a sour face, and she squealed laughing at the sight.

He sat back in his chair eating from a large chunk of bread, hoping to get rid of the awful aftertaste of fermented oats and sheep guts. He scanned the crowd, which had already started to show signs of heavy drinking. Gustavo was right in the middle, carrying two bottles, one scotch and the other gin. He poured liquor into any glass that looked like it had room for more liquid.

He then spotted the bride's maid standing at the far corner near the bar. Now that he could see her in proper light, she reminded him in every way of his mother when she was that age. Her dress. Her dark hair. Her pale skin. Even her mannerisms reminded him of his mother. She walked through the crowd with a singular confidence. She seemed to be most at ease around the men. She was cordial to the married men, but with the single men she found reasons to touch them as she approached.

He suddenly realized that she was a prostitute. Not a whore from the street, but a proper lady of the night. Someone who likely worked in a brothel and that likely escorted gentlemen to social affairs on occasion. He had seen too many professionals in his lifetime not to recognize the signs. He was fascinated by her presence. She was different than the other women in the crowd. More refined, more social, and certainly more beautiful than the others.

She looked back in his direction and he quickly averted his eyes. He pulled back up to the table and started eating the soup. Marcus came up to the table and sat across from him.

"This will be the easiest service we have had in a while. There are even two girls in there washing dishes right now. I tried to talk them out of it, but they just laughed at me, handed me a bowl of soup, and kicked me out of the kitchen."

Octavius agreed, "Gustavo looks like he is enjoying himself. I have a feeling we will be carrying him to his office tonight. And he might have company by the looks of this crowd. They don't look to be slowing down anytime soon."

"Speaking of company, I could do with the company of that Mary Jane girl." Marcus was looking across the bar at the bride's maid.

"Who is Mary Jane?" Octavius asked without following his gaze.

"She was that girl in the red dress standing next to Margaret. Her name is Mary Jane Kelly. Victor says she's a working girl over in Spitalfields. She grew up with Natasha and Margaret, and now she is one of those registered girls with a health certificate and all."

"I see," The chef continued to eat from his bowl. "Sounds expensive to me."

"You are probably right about that. But maybe she will be feeling charitable tonight with all this love and celebration going on."

"Well best of luck to you. I am going to get that dreaded wedding cake ready. Why anyone would want to eat fruitcake at an occasion like this is a mystery to me. The Scottish have some odd traditions."

A few minutes later, the wedding cake was served and a few toasts were made in honor of the bride and groom. Octavius found himself growing more uncomfortable at the raucous party. His kitchen had been overrun with ladies cleaning and threatening to cook more traditional foods. The dining room became louder as more drinks flowed, and it was hard to hold a conversation with anyone who wasn't within an arm length.

Knowing that they would have a full day tomorrow to put the bistro back together, he decided it was time to bow out for the evening. He told Marcus to make sure Gustavo made it to his office at the end of the night. He then found Victor and Natasha and offered his congratulations before heading for the back door.

As he grabbed the doorknob, a soft voice called after him. "Excuse me, chef."

Octavius turned around to see the woman in the red dress standing in front of him. She grabbed his arm and moved in uncomfortably close. "I just wanted to thank you for a wonderful evening. Natasha loves working here and says such wonderful things about you."

He wasn't sure how to respond. Instead, he turned shy and averted his eyes from her and spoke in a soft voice, "Natasha is a good woman. She will make a good wife to Victor."

"Yes, she will." She did not let go of his arm and instead shifted her grip so that she could pull in tighter. "Well, I just wanted to say thank you again for all you have done for the happy couple." She then moved in and kissed him on the cheek. It was a slow sultry kiss that sent goosebumps throughout his entire body.

"Good evening, chef." She gave him a sly smile and turned around in one graceful motion. He watched her as she walked away before pushing himself through the door.

Sarah stood in the study behind her father's old wooden desk. It was the one piece of furniture of his that she wanted to keep when moving into their new house in the city several months ago. She had watched him work at the desk for years as he built the company she loved from a small print shop into a full-fledge printing operation.

Johan was so proud when he had finally scraped up the funds and the nerve to start the *East End Observer*, and Sarah had been with him through every year of that journey. It wasn't always an easy road, especially with the expansion of competition throughout the city. When her father started the paper, there were only a half dozen papers in all of London. Now there were nearly thirty papers of varying sizes, with more popping up every year.

Even before he father's death, the newspaper had struggled to remain relevant. She was not naive to the numbers and she and her father had spoken often about ways to keep the paper going.

Johan, Sarah, and Thaddeus had all been a part of the decision to reduce the paper to three days a week in order to take on more outside jobs. It was a move that especially disappointed her husband, but it was necessary in order to keep revenue flowing and save the company. It also kept the newspaper going without having to fire any of the journalists or other employees.

She had been studying the company ledger all morning. Thaddeus had certainly done a wonderful job of turning around the numbers. The company was more profitable than it had ever been. They were now selling out forty thousand copies every day, and advertising revenue had quadrupled.

In just six months her husband had taken the paper from near bankruptcy to record profits. But at what cost? Journalistic integrity was one thing, but the letters her husband had written went far beyond a lapse in ethics. It was a moral failing. A failing that had likely led to the death of an innocent woman.

All the newspapers, even her paper, had painted a picture of Catherine Eddowes as unworthy. Like all the Whitechapel murder victims, she was deemed as a lowly prostitute. A vagrant that walked the slums begging men to pay her for sex so that she could buy more alcohol. To some who read Catherine Eddowes story, it was seen as a mercy killing.

Sarah knew there was truth to this, but she also understood that Catherine Eddowes was a human being and a citizen of Great Brittan. A woman who had been forced to sleep in the streets when she could not earn enough money for a warm bed. Sure she was flawed, but how many other women and men in the city suffered those same flaws. They did not deserve to die any more than she did.

She did not know who to blame. Was it the politicians who had not done enough to clean up the slums? The local authorities who had not taken the first murders seriously enough? Was it the detectives at Scotland Yard who had whipped the city into a frenzy without any viable suspects? Was it her husband who had given a salacious name to the killer and thrown fuel on the fire? Or was it her?

Her father had wanted her to take over the company and run it as the publisher. She had the experience and the education. She had the journalistic ethics that he had instilled in her. She thought of herself as a person of decent moral standing.

She had considered it at first, but decided against it. Her husband loved the newspaper and wanted great things for the company. She desired to make him happy and give him the opportunity to learn from her father. Maybe if they would have had more time together, Thaddeus would have picked up more of her father's ethics and love for the truth.

Sarah had promised her father that she would keep her husband under control. That she would keep him focused on the business and not let his ambition affect the company or the integrity of the newspaper. She had now broken that promise, and it hurt her deeply.

She contemplated all of this as she looked out the window at the gray clouds and soft rain as it fell onto the street. She heard the front door open and close and the footsteps heading toward the parlor. She did not turn at first. She did not want him to see her face yet, and she did not want to see his.

"Good evening, Sarah. I know you are still not speaking to me, but I have something I need to tell you," Thaddeus waited a second before continuing. "Another letter arrived today. This one was different from the others. It was sent to all the newspapers from Scotland Yard. It was also accompanied by a box containing half of a woman's kidney."

It was awkward speaking to the back of her head, and he felt ashamed for some reason as he spoke the words. "I know I promised that we would not print anymore letters, but this one is quite different. I thought I should talk to you about it first."

She turned around and looked him in the eyes. He did not recognize the expression. It looked like a mixture of both anger and sadness. "So has Walter started to typeset the story?"

"Well, yes. Frank... I mean Frank and I thought it would be prudent to get things moving just in case."

"Since the paper starts printing first thing in the morning, I assume you are not really here to 'talk to me' about printing the story. You are just here to 'tell me' that you are printing it."

"Well, yes, Frank and I just thought that it was something that had to be reported given that it came from Scotland Yard and the kidney and all."

She continued to look at him with that same unreadable expression without saying a word. He thought maybe she was having doubts about his motives. "Sarah, I swear to you. I had nothing to do with this letter. It came from the Yard by way of the Whitechapel Vigilance Committee. I promise you, I would not do anything like that again."

"I am not interested in any more of your promises right now." Her eyes flashed a moment of anger. "I guess I will read about it tomorrow in the paper."

"Yes, would you like for me to bring you a copy?"

"No, that will not be necessary, Thaddeus. I will be coming into the office tomorrow. I think it's time that I got back to working at the paper again."

He felt a glimmer of hope. "That is great news. I know Walter would appreciate having you back in the typesetting room."

"No, Thaddeus, you misunderstand me. I am coming back to work at MY COMPANY tomorrow."

The start of November had brought a bitter cold to London. A heavy frost lingered each morning causing the thick morning fog to linger longer than usual. The city markets were slower at this time of year, and all the vegetables had lost most of their color.

Marcus and Stephane returned from the market with only root vegetables. Everything else was either rotten or mushy with frostbite. Octavius did what he could to use spices and herbs to enhance the taste of their signature boiling pots.

He asked Victor and Tom to come up with something warm and aromatic for the dining room to help brighten up the place. They decided on a spiced mulled wine with brandy, which smelled of heavy cinnamon and cloves.

It had been over a week since the wedding, and everything in the bistro had returned to normal. Octavius had let his sous chef do most of the cooking that week, while he worked with Stephane on how to store certain ingredients to keep them usable throughout the winter.

The crowds continued to thin a bit, but not to an alarming rate by any measure. They still had nearly a full seating for most lunch and dinner services, but the off hours were much slower now.

Victor was able to let some of the staff go early in the evening on most nights, just keeping one bartender and a server in the dining room. In the kitchen, Octavius and one of the boys would come in during the morning to start the pots and pies, then they would leave after the dinner services was nearly finished. The other cook would then stay until the restaurant closed at night to clean and prep for the next day.

Some days, the chef would leave early to check out the market or travel to the countryside to see what ingredients he could find. At night, he would still make his walks to the slums, but he rarely stayed out much past eleven. The police officers were still posted on nearly every other corner, and they routinely approached people that were walking by to ask about their business in the area. This questioning increased later in the evening when the lamps were extinguished.

He understood that chapter of his life would need to come to an end, at least for a while anyway. It was too dangerous for him to walk the streets now.

Many evenings, Octavius would sit in his room fantasizing about his nighty activities. Sometimes he would pull out his stack of newspapers and read over the articles. He would often take the top hat out of its case and wear it while he read the papers to heighten the memories.

The "From Hell" letter, as the newspapers kept calling it, had been especially entertaining. He couldn't believe the audacity of the author to actually send a piece of a woman's kidney with the note. He had decided to cut the kidney out of Catherine Eddowes as a lark. He never imagined that someone would respond by sending a new letter and placing the specimen in the jar of alcohol.

Henri had shown him how to properly cut kidneys from pig carcasses in order to make rognocini trifolati, a dish made from sautéed pork kidneys. It was important to remove the kidneys before gutting the animal in order to ensure that the meat was not spoiled by the removal of other internal organs.

Eventually, the exploits of Jack the Ripper began to lose their luster. Even the doctor's reports no longer fueled his memories or fantasies. Those stories seemed to describe events that happened a lifetime ago. He had even lost the ability to relive some of the vital moments of the murders. Something he thought would stay with him forever.

Something had begun to change inside him. The killing of the whores had been a necessity. A message needed to be sent. Sure, he enjoyed the acts, but they were not something he felt compelled to continue. The constant barrage of newspaper articles, along with the updates on the investigations would keep Jack the Ripper in the minds of the public for months to come.

But ever since his encounter with the doctor's wife in the hotel room he could only see one moment when he closed his eyes. It would start with blackness, then he could see the sultry hazel eyes of Dinah looking up at him. He could feel her chest against his and smell her sweet perfume. He could feel his hands slip around her neck and begin squeezing tighter and tighter. He could see her eyes widen and her pupils dilate. He would then lay her gently on the ground and look at her beautiful body shimmering in the pale light wearing nothing but her shear slip and open bustier.

He would relive this moment over and over each night. It aroused him every time. He longed to repeat the sensation in person. It had started as a fantasy, but was growing into an urge.

After the wedding, a new image started to appear in his mind when he closed his eyes at night. Most nights he would still see the doctor's wife, but occasionally he would see an image of Mary Jane Kelly standing in front of him at the bistro. He could see her wearing her deep red dress. See her dark hair fixed with the blue ribbons. Her pale skin. See that look of wanting in her eyes.

As the nights went on he started to see Mary Jane more often. Sometimes she would appear before the image of the doctor's wife. Then the images started to show up together. After a while, Dinah was replaced by Mary Jane as the two memories melded together.

The fantasy became more clear. He could see Mary Jane wearing her deep red dress and looking up at him. She would kiss his cheek as she did that night. Then he would wrap his hands around her throat and squeeze. He would lay down her slim, pale body and look at her for hours as she radiated in the dim light.

Octavius enjoyed this new fantasy immensely. It excited him more than ever, and he found himself lying in bed earlier and earlier every night in hopes of reliving the fantasy as many times as possible.

Sarah was standing in the publisher's office looking around at the full decanters of whiskey. She didn't mind a little drink now and again, but she had never approved of drinking on the job. Those would have to go.

Frank walked in the door. "Um, good morning Missus Donleavy. Have you seen Thaddeus this morning? We were just getting ready to start the editorial meeting, and he usually weighs in on things before the guys hit the street."

"Good morning, Frank. Thaddeus has decided to take a sabbatical. I'm not sure when he will be coming back just yet."

Frank looked at her with his mouth hanging open.

"Oh don't give me that look. You know this company has always been in my family, and it will always stay in my family."

"Yes, ma'am. I just didn't... I, um. Would you like to come to the editorial meeting this morning, Missus Donleavy?"

"That would be great Frank. And please, for heaven's sake, call me Sarah."

They went downstairs and met the other reporters at the table. Frank delivered the news about Thaddeus and moved on quickly so that no one would have time to start asking questions. He went around the table and listened to the pitches.

Every story pitched had spin related to the Jack the Ripper murders. Frank listened to them all before shaking his head. "We are going to need to do better than that today guys. Why don't we shake the trees this morning and come back in an hour to see what turns up."

He looked over at Sarah who was sitting at the table. She smiled and stood up. "I am not here to undermine Frank. He is the one who will be making the decision about what stories go in and what gets kicked out. But today, I would like to do a little shaking on that tree myself."

Everyone sat back down at the table and leaned in. "O'Conner and Sam, I would like for you guys to stay on the Ripper case. We should run an update in every edition, along with anything else you think needs to be covered. We just don't need to go out looking for something that isn't there. Only report the news and not the rumors."

Both men nodded in agreement.

"Peter, I would like to see some real political stories again. I know the Bill of Rights issue is back on the table, and the new

Prime Minister is causing a fuss in the House of Commons with his new agenda. Why don't you take a couple of these new guys and show them around Parliament."

Peter was grinning as she spoke. It was obvious he was ready to get back to some real political reporting.

"As for everyone else, let's see what's going on at Buckingham Palace. Check on the social scene and find out what's coming up for the holidays. Bottom line is we need to turn this back into a full-service newspaper and not Jack the Ripper's journal."

It was clear from the expressions around the room that everyone was welcoming the new direction. They were all released from the meeting and told to come back by three with whatever they could find.

"Thank you, Sarah," Frank looked relieved. "We needed that. I needed that. Thaddeus knows how to drive circulation, but we were running on fumes trying to pull out more Ripper angles."

"It's not going to be easy, Frank. Everyone else is going to ride the panic storm until the public loses interest. We might lose some circulation and maybe even some advertisers, but we are in this for the long haul. And we are in it for the right reasons. I will take us back to three papers and week and print a wagon load of catalogs if that's what it takes to keep our journalistic integrity intact."

"Understood. What else can we do to get back to reporting real news?"

"Well for starters, I want to see a woman other than me at the table at tomorrow's meeting."

On Thursday, after a particularly long day at the café, Octavius returned home late in the evening. He did not feel like looking through his newspapers. Instead he rushed to take off his clothes and climb into bed. He lay down and closed his eyes waiting for the fantasy to begin.

He lay there for hours, but nothing appeared. He saw only blackness. As the night went on he tried everything to get the image back. He opened the newspapers and read every article. He tried putting on the top hat, but it failed as well. He finally laid back down and tried to sleep, hoping that the fantasy would find him in his dreams.

He awoke the next morning still feeling anxious that the fantasy had not come. He got dressed and headed out for work. Throughout the morning he labored in silence, avoiding the staff and customers as much as possible. After the lunch hour he decided to leave early for the day. He left the bistro and headed back to his apartment.

He sat on his bed for a while contemplating his next actions. He had decided somewhere during the day that he had to see Mary Jane again. Not talk to her or meet her again. He just wanted to see her. He was sure that was all it would take to fuel his imagination.

After the double event he had been forced to purchase a new suit. He had worn the suit a couple of times, and he was much happier with the new design. He had asked the tailor to allow for more fabric in the armpits and to make the waste line a bit larger this time. This did not look as slimming, but it allowed for a better range of motion.

He had also purchased a new overcoat. This one was also a better design. The collars were fitted with higher peaks that shielded him more from the wind. They also helped to conceal his face better when needed. Best of all, he had managed to sew in a full leather sheath for his eight inch chef's knife, which he always carried in his right breast pocket.

He donned his new outfit and put on his top hat before leaving his room. He wasn't sure exactly where Mary Jane lived, but he remembered Marcus saying she worked in the Spitalfields area. He headed that way and see what could be found.

He arrived at the Spitalfields Market and decided to start in that area first. It was a slow afternoon, and he took his time wandering through the vendors, scanning the crowds as he walked.

It was a gamble, but he had hope that something might turn up. Markets were a hub of activity for those living in the city, and most people found a reason to stop by every day on their way home.

He spent a couple hours trying to map out the area in his mind and guess where she may live. There were apartments scattered throughout the region, and she could be in any one of them. Plus, he couldn't be certain that Marcus was even correct about where she lived.

He started to doubt his plan, when he saw a flash of dark hair fitted with blue ribbons walk across the street at the far end of the market. He hurried to the edge of the street and saw a lady walking his way. He wasn't sure it was her, but he ducked into a basket weaver's tent just in case. As she passed by he could see that it was definitely Mary Jane. She was wearing a green dress but no bonnet.

He quickly fell in behind her keeping his distance. He watched as she stopped at a market to grab a loaf of bread and a few other items. She then headed down the street and turned onto Dorset Street. He was careful turning the corner when he saw that she entered the small apartment located at Thirteen Miller's Court.

He found a bench at the corner of Dorset Street that gave him a good view into Miller's Court. He decided to sit there for a while to see if she came out again. He wasn't sure what he was hoping to see, but he had made it this far, so what would a little more investigating hurt?

A few minutes later another lady showed up and knocked on the door. This woman was not as pretty as Mary Jane, but she did have clean clothes and looked to be in decent health. She was let in the room. Soon after a man wearing fisherman's boots and a heavy soiled coat arrived. Octavius thought he might be a customer; however, minutes later an older lady arrived and knocked at the door. The three visitors did not stay long and soon the older lady left carrying a bit of the bread with her. Then the man and the first lady departed together and walked off in separate directions when they got to Dorset Street.

Octavius found all this activity to be interesting. It looked as if Mary Jane was quite the social butterfly. He waited a few more minutes reading from a newspaper he had purchased in the market. Then he saw her leave the apartment still in her green dress. She headed down the street and stopped at Ten Bells public house, no doubt to get a drink. Octavius thought about going in but decided against it. He wasn't ready for another personal encounter.

Instead, he stayed at the bench reading his paper. The lamps were still lit so he had a little time before he would start being accosted by the police. After about an hour he saw Mary Jane exit the public house and walk down Dorset Street. He followed her for a while until she walked in to the Horn of Plenty pub.

It was getting later, and he now had to make a decision. If he stayed on the street, he would start to look suspicious. He decided he would take a chance and enter the pub. He waited a few minutes to make sure his collar was fixed high, then entered the door.

To his advantage, the bar was filled to capacity. He found a secluded seat in the corner and sat down. From his vantage point he could see most of the patrons and found Mary Jane at the far end of the pub speaking with a group of men and women she obviously knew. He ordered a tonic water and tipped heavily so that the waitress would not bother him about taking up a seat.

He watched her as she glided in and out of conversations much like she had done at the wedding. But in this setting, she had more freedom from social conventions. Instead of lightly touching men's arms she was holding them with both hands as she laughed at their jokes. She played off the other women in the crowd, using them as props to further excite the men. He had seen his mother play this game hundreds of times, only in more luxurious settings and with richer targets.

It did not take long before Mary Jane had secured her mark. He was a stout, ginger-haired man with a dark bowler hat and a thick moustache. He was drinking beer from a bottle and looked fairly tipsy. She sat with him at the table as they sorted through round after round. At about eleven-thirty she helped him out of his chair, and they headed for the door.

Octavius pulled down his top hat as they passed him by. He got up a few seconds later and followed them out the door. As he walked behind them, he noticed that Mary Jane appeared quite intoxicated. This disappointed him. His mother would feign intoxication at times in order to impress a client, but she was always measured with her drinking.

They reached Millers Court where Mary Jane was greeted by another lady who was standing outside her apartment. She also looked to be working as a prostitute, but she had no customer at the moment. Mary Jane hugged her as she passed and said, "I am going to have a song."

She then took the man by the arm and pulled him into her room. Octavius searched the area for a place to stand out of the way. He had seen an alcove down the alley at the back of Mary Jane's room and made his way to the corner. As he passed by her door, he could see that the window was broken, which would make getting into the room very easy. He tucked himself away in the alcove and waited in the shadows.

He could hear everything in the apartment. There was laughing followed by Mary Jane singing an old Irish song called "A Violet I Plucked From Mother's Grave When a Boy." Her voice was beautiful and filled Octavius' heart with joy. He closed his eyes as he listened to the wonderful ballad. This time the fantasy returned, and he let it wash over him.

He wasn't sure how long he had been standing in the corner letting the images fill his mind, when the sound of the front door opening broke his trance. He pushed himself back into the darkness as he watched the stout man stumble out the door.

He contemplated knocking on her door at that moment. He did not know what he would say. He might just ask to pay her for her time and just sit with her for a while. She would no doubt take his money for a little conversation. His thoughts were interrupted when she walked out the door and pulled it closed behind her.

She walked out to Dorset Street, but this time turned toward the market. He followed her again, this time staying closer because she had entered Commercial Street, which was a much larger and busier street with plenty of people to hold her attention.

He quickly realized that she was heading toward Flower and Dean, which was an area of the slums known for its sordid activity. He had walked the area several times in the past and knew it was popular with the whores. He did not understand why Mary Jane would need to go there.

His suspicions were confirmed when she turned down Thrawl Street. He had to work harder to hide his presence once he followed her down the narrow street. He stood out in this new area since he was wearing a nice suit with an expensive top hat. He saw her approach a man and start a conversation. They obviously knew each other and he was afraid that she had found another customer.

After a while, she wished him goodbye and continued walking toward Flower and Dean. As they approached the busy street, he could see that there were several factory workers walking the area. He had to act fast because he knew a prostitute of her caliber would not stay alone for long.

He walked up to her and pretended to be lost. "Excuse me, ma'am. Do you happen to know the way to Commercial Street?"

She turned to him and sized him up in a moment, at least his worth anyway. She was drunk but had most of her wits about her. However, it was clear that she did not recognize him.

"It is just around that corner there, my good sir. I could show you the way if you like?"

"That would be kind of you."

She took him by the arm and led him back out the way they had entered. They passed by the man she had been talking to earlier, and Octavius pulled down his hat in an attempt to shield his face from view.

Once they got to Commercial Street she decided to make her pitch. "I say, sir, you wouldn't perhaps be interested a little company this evening would you? I have a nice warm bed just down the street there."

"I don't know. I like to be discrete. I might be interested in having your company for the rest of the evening."

"That would cost you a bit."

"Would this be acceptable?" He held up a few pound coins so that she could see them shining in the moonlight. He knew it would be more than acceptable, as it was a week's pay for any hardworking prostitute in London.

She grabbed him by the arm and led him toward her apartment. She tried to engage him in conversation, but he only responded with one word answers. He was still trying to figure out what he was going to say when they got to her room. She had not recognized him yet, and that revelation would change the dynamics in a flash.

Once they got to her apartment, she lit a candle and offered him a drink of whiskey, which he refused. She drank it down herself, then started undressing. She looked back to see that he was not moving. Instead he just stood there staring at her. She finished removing her dress and now stood there in her bustier and white slip.

She walked up to him and took off his top hat. She stood frozen for a moment as she looked at him with slight awareness. Her gaze made him avert his eyes and he bowed his head. That is when she recognized him.

"Ah. You are the chef. Why didn't you say something?"

"I thought it best to be discrete, Mary Jane."

She was surprised that he knew her name. She moved in closer and kissed his cheek the same as before. She then started unbuckling his trousers. She pulled them down to his feet and slowly rose to kiss his cheek again. Then his lips. He closed his eyes as she kissed him again, fuller this time.

He could taste the whiskey on her lips. He could smell her perfume. He stood there kissing her, awash in a wave of emotion. It was an exhilarating feeling that he never wanted to end.

They kissed for several moments before she started to pull back the sides of his overcoat. He opened his eyes to look at her beautiful face. But something was wrong.

She was looking at him, but he did not see her beautiful eyes. Instead, they were replaced by his mother's hazel eyes. He stood frozen not understanding what was happening.

Mary Jane turned her back to him and pressed her now naked body against him. He looked down and saw the ribbons in her braided hair. But again they had been replaced by his mother's thick blue ribbons. He couldn't understand why his mother's ribbons were flowing through the intricate French braid.

He closed his eyes tightly and shook his head hoping to correct the image. He knew it was just his mind playing tricks on him, but it felt so real. He took a deep breath before opening his eyes again.

This time when he opened his eyes he did not see Mary Jane's face. He only saw the face of his mother and those piercing hazel eyes were staring at him.

It was wrong. It was ALL WRONG!

It was Friday morning and Frank was meeting with the reporters at the assignment desk. There were now two female reporters at the table. Sarah was standing to the side just listening to the stories being pitched.

O'Conner came into the room late and held his notepad up near his face as he wrote, a sure sign that he had a big story. He looked ashen and a bit sad. He sat down at the table and plopped down set his notepad.

"There has been another murder. Most likely Jack the Ripper. But this one is bad. Really bad."

Frank walked over to him and put his hand on his friend's shoulder.

"I got to the scene quick, about the same time as the doctor. It was over on Miller's Court. I saw in the room. It is nothing like the other girls. This one was done by a monster."

Frank released the other reporters. "Go ahead and get to your stories. Stay on the political news, the world news, and the stuff at the palace. Let's hold off on the social scene for now."

"Sam is at Scotland Yard. I got all I needed at the scene. I spoke to the doctor and a few witnesses. The story is the same as the rest, only he spent a lot of time with this one."

Frank and Sarah both had an idea of what that meant.

To everyone's surprise Sarah sat down at the typewriter. "Give me what you have so far, O'Conner. You guys have had to deal with this stuff for too long, why don't I get this one started and you and Sam can finish it when he gets here."

O'Conner turned over his notepad and started reading off the details.

The victim's name was Mary Jane Kelly. She was twenty-five years old and had an apartment at thirteen Miller's Court in the Spitalfields area that she had resided in since 1886.

All the witnesses said she was a pretty and friendly woman from Limerick, Ireland who had a penchant for strong drink. Like all the other victims, she was a prostitute.

Her body was found inside her apartment this morning at ten forty-five by her landlord's assistant Thomas Bowyer who had stopped by to collect the rent. He saw her body through the window and reported it to his boss John McCarthy. Mister McCarthy then verified the claims and sent Bowyer to the Commercial Road Police Station.

Inspector Walter Beck reported to the scene and called for Police Surgeon Doctor George Bagster Phillips. The doctor declared her dead immediately by way of a cut throat, the same as the other victims. He said that the other mutilations of her body would have taken at least two hours to perform.

Sam arrived and verified that Scotland Yard had been notified and Detectives Frederick Abberline and Robert Anderson were now at the scene.

Sarah pulled the story out of the typewriter and handed to Frank. He read it over and noted the difference in style from what they had been printing. She had covered all the facts and details, but she had also covered more of the personal aspects of the story.

Sarah noted that Miss Kelly was from Ireland. That she had her own apartment which she had lived in for two years. She mentioned that she was liked by her neighbors. That she was pretty and young. The story was news, but it was also relatable. The stories about the other victims had seemed clinical and dark. This one was horrific but felt like it had happened to a friend or acquaintance.

Frank showed the story to O'Conner who then passed it on to Sam.

Sam handed the letter back to Frank who read quickly for a second time. "I think you should keep the byline on this one, Sarah. It's about time people in this city started reading real news from a female publisher."

Sarah nodded her head and asked O'Conner for a piece of paper out of his notebook. She grabbed a pen and wrote out something and handed it to Frank. "If it's going to be my byline then I might as well write the headline.

JACK THE RIPPER CLAIMS ANOTHER VICTIM
IRISH MAIDEN MURDERED IN SPITALFIELDS AREA

Octavius sat on his bed staring at the top hat. He did not understand. Who had he become in that room with that beautiful woman? He had killed before, but as a means to an end. As the Liberator. As Jack the Ripper.

He had gone to that side of town just to see her. To see her as Octavius. To fuel his imagination. To find his lost fantasy. He had not gone for violence, or murder, and certainly not to send a message.

He felt as if there were two men in that room with Mary Jane that night: The simple chef who wanted the woman from his fantasies and a mad man trying to expunge the demons from his past.

Octavius was not naive to some of the bitterness he felt

towards his mother and the way she had treated him, but he had always respected her. Her strength. Her poise. Her ability to manipulate others, especially men. He respected the way she protected the girls that worked for her and all the other respectable prostitutes. He respected the way she admonished the girls that did not act properly and punished the whores that brought shame to the craft.

He had never viewed her occupation as unsavory or vile, or even inappropriate. She brought dignity to the craft. She made sure her girls had clean rooms, warm beds, and proper clothes. She paid them well and protected them.

So why then did her image cause him to react in such a chaotic manner? Why did he feel the need to mutilate Mary Jane?

He lay back in his bed. At first, he was afraid to close his eyes for fear that he would relive the moment again, but he had to find answers.

When he closed his eyes this time, all he could see was the face of his mother. The image made his stomach lurch. He felt the anger boiling inside him again. He opened them quickly, then forced himself to go back. He had to find answers.

This time when he closed his eyes, he saw his mother again standing in her brothel. But he did not focus on the clean rooms and warm beds. He did not see the well cared for girls. Instead, he saw himself in the background.

He was scrubbing filth from mattresses that had been used the night before. He was sewing stitches into a woman's arm who had been taught a lesson in manners by his mother.

He was filling bottles with warm water in preparation for his mother to perform abortions. He was holding a screaming woman down while his mother injected the solution into her uterus.

He was sitting on his bed holding his hands over his ears trying in earnest not to hear the exploits of his mother with her latest customer. He was washing dirty sheets covered in all manner of human filth.

Then he saw Augie hanging from that rope in his apartment.

He saw himself loading his oldest friend onto a dirty cart and wheeling him to the undertaker. He saw himself shoveling dirt on the casket. He saw his mother standing in her black dress and holding an umbrella. He saw her pursed lips in and stern eyes as she told him he had suckled at her breast for far too long. Her awful piecing hazel eyes.

The sights, sounds, even the smells circulated vividly in his mind. He could now see clearly what his mother had done to him. What she had created in him. He hated this feeling. He needed to purge it from himself.

Octavius stayed in his room all morning and into the afternoon. Even after his mental anguish had subsided, he was still in no condition to go to work. At two o'clock Victor knocked on his door.

The chef thought about pretending he wasn't there but knew that would only cause the maître d' to go find his landlord. He told him to wait a minute before putting on an undershirt and pulling on his pants.

He opened the door a crack and forced himself to stand up straight. Victor looked worried when he opened the door, and he looked even more worried after seeing his boss' condition.

"It's fine, Victor. I just ate something that didn't agree with me in the market yesterday. I was trying to find some better vegetables for the bistro, but it did not work out very well."

"Chef, you are drenched in sweat and look so pale. Are you sure you shouldn't get to a doctor?"

"No, I'll be fine. I just need to get back to bed."

"Can I at least get you some food and water?"

"No, I am fine. I have plenty of water and some bread. Get back to the bistro and make sure the boys haven't burnt it down."

Victor reluctantly shut the door and Octavius returned to his bed. He closed his eyes and tried to rest, but the images started flooding back again.

Octavius knew with certainty that these images were not going to leave him. The feelings were not going to leave him. Not until he found a way to purge them. And to do that he would have to purge the one who created them in the first place.

It was time for him to go home. It was time for his mother to meet the man she had created. It was time for her to meet Jack the Ripper.

He used the rest of the evening to start working out a plan on how to best leave the Café Langham. He did not want to leave Gustavo in a bad way with his departure, especially given all that he had done for him. Plus, the boisterous hotel owner was a very influential man throughout Europe, and it wouldn't be a good idea to spurn him.

Thaddeus sat at the bar at the Café Langham. It was two in the afternoon and he had nowhere else to go. He had given up on the idea of resisting the bottle ever since Sarah had sent him away on a sabbatical, whatever the hell that was supposed to mean.

Basically, she had paid him six months of salary and told him to go travel for a while. He had been staying at the Langham Hotel for a few days, but he planned to check out in the morning. He would head to Paris to catch the Orient Express and travel down to Istanbul to get lost in the mountains for a while.

He supposed it was Sarah's way of telling him she wanted to take a break in their marriage. She did not want a divorce, not yet anyway. She said that after Thaddeus cleared his head, and his liver, she might be willing to take him back.

For now, he figured he would work on the head clearing part. The liver clearing would have to come later. He signaled Tom for another pour of whiskey, as he opened a copy of the *East End Observer*. He had been keeping tabs on the paper over the past few days, interested to see how his wife would go about implementing her vision of journalistic integrity.

For the most part, it meant cutting back on Ripper stories. She had leaned heavy into politics and royal shenanigans. He knew that wasn't going to drive circulation for long.

She was smart enough to print extensive coverage of the Mary Jane Kelly murder, which was the most sensational event he had known of in London. He was surprised to see her byline connected to the lead story, and he had to admit that she had written a far better article than he would have been able to produce. However, the *Observer* didn't get out until the afternoon that day, long after many of the other papers in town.

He guessed that was her definition of journalistic ethics. Write a better story but put it out late so that you can't sell as many papers. *Oh well*, he thought. *It was her problem now.* She might be more willing to take him back in a few months after the circulation tanks and the bills start piling up. Sarah was too good hearted to start firing people, which is a must in business when the revenues dry up.

He swallowed the drink in front of him and signaled for yet another. Then he went back to reading the paper. Politics, politics, royal family, blah, blah. He got to page four before there was any mention of Jack the Ripper. To his surprise, Sarah had allowed them to print the entire coroner's report. It was buried deep in the paper, but at least it was there in all its gruesome glory.

He read through the report, slammed another drink, and set the paper down. He called for another drink and Tom asked if he wanted anything to eat. After reading the details of the murder, he decided it best to wait a bit before putting anything any his stomach.

A few minutes later, Octavius appeared from the kitchen. He walked up to the bar and asked Victor to pour him a tonic water. He glanced over and recognized the man at the bar from the night Gustavo had introduced him as the publisher of the newspaper.

"Hello… Thaddeus, I believe. From the *Observer*?"

"Why, yes. And you are Chef Octavius. Purveyor of fine stews and soups I believe."

"Yes, sir. It looks like you are finished with printing today's paper."

"Yes, I'm finished with the paper alright." He held up the newspaper and waved it around.

Octavius could read the headline on the folded page showing the coroner's report. His heart started pounding, and he had to calm himself with a drink of tonic water. "I was planning on picking up a copy on my way home. I have made it a point to read the *Observer* every day after meeting you and your lovely wife."

"That is very kind of you to say. Why don't you take this copy? I have had my fill of this paper for a while."

"Thank you, sir. Have a nice day. And give my best to your wife." Octavius folded the paper to hide the headline.

Thaddeus pulled out a few coins from his pocket and tossed them on the bar. "Thank you, gentlemen. Have a good evening."

On Sunday, Octavius went to the market and purchased two notebooks. He walked to the bistro and sat in the kitchen with the first notebook. He wrote out the recipes for the signature dishes they had been making: the cassoulet, the Coq au vin soup, and the various pot pies. He also added notes on how to change the recipes for each season as new ingredients became available.

He wrote out checklists for prepping in the mornings and evenings and other detailed lists for shopping and cleaning. He wrote out lists and directions for nearly every task that involved the kitchen. He wanted to be as thorough as possible.

He went to the dining room and took out the second notebook. He wrote out notes for the maître d', including how best to interact with Gustavo. He described how to manage the kitchen staff and how to deal with the vendors. He also outlined basic ledgers showing the payroll amounts, vendor payments, food costs, and other expenses. He then gave samples of a full monthly accounting showing expected daily revenues and expenses. He described what the margins should be each week and outlined what amounts would make Gustavo happy and which amounts would be cause for alarm. He provided tips on how to manage the kitchen staff when things got too busy.

On Monday Octavius showed up at the Café Langham early. He wanted to be there when the boys arrived. He was pleased to see that Marcus arrived early and immediately started the pots before moving to the prep tables. He then went out to the dining room where he greeted the chef and made sure he was feeling better from his illness.

Stephane arrived a few minutes later and joined the sous chef in the kitchen. Both men were fast at work preparing the meals without any expectation of direction from the chef.

Victor and Natasha arrived soon after and said hello to the chef before starting to prep the dining and bar areas for service. They worked quickly without saying a word to each other.

Satisfied that things were well in hand, Octavius climbed the stairs to Gustavo's office. He rehearsed his speech in his head on the walk. He reached the office and could see the owner sitting at his desk looking over a stack of letters.

"Good morning, Gustavo. Do you have a minute this morning."

"Always, Octavius. I have all the time in the world for the finest bistro chef in London."

"Sir, I wanted to say thank you for all that you have done for me here at the Langham. Starting up the bistro has been a dream come true for me. I am really proud of how much the staff has grown and how much responsibility they have taken on over the past few months."

"Oh no. I don't like where this is going. The only time someone says such things is when they want more money or they are trying to sell me something."

"No, sir. Nothing like that. I am afraid I have received word from America that my mother has fallen ill. She does not have anyone to care for her, and I have been asked to come to see after her. Otherwise, she will be sent to an infirmary, where there is little hope that she could recover."

"That is horrible news. Now, I wish you were asking for money. I am so sorry to hear about your mother's condition. Is there no one else who can respond to her?"

"I am her only child and her only family. She does not have a husband, so I am the only one that can look after her and handle her estate."

"But what will happen to the bistro, the wonderful restaurant that you built?"

"It will be fine. The boys have learned to make all the signature dishes and they have handled several services on their own now. Marcus may not be completely ready to be a head chef, but he is more than capable of running a little bistro kitchen."

He held up one of the notebooks. "I have copied down all the recipes and provided them with checklists and notes on everything they need to remember in the kitchen."

"I know they are good cooks, but they are so young."

"They are responsible young men, but I agree that they are very young. That is why I think you should promote Victor to general manager. He has been an excellent maître d', and he has a calmness about him that would serve him well as the head of the restaurant. The boys respect him, and so does everyone else."

"Yes, that does make sense. I do like Victor. He is a strong man. Any man who can tend a bar and not drink all day must be a man of strong character."

Octavius held up a second notebook. "If you agree to making him general manager, then I can show him everything he needs to know, and he can always come to you or Chef Simon if he gets in over his head."

"Okay, okay. I see that you have a good plan. I just don't want to see you go. When do you leave?"

"I plan to leave Saturday, if possible, to head to Hamburg to see if I can find passage to America. I am hoping they could use an extra cook on one of the ships."

"Well, you are in luck there, my boy. I happen to know that the *Frisia* was just sold to Rolland Gillcrest here in London. He is a friend of mine who owes me a number of favors. I will make a point to visit him and tell him he simply must hire you as his head chef."

"That would be very kind of you, sir. But I wouldn't want to put you out."

"Nonsense, it is the least I can do. Now, you haven't any time to waste. Go make sure my bistro staff are ready to handle things on their own. Let me worry about securing your passage back to America."

Octavius left Gustavo's office and headed for the bistro. He was relieved that the meeting was over and pleased with the results. He had expected more resistance, but then again, Gustavo always seemed to find a way to turn bad news into an opportunity.

He went to the kitchen to deliver the news to the staff. He started with Victor and pulled him aside to tell him in private. The maître d' was apprehensive about taking over the reigns as the general manager. He had only been running the front of the house for a few months and that was a big step for him. Now he would have to balance the ledger and watch over the kitchen staff as well. Octavius assured him he would be fine, as they reviewed the notebook together.

The chef then told the boys in the kitchen. He told them both together, and like most young men they took the news as an opportunity to improve themselves. Marcus was most appreciative of the written recipes and immediately started barking orders at Stephane in jest.

On Tuesday, Wednesday, and Thursday Octavius worked with Victor and Marcus to ensure that they understood their new duties. By Friday he was convinced they were ready, and he let them both manage their areas. He watched as Marcus prepared the meals for the service and made out the lists for a trip to the market that afternoon.

He also watched as Victor worked on the ledger and dealt with two vendors who arrived to collect payments. One of the vendors tried to take advantage of his new contact by charging him extra for his deliveries and Victor quickly put him in his place.

By noon on Friday, Octavius was confident things were

settled at the bistro. He told Victor that he was heading to his apartment to pack his bags and let him know that he would be back in the morning to say goodbye to everyone.

As he left the bistro, he had a strong urge to read the paper, but knew that would cause him to lose focus. He had a long journey ahead of him and he couldn't let his inner urges derail him.

Once he got to the apartment, he opened the hat carrier containing his top hat. He placed the newspaper inside the carrier, closed the top and buckled the straps tight. He vowed to himself in that moment that he would not open the carrier to don the hat or read the paper until he reached America.

If he could keep the hat locked away, then he could also keep Jack the Ripper locked away. At least until he was needed again.

Sarah sat at her desk sorting through her mail. It had taken her a while to get a handle on the company ledger. Thaddeus had left the company in great financial shape, but he was behind on entering revenues and noting which payments had gone out.

Luckily, Frank had stayed on top of paying the vendors and Walter had a log showing which advertisers still owed money.

This was the first day that she felt comfortable enough to step away from business and sort through all her personal mail.

The first several letters were from readers. Most were negative, which she understood was common for newspapers. Readers complained that the Ripper coverage was too gruesome. Others complained there weren't enough gruesome details. Readers from both parties complained about the "obvious" political bias of the paper. More than a few people complained about the paper now giving women bylines, especially in the news sections.

She was rather happy that the letters were arriving. It meant that they were doing something right. At least people were still reading, which was a relief to her. She had made her speech about journalistic ethics, which she meant, but she knew that all the ethics in the world wouldn't pay the bills. Circulation and ad revenue had remained steady, which was all she could hope for at the moment.

She read through a few more letters before seeing one that caught her attention. It was a letter from Thaddeus that she must have missed during the first pass. It was in a small envelope that looked tattered and dirty and was post marked Istanbul, Turkey.

She opened the letter and read the short note.

My Dearest Sarah:

I don't know how many times I can say I'm sorry. I don't know if I will ever be able to say it enough to gain your forgiveness. I am even more worried that I will never gain your confidence again.

For now, I have decided to embrace this sabbatical, as you call it. I am currently in Istanbul and will soon be traveling deep into Africa on safari. I honestly don't know what adventures await me. I was in need of a change more than even I understood.

Maybe I will find myself in all this. Find the curious journalist that I was as a younger man. Find the man that you married. Or maybe I will be eaten by a hippo somewhere along the Amazon River. Either way, I am eager to find out.

I think of you every hour, and I will write you often. I wish the best for you in your new role. I read all the papers I could before I left. It was good to see your byline. A woman's perspective is just what the Observer needed after suffering under my brutal hand.

Give my best wishes to Frank, O'Conner, Walter, and the rest of the group.

All My Love,
Thaddeus

After reading the letter she sat back in her chair not quite knowing how to feel. A big part of her missed him. But she knew it was for the best. She hoped he would find himself during his travels and come back a better man. A sober, less ambitious man would be all that she ever wanted. She folded the letter and stuck it in the front drawer of her desk.

She went downstairs and walked into the typesetting room. Walter was already working on the next day's paper. "Good afternoon. I didn't think you were ever going to get out from behind that desk today."

"That makes two of us, Walter. How are things going?"

"We have most everything set. Do you want to help me work on the headlines?"

"You know that has become my favorite part of the day."

Octavius stood outside the front entrance of the Langham Hotel. He rarely used the front entrance anymore, but he thought it would be fitting for his last day. He looked up at the grandeur of it all.

It had been a once in a lifetime opportunity to work in such an established hotel. He had truly enjoyed the work and being able to create something that was his own. If it weren't for his other urges, Jack's urges, then he could have happily stayed at the hotel for many years. He could have undoubtedly convinced Gustavo to invest in more bistros and other restaurants around the city. But that was not in the cards.

He pushed through the heavy entrance doors and spun around the lobby taking it all in. Then he walked to the back of the hotel and down the stairs to the bistro. The staff were already there working on preparing for the lunch service.

As soon as Victor saw the chef walk into the restaurant, he signaled for everyone to come out. They all stood around him in silence.

"I guess there isn't much to say. Just remember your training. Always care about the food. Care about the customers. But above all, care about each other. If you do that you will be successful for a long time. Be good to Gustavo and he will be good to you. He gave me a wonderful opportunity, and now I am giving it to you. Especially you Victor and you Marcus."

"Yes, chef," was all anyone could say.

Natasha handed him a notebook that was bound in nice thick leather. She was fighting back tears. "For your recipes, chef. We know how much you like to keep notes."

"Thank you, Natasha. Thank you all."

With that, Octavius walked back up the stairs. He stopped at the top of the landing and watched as they all returned to their work. He knew it was going to be a rough month for them all, especially Victor. But he was sure they would make it through.

He headed down the hallway where Gustavo was standing in his office. "There is the chef who is going to abandon me. Leaving me with a bunch of young boys who just learned to boil water."

"As long as people are willing to buy it, I am sure you will still sell it to them."

"You can bet your hat on that. Come into my office, I have something for you." The owner was as jubilant as ever. He opened the safe in his office and took out a money pouch and threw it to Octavius.

The chef could feel that it was full of money and lots of it. "This is too much, Gustavo. You have paid me well already."

"I was planning on giving it to you at the end of the year anyway. It is your share of the profits. Don't get too excited, it's all in American dollars. A man from Rhode Island owed me money a few years ago and he paid me in dollars. I never took the time to get it to the bank. Who knows what the exchange rate is like now. You might not be able to buy more than pair of boots with what is in that bag."

Octavius knew that wasn't true. The pouch was obviously full of bills and coins. "You are too generous, Gustavo. I can never repay you for your generosity."

"You have no debts with me my friend. I will be making money from the bistro long after you are gone. Plus, I expect you will come crawling back to London in the future ready to start a new adventure. And I will be here waiting to let you make me more money with another restaurant."

"You are probably right about that. I am going to miss this city and the Langham."

"Now, you should get on the road. Old Mister Gillcrest will be waiting for you in Germany."

The two men exchange another round of goodbyes and Octavius left the hotel and headed toward the train station. He was carrying all his belongings, which consisted of his knife role, a single large suitcase, and the carrier for his top hat.

A few days earlier Gustavo had introduced Octavius to Rolland Gillcrest, who was the principal owner of R.L. Gillcrest and Company. The company had recently purchased the SS *Frisia*, as a short-term deal in order to upgrade the ships engines and reconfigure the top masts. The company planned to resell the vessel within the next year.

The old ship had made its last official passenger tour three years ago in 1885. It was common practice to convert passenger ships into cargo haulers once they had grown long in the tooth, and at nearly twenty years old the *Frisia* was at a prime age to be converted into a coal hauler.

Rolland had business in Virginia, so he scheduled to sail his company's new acquisition to New York City in early spring. Gustavo knew that the rich old man loved his fine food, so he introduced him to Octavius and told him he would be a fool not to hire Octavius to serve as a proper chef during the voyage. It was the kind of extravagance Rolland was known to flaunt.

Gustavo played the situation perfectly by saying he doubted his formally trained chef would even consider such a mundane task but would try to convince him if the businessman could afford such a luxury. Rolland took the bait and told him to offer the chef twenty pounds a day for his services, as well as a first-class accommodation for the voyage.

Octavius couldn't believe that he was going to receive free passage to America, as well as being paid a year's salary during the twelve-day journey. His debt to Gustavo continued to grow, as the man's generosity had no bounds.

The chef walked out of the Langham and crossed the street. He looked back for a minute and tried to sketch the building into his memory. He knew there was little chance that he would ever return to London. He had done all he could for this city, and now it would have to fend for itself.

He picked up his luggage and headed to the train station. He wasn't expected in Hamburg until mid-March, but there was another city in Germany that he always wanted to visit called Solingen, the legendary City of Blades.

Sarah sat in the typesetting room looking at the blank spot on top of the lead story that was reserved for a two liner. It was yet another Jack the Ripper update, and she tried to force herself to come up with another headline.

Walter stood over her shoulder attempting to "help." He just watched as she tried out different word combinations and made guttural sounds every time she came to the end of a line.

After the last clearing of the old typesetters throat, she called out for assistance. "Frank, it's your turn to write a headline for one of these blasted stories. I've done the last four. I will write the headlines for everything else, but I just can't handle any more of this Ripper business."

Frank shared her frustration. They had written a least a hundred stories about the Whitechapel murders in the past several months, and it was becoming impossible to come up with new headlines.

Walter had a memory like an elephant and would notice right away when any lines had been repeated. It was grating on everyone's nerves to have the old man stand behind them grunting after each attempt.

Frank took Sarah's seat after she moved over to another roller to work on a different set of stories. "Walter, why don't you go get us some coffee?"

The typesetter gave him an ugly smirk and headed out of the room. He tried out a couple of lines, but knew they had all been done before. He sat back in his chair and sighed. "It's been a week since the last murder. I sure hope that was the last of it. I know it has been good for business, but I can't believe what it has done to this city. My wife is afraid to even go to the market in the afternoon for fear that she won't make it back before the sun sets."

"We have been a part of that you know," Sarah said it as a matter of fact and not an accusation. "I guess that is always a danger when reporting the news. It is always the ugly stories that makes the headlines."

"I know it, but this Jack the Ripper stuff is different. Reporting ugly news is one thing. But the Ripper coverage has just been oppressive."

"Well, as managing editor, you pick what articles make it into the paper. It won't be easy finding subjects more interesting than the Ripper, but I think there are more stories out there than just murders and updates about murders. You just have to find them."

Frank sat back for a moment and contemplated his publisher's comment. She was right of course, but he doubted there was much out there that could supplant the Ripper for headlines.

When Octavius was a child, Augie had shared newspaper clippings and pictures with him about Solingen, Germany and its amazing history. He had dreamed about visiting the famous city all his life.

Solingen had been renowned since the Middle Ages for its fine blades. Originally, the craftsmen had created the finest swords, but now it was known more for its knives, axes, scissors, and straight razors.

The city was located near the western edge of Germany, and the train ride from London took less than a day. Octavius arrived in the evening and secured lodging at a small inn located near the center of the city.

The next day, he arose early and walked the streets looking at all the shops. The city had more than a dozen large knife shops, most with names he recognized. There were also nearly twenty smaller shops circling the outskirts of the city. Octavius used his new notebook that Natasha had given to him to draw a map showing the location and size of each shop.

That night at the inn, he spoke to the keeper about renting the room for the month. He then wrote out the order in which he would visit the shops by placing a single shop name on the top of each page. He wanted to start with the smaller unknown shops before moving on to the famous bladesmiths.

He spent the next month visiting every shop on his list. He only visited one shop a day and spent as much time in each location as was allowed. Most of the owners were very friendly and even showed him around their forges and operations. Octavius was in awe of the skill and craftsmanship displayed by even the smallest of shops.

He enjoyed watching the blacksmiths in the forges and took notes on the quality and unique techniques employed by the different operations. He personally had little interest in metalsmithing, but he understood its importance in the crafting of fine blades.

What fascinated him most about the craftsmen in the city was their innovations in grinding and sharpening techniques. Nearly every shop was located near a river or creek and used water as a means to power their grinding wheels. Octavius had only used foot powered grinders, which were inconsistent in their motions and exhausting to operate. He drew diagrams of several of the water grinding setups for future reference.

The shops in the area also used a variety of large and small wet stones to sharpen the blades. They could get complex hollow and convex edges using these stones. For larger ax blades and kitchen choppers they used grinding wheels that rotated in water.

After twenty-eight days, Octavius had filled his entire book with notes and diagrams and had started on a second notebook. A plan started to develop in his mind. He understood blades. He knew how to use them. How to sharpen them. What edges worked best for certain tasks. Maybe he could use that knowledge to make some money on his next venture.

He had already purchased several knives from every shop he visited, sometimes dozens at each shop. The prices were amazingly low compared to anything he had ever seen at the stores or even from street vendors, and the quality was unparalleled. He returned to some of his favorite shops and purchased even more blades. He even hired a carpenter to build him a reinforced crate suitable for carrying the load.

It was early on Wednesday, and Frank was tired. He had been working long hours for the past month. Once the stories about the Ripper started to subside he had to work even harder to find news that was worthy to print.

World news and politics had started to dominate the front page again, and the Royals always provided good fodder. But circulation was waning. They had moved the *Observer* from forty thousand copies down to thirty-five last Wednesday, and he was now planning to move down to thirty thousand for the next run.

So far, he hadn't had to fire any of the reporters or other staff, but he had stopped hiring anyone to replace those who had left the company. He knew the next step would be to start letting people go, but he was a few months away from having to make those sorts of decisions.

He just needed a little more time. He had a decent group of seasoned reporters, but they were attuned to working the three stalwarts of London journalism: police, politics, and the palace. Where his team was lacking was in its ability to cover world news and social interest stories. Those were the kind of articles that would carry them into the future.

He had the right young talent in place, but they were inexperienced and needed more training. He just needed to prepare them for life after Jack the Ripper. God knows, he was ready for that chapter to be over.

Unfortunately, O'Conner walked in just as that thought entered his mind and told him that his dream of a Ripper-less future would need to be put on hold.

"Sorry, Frank, but there has been another murder. It happened about two miles from Whitechapel, so they aren't saying it was the Ripper yet. But she was definitely a prostitute, so I am sure the public will jump to that conclusion."

"Damn it. It's been six weeks since Mary Jane Kelly. I had hoped he had fallen into the Thames or something worse."

"I know, but at least it will sell more papers." O'Conner pulled out his notepad and sat down next to the managing editor who had stuck a sheet of paper into the typewriter.

Frank called for his brother who came out of the print room wearing overalls. "Peter, tell Walter we are going to have to pull the first roller and change out the lead story. And pull another three rolls of paper out, we are going to push the run to forty-five thousand."

"Damn it all to hell. I take it the Ripper has stuck again?"

"It looks that way. Even if it wasn't the Ripper, another woman has been killed."

Peter ran off to inform Walter. Frank turned back to the typewriter, and O'Conner started reading off the details he had gotten from his visit to the police station.

The victim's official name was Catherine Mylett, but everyone knew her as Rose Mylett. She was last seen alive by a lady named Alice Graves outside of The George Tavern on Commercial Road at around two-thirty in the morning. She appeared to be drunk at the time.

Her body was discovered at four-fifteen that morning by Police Sergeant Robert Golding who was walking his beat down Poplar High Street. He found her lying in Clarke's Yard, which belonged to local builder's merchant George Clark.

An assistant to Divisional Surgeon Doctor Matthew Brownsfield was the first to arrive at the scene and pronounced Rose Mylett dead, but the cause of death was not immediately discerned. Doctor Brownsfield reported to the scene a short time later and determined that she had been killed by strangulation. The body was not mutilated like the others. In fact, the only indication of murder was the thin line created by some sort of cord that was used to affect the strangulation.

Frank pulled the page out of the typewriter when he was done and handed it to Walter who was now standing behind him waiting for the article. "This does not sound like the work of the Ripper."

O'Connor nodded in agreement, "There was no cutting of the throat. No mutilation. There wasn't even a knife involved. How can it be Jack the Ripper when there was no... Well, no ripping."

Walter did not care about any of that nonsense. He had work to do. "I need to get this to the typesetter. You can argue about all that while you come up with a headline."

Sarah arrived a few minutes later and saw Frank and Sam looking over a few lines written on a piece of paper. She greeted the men and looked down at the headline.

"Damnit. I thought we were done with all this nonsense."

WOMAN FOUND STRANGLED ON POPLAR HIGH STREET
MURDER DOES NOT FOLLOW JACK THE RIPPER PATTERN

During his short time in the Solingen, Octavius had grown in notoriety as the American who was in town to purchase knives. He had told many of the owners that he was a purchaser for a company in America and that he had been sent to the city to bring back samples. He had hoped to capitalize on that notoriety when he visited the final two manufacturers.

He saved the two largest manufacturers for last. They were both companies he knew intimately, as their blades had filled his knife roll for years.

The first manufacturer he visited was Wüsthof, a family owned operation that started in the early 1800s. The company had recently moved into a large factory that was powered by a collection of large steam-engines. He was given a tour of the facility where he saw dozens of metalsmiths producing shears, pocket knives, daggers, forks, axes, scissors, and all manner of kitchen knives. For such a large volume of production, quality control remained high throughout all areas.

At the end of the tour, he was taken to a smaller forge where a master blacksmith created their prized chef blades. He did his best to hide his excitement. He managed to procure a number of free samples from the Wüsthof company, and purchased even more at greatly reduced prices. He also splurged on a new boning knife made by the master blacksmith.

The final manufacturer he visited was the Zwilling J. A. Henckels company, which was the largest and oldest manufacturer in the area. The company was founded in 1731 by Peter Henckels and remained a family-owned company like most other knife makers in Germany.

The company had a special place in Octavius' heart because it was the company that made his prized possession, the eight inch chef's knife that Tumas had given him. Tumas had raved about the company's legendary craftsmanship, and he was excited to see it in person.

The Henckels operation was every bit as impressive as the Wüsthof company, only more focused on kitchenware, straight razors, and fine knives. The companies were also similar in size and number of employees, but it was clear that Henckels was an older company with more experienced craftsmen. Wüsthof had compensated for this by using more modern equipment.

For Henckels, this meant that they produced blades at a much slower rate, but the quality was superior. At least four of the company's blacksmiths wore marks showing that they were master class level. These were facts that Octavius noted during his tour of the factory, which helped him to score a large number of free samples. Between samples and purchases, he had left the facility with forty blades.

At the end of his visit to Solingen, Octavius had amassed nearly four hundred blades, while spending less than two hundred pounds.

He had planned on leaving the area by early March in order to get to Hamburg in time to explore the city. But he ended up staying an extra two weeks and was now pressed to get to the ship in time for its departure.

He packed his bags and had the hotel bellhop help him load the heavy crate of knives onto the back of the carriage. As he checked out of the inn, he noticed a stack of newspapers sitting on the counter. He had read all the articles about Jack the Ripper during his first couple weeks in the German city, but they started to become mundane after a while. He hadn't read a newspaper now in almost a month. However, the new headlines caught his attention. Apparently, the Ripper had struck again.

He grabbed the last few editions of the *East End Observer* as he left. After climbing into the carriage, he read through the articles about another prostitute being murdered in London. He though it odd that anyone would think that the killing was done by the Ripper. The event was not even close to anything that had been perpetrated by his hand.

There was even debate among varying doctors as to whether or not the woman had actually been strangled. Some in the medical profession speculated that she may have died from suicide, but there appeared to be no solid proof either way.

He sat back and laughed to himself. The legend of Jack the Ripper had taken on a life of its own. He wondered how many more victims would be credited to the Ripper over the next several months, maybe even years.

Sarah was excited to read the headline that Walter had just typeset. It was announcing France's failure to complete construction of the Panama Canal.

It had been weeks since the murder of Rose Mylett, but news about Jack the Ripper continued to dominate the headlines in most newspapers, and the *East End Observer* was no exception. Finally, Frank had found something that was worthy of knocking the Ripper off the front page.

The only thing that could possibly draw the British public's attention away from murder was news about the embarrassing French debacle that had cost the country a staggering two hundred eighty-seven million pounds. The failed endeavor had gone on for nearly eight years and cost the lives of more than twenty thousand men. The country had finally called the project a total loss, and all of England was reveling in the disgrace of their rival country.

By mid-day the paper was on the street and Sarah told her managing editor that she was going to spend the rest of her day working from home. When she reached her home study, she dumped out a box of mail on the desk. Sorting through the mail, she saw a letter from Thaddeus.

She pushed everything aside and sat down to open the letter. She had received a few letters from him over the past several days. He had gone from Turkey to Egypt to Kenya. He was last planning to travel to South Africa.

She knew that would be the last leg of his journey, and she was not sure how she felt about him coming back to London. She missed him, but the dynamics of the company and even her social life had changed so much in his short absence.

She took a deep breath and used a letter opener to break open the seal.

My Dearest Sarah:

I hope all is well with you in London. My travels through Africa have been amazing. I have seen all manner of wildlife. We even encountered a herd of giraffe the other day. The sight was breathtaking.

The nights are not always the most comfortable. The heat is oppressive, and the mosquitoes are insufferable at times. A bout of malaria went through our camp for a short spell. Luckily, I was able to escape the dreaded disease. The event caused us to hurry our travels, and I am now in South Africa waiting for my ship to arrive.

That brings me to the main reason for this letter. I will not be sailing back to London as planned. I have been offered a job in New

York City with a newspaper that will be starting upon my arrival. It wasn't something I had ever considered, but the opportunity presented itself during this journey. I feel this is something I need to do. I need to see if I am really cut out for the newspaper business. Your father only handed me an opportunity because he knew you would be there to catch me when I fell. Now I have the chance to prove to myself and to you that I can do this on my own and do it the ethical way.

I hope someday in the near future we can see each other again and share our stories about being successful publishers. I wish nothing but the best for you. Tell the staff I said hello and let them know they have jobs waiting for them in America if they ever want to visit the New World.

With Love,
Thaddeus

Sarah was saddened by what she read, but also relieved. She had resigned herself to the idea of taking her husband back upon his return. Maybe even sharing the publisher title with him and running the newspaper together. It would have been a complicated matter, but she understood that social norms would have warranted her making the gesture.

Now Thaddeus had removed that burden from her. He was smart enough to know the complexities involved with his return, and she was thankful for his willingness to avoid the awkward situation. However, she would miss him dearly.

But now she could move forward with her vision for the newspaper without worrying about how it would affect their future together. She had only one future to worry about now. Her future, her legacy, and the legacy of the company that she loved.

Octavius made it from the Hamburg train station to the dock where he could see the SS *Frisia* was being fitted to sail. The last time he had seen the vessel it was the largest ship in the fleet. Now the aged boat was engulfed by a larger migrant ship and even a few cargo carriers sitting in the bay.

He had no problem locating his new temporary employer. Rolland Gillcrest was standing in the center of eight other well-dressed men giving directions. He was a very tall man in his late sixties with slicked back white hair and a white shortly cropped beard.

The chef approached the group of men and waited for the lecture to end. When the men were dismissed most walked off quickly heading in different directions. Only two men stayed speaking with Rolland. Octavius approached the small group and waited to be noticed.

The old man saw him and waved him in closer. "Ah, I see my chef has arrived. You are right on time. How do you prefer to be addressed, young man?"

Octavius considered the question for a moment and decided his new boss would likely appreciate formality. "Chef Octavius or chef, sir. Either are acceptable."

"Very good then." He turned to one of the men standing next to him. "Dexter, why don't you show Chef Octavius to his cabin so he can stow his luggage. Then you can escort him to the kitchen and help him secure the rest of the ingredients and tools he needs for the journey."

Dexter jumped into action immediately pointing out the way. He signaled for two dock workers to grab the chef's crate and told them to follow them as they boarded the ship using the old first-class gangway. Octavius looked down the length of the ship. He could see the doorways for where the second class and steerage passengers once boarded.

The two men boarded the nearly vacant ship and headed toward the first-class cabins. The ship would only be sailing with a modest crew of forty, so only the first-class cabins would be needed. Octavius was shown to the cabin closest to the first-class galley, where he dropped his suitcase and hat carrier in the closet.

The men went to the galley, which was much larger than he

needed and fitted with more than a dozen stoves. There were two other men in the kitchen wearing aprons and sorting through pots and pans. They stopped what they were doing when they saw the chef walk in.

"Good morning, chef," they said in unison. After a short round of greetings, the two cooks returned to their task. The kitchen had a thick layer of dust covering most areas and the cooks had already cleaned off four stoves and two large prep stations. They were now finding enough pots, pans, and other items needed to prepare meal services for the voyage.

Octavius then asked one of the cooks to show him around the storage areas. He was surprised to see that most everything had already been stocked. He sorted through the shelves full of beans, rice, vegetables, and other ingredients. He also looked at the livestock pens, which were stocked with crates filled with chickens and a variety of other fowl. The meat locker had five cows, eight pigs, and a few lambs hanging on hooks. It was clear that the crew expected to eat very well over the next several days.

The chef complimented the cooks on the work they had completed and gave a few directions regarding the types of large pots and frying pans he would need. He left with Dexter to visit the local market to grab a few more ingredients.

By early afternoon, the chef and cooks had the galley ready to start the dinner service. The ship left promptly at five, and they served their first meal at seven that evening. Octavius felt silly serving cassoulet for his first meal, but Rolland had requested it after hearing Gustavo rave about it during their meeting.

The service went even smoother than the chef expected. He continued to be quite pleased with the skills of his assistants, and he was especially pleased with their knowledge of shipboard cooking. Both men had worked as line cooks aboard the vessel over the years, so they needed very little direction.

Except for Rolland and a few of the company managers, the rest of the crew did not require any serving. They would simply arrive in the galley to pick up their meals whenever the dinner bell rang. Even the ship's captain, an older man who didn't care much for the trappings of authority, would often eat with his crew in the dining room.

Octavius found the work on the ship to be calm, almost to the point of mundane. To stave off boredom and keep his mind from wandering to dark places, he spent time experimenting with dishes in the kitchen. He passed the time showing his assistants how to prepare French recipes, which they found intriguing.

Rolland remained in his cabin for nearly the entire voyage, only coming out occasionally to walk the deck on sunny days or to visit with the captain. He would usually pass through the galley once a day to make a suggestion about a preferred meal or dessert.

It was hard for Octavius to tell if the stoic man appreciated or even liked his cooking. But he decided that men like Rolland don't usually keep their displeasure to themselves. If he was not happy with the meals, he would likely let the chef know right away.

On the morning of the tenth day, the captain informed the crew that they were ahead of schedule. The ship was now expected to arrive in New York City the next day. Rolland met the chef outside his cabin that morning and told him he would like to have a grand feast prepared for the night. He told him that the ship would not be leaving for a return trip to Europe for at least two months so he should feel free to use whatever livestock and fresh vegetables he wanted.

The prospect of making a formal dinner appealed to the chef. He had made a few nicer meals for Rolland and his guests during the trip, but most of the crew preferred heartier peasant meals. He went to the galley to find the cooks and told them about the plan.

They sat around the prep table discussing options and settled on using the last cow and two pigs that were hanging in the aging locker. They would serve steaks and chops with roasted vegetables. It wasn't nearly as fancy as the chef would have preferred, but he knew it would be well received by the crew. He could add a little more refinement to the sauces he used for the dishes served to the few on board with more discerning palates.

Even with recruiting two crewmembers to assist, it still took them all day to prepare the meal. The two cooks started by quartering the cow and pigs and bringing sections out to the meat prepping table. There Octavius begin breaking them down into steaks. The two cooks had never seen anyone wield a knife with such speed and precision. The chef was able to slice up an entire quarter before the next one was carried out.

The chef told the men to clean the beef bones as much as possible and throw them into pans. He placed the two largest pots he could find on the stove and filled them a quarter full with water. Next, he carried out a case of red wine and began pouring full bottles into the pots until they were half-full. Handfuls of spices and herbs were added to the mixture.

The cooks brought the pans of bones into the galley, and the chef began picking out the largest, cleanest bones and adding them to the pots. These bones cooked in the pots for several hours until the aroma engulfed the entire galley. Even outside the kitchen, crew members could smell the intoxicating mixture.

Octavius set about making a variety sauces while the cooks prepared the trays of roasted vegetables. He also asked the two volunteers to knead some dough for the bread. Once the bread and vegetables were in the ovens, the chef pulled the bones from the broth and set them in pans to begin cooling. He had everyone start arranging the plates on a large table in preparation to begin cooking the meats.

Once everything was ready, the two cooks started grilling steaks and chops on their stoves, while the chef monitored the process and directed the assistants on how to plate each dish.

Once the meats were plated, he added the sauce and started scooping out lumps of bone marrow to place on top of the meat. The marrow immediately began to melt just like soft butter covering each steak.

The chef waited until the last minute to finish cooking the final steaks for Rolland and the captain. He then finished their plates personally and placed them on a tray. He signaled the others to start grabbing trays and they headed out to the dining hall.

The meal was well received by everyone, and even the stoic Rolland stood up and toasted the chef and the rest of the cooking staff for such an excellent meal. Satisfied that everyone was well fed, Octavius and the cooks retreated back to the kitchen.

The chef told the two cooks and their new assistants to sit down while he cooked them each a steak of their own. He pulled a tray out of the oven that was warming the last of the large bones. He served them each the finest cuts of steak topped with large helpings of bone marrow. The cooks had never experienced a meal quite like it before. They had never heard of such a thing as using bone marrow to butter a steak. The spongy marrow had soaked up all the flavor from the wine reduction and enhanced every bite.

Later that evening Rolland came into the galley to congratulate the men again for the fine feast. He thanked them all for their service over the past several days and told him he would not see them again on this voyage. He would be leaving the ship as soon as possible when they arrived in New York the next morning. His business in Boston was urgent, and he was eager to be done with it.

The next morning, the cooks got up early and prepared breakfast while Octavius packed his bags. He met them in the galley and helped serve the meal and clean up. The two cooks would be staying with the ship over the next couple of months to prepare meals for the workers that would be retrofitting the ship for service as a coal hauler.

At mid-morning, Octavius along with several other crewmembers went to the bow of the ship to watch as it sailed into the bay. All eyes were on the magnificent statue standing more than three hundred feet high in the middle of the harbor. The last time Octavius had been in New York City, they were just getting ready to start erecting the statue the papers were calling Liberty Enlightening the World.

The structure was the most magnificent piece of architecture any of them had ever seen. As the ship sailed by, they could see the people waiting in lines to enter the statue and noticed people walking around the observation platform in the figure's crown.

Less than an hour later, the ship pulled into the dock and the gangway was lowered. Rolland and a group of well-dressed men wasted no time before heading off the ship. They spoke briefly with an official on the dock before climbing into a carriage.

Octavius said goodbye to the two cooks before heading to his cabin to grab his luggage. He met Dexter on the deck of the ship. Transportation had been arranged for both men to Grand Central Station in Manhattan. Dexter had business in Philadelphia, while Octavius was eager to start his journey westward as soon as possible.

The two men stood in line at the payroll desk where they could see workers on the dock preparing to bring aboard large crates of engine parts. The chef reached the front of the line and provided his name. The clerk made a notation in his ledger and counted out a stack of paper bills. The currency looked odd to Octavius. He had seen a few paper English banknotes in Gustavo's office for large purchases, but he had not seen much American paper money during his time in Seattle.

He folded the bills and secured them in a pocket in his chef's jacket and stepped out of line. He waited for Dexter to finish his turn, then the two men walked the gangway off the ship. A small carriage was waiting for them on the road next to the dock and they climbed in as their luggage and the wooden crate was loaded on the back.

As the carriage pulled away, Octavius looked back at the SS *Frisia*. He knew it would be the last time he would see the hulking ship.

Sarah, Frank, and Walter sat in the typesetting room reviewing the latest edition of the *East End Observer*. The front page headlined four stories, and none of them were about Jack the Ripper.

It had been a month now since the death of Rose Mylett, the

last prostitute to be murdered near the Whitechapel District. Her death had been widely debunked as a product of the Ripper, so there had not been any verified activity from the killer since early November.

Many of the newspapers were still trying to keep the story alive, but Sarah and Frank had agreed to take the *Observer* in a different direction. They now only reported on solid facts regarding the murder cases and stayed away from the manufactured and sensational stories reported by many of the other papers.

This policy had hurt them only slightly the first couple of weeks, but eventually the public began to tire of hearing about the hysteria surrounding the Ripper. By late January, the change in policy started to pay off. The *Observer* actually increased in readers and ad revenues while other papers saw reductions.

By the middle of February, the *Observer* was again consistently printing forty thousand copies a day and fifty thousand copies on Saturdays and Sundays. This officially made them the third largest newspaper in London, and solidified Sarah as one of the most successful female publishers in the world.

She felt a twinge of sadness when she heard the news. Becoming one of the largest newspapers in the city was a big accomplishment, but that had always been Thaddeus' goal. Ambition had never been something she put much stock in.

However, she did put stock in her family legacy, and she felt proud to be keeping that legacy moving forward. She understood that growth and success were a big part of that legacy, and she had no intention of letting go of the progress they had made.

She now had a reputation of her own to protect. She just intended to protect it in an ethical and moral way. And hopefully, she would not have to hear the name Jack the Ripper ever again. However, she found herself missing Thaddeus a little more every day. She hoped he was finding success in America.

The carriage ride to the train station happened in a blur. Octavius and Dexter barely spoke during the trip, as they were pressed against the windows looking up at the huge brick and wooden structures lining the streets. This was Octavius' third trip through the city, and he couldn't believe how much it had grown in such a short amount of time. It had more than doubled in population since his last trip through the area nearly three years ago.

He longed to spend time in the city sampling its famous restaurants and ever changing architecture. The newness of the city stood in stark contrast to the history of London. He promised himself that he would return to the city as soon as his business out West was finished.

The two men arrived at Grand Central Station, which was a sea of people. Dozens of trains lined the tracks running in every conceivable direction. Octavius helped the driver unload their luggage along with his heavy crate, while Dexter went to the ticket window to secure their passages to Seattle and Philadelphia.

Dexter returned a few minutes later and handed Octavius his tickets. "Here you are, chef, a first-class ticket to Seattle, courtesy of Mister Gillcrest. It looks like you have just a few minutes to use the facilities before your train leaves at the top of the hour. I will have the porters take your crate to the cargo hold."

Octavius was surprised to see that he would be changing trains in Wyoming and push north to Portland. He was even more surprised to discover that they now had tracks running north all the way into Seattle. He had planned on spending at least ten days on the train, followed by another few days of travel by carriage. His itinerary now had him arriving in Seattle in less than six days.

"Thank you, Dexter. Best of luck in Philadelphia. I hear it is even colder there this time of year."

With the goodbyes said, the two men headed to separate ends of the station to catch their trains. Octavius walked up to a conductor and showed him his ticket. The uniformed man pointed toward a car at the front of the train.

He found the first-class entrance and showed his ticket to another sharply-dressed conductor. He confirmed that he was traveling alone and the conductor showed him to a single bench near the rear of the Pullman sleeper car.

Octavius inspected his seat and noticed that his bench folded down into a bed and that he had room to store his luggage overhead. He also had a curtain that could be closed for privacy. He had traveled in first-class as a boy with his mother, but that had been a very different trip. Now he had a full-service ticket, and he liked the benefits it provided. He especially liked being able to seclude himself away from the other passengers.

The train left promptly at four in the afternoon. Octavius took in the sight of the city as it rolled westward. In less than thirty-minutes, the train had cleared all signs of buildings and people. The land was covered in thick forests and occasionally they traveled near to rivers and lakes. It was tranquil beyond the city, which unnerved him a bit.

After eating dinner at his seat, he decided to close his curtain and take stock of his belongings. It occurred to him for the first time that he was now unemployed. Everything he owned was in his possession, except for the crate of knives in the cargo hold. He had two fine suits and an overcoat. Two chef's jackets and other assorted clothing items. He had plenty of notebooks and pencils. He also had his knife roll, along with his pocket watch and some other finery. Plus, there was the top hat and the newspaper. They called to him, but he knew he needed to wait a little longer before visiting either of them.

He also had money. Before Solingen, he had never spent much of his earnings from the past few years, neither in Paris while working for Henri or in London at the Café Langham. He had splurged on a bit of clothing, but otherwise he had lived modestly in his apartment. He never had the need to spend much on anything else. He had all the food and drink he needed at the bistro, and he had spent his nights walking the slums. He decided he should probably make a proper analysis of his funds.

He asked the porter if he knew what the current exchange rate was for British pound. After a moment, the man returned holding a newspaper. He flipped to the financial section and told him it was one point thirty-four as of this morning.

This was pleasant news, as the dollar had increased significantly in buying power over the past few years. When he had arrived in London, the exchange rate had reduced the cash he had on hand by half.

Octavius started by counting his earnings from the voyage and discovered he had been paid three hundred dollars. It was a staggering amount for such a short period of time. He couldn't believe the amazing deal that Gustavo had negotiated on his behalf. He was paid well in London, but never to that degree.

He then pulled out the money pouch that Gustavo had given him at their final meeting. He opened it to reveal a number of American bills, as well as a collection of gold coins. He totaled up everything in his bag and realized it added up to more than a thousand dollars.

He then removed his money bag from his suitcase, which contained the British pounds he had saved over the past few years. It took him longer to count up the large stash of coins. It all added up to one thousand six hundred pounds. With the exchange rate, it pushed his total to over three thousand dollars. He was sitting on a small fortune.

Victor had been his highest paid worker, and he made just over two hundred pounds a year. The other staff were closer to one hundred fifty pounds.

Octavius had no great desire for wealth, but it did provide him with a modest amount of comfort and an even larger amount of freedom. He had the means to travel now and could afford some niceties. More importantly, money could buy privacy, which was paramount.

He unfolded the bench on his seat and laid down. He had a lot to consider with his new life in America. As he drifted off to sleep, he looked up at his luggage in the rack above his head. He could see his hat carrier through the slats. He knew he couldn't resist its call for much longer.

New Horizons

"Everyone thinks of changing the world, but no one thinks of changing himself."

– **Leo Tolstoy**

By 1889, the city of Seattle's population had grown to nearly forty thousand people, overtaking Tacoma as the largest city in the territory. That number did not include the thousands of people who routinely traveled through the city on their way north to mine gold claims or south to sell their goods in Oregon and California.

Milled timber was still by far the largest industry in the area. Whatever lumber that was not being used to build the ever growing city, was loaded onto trains headed for San Francisco. The railroad system in Seattle was constantly expanding in order to accommodate the freight demands. Nearly a dozen full trainloads left the city every day heading south.

Seattle now had all the trappings of a big city including a university, library, opera house, and a bustling central business district that encompassed more than thirty blocks. It also had all the typical big city problems including political unrest, inadequate infrastructure, and growing tensions between the Chinese and white immigrant populations.

A loud whistle blew in continuous pulls, followed by the screeching of breaks as the train pulled into the Seattle station. The large wooden structure was under construction as dozens of new platforms were being added to the already impressive structure.

Octavius stepped out of the train and looked out at the city, which had completely transformed in his absence. He guessed that the population had tripled from when he left nearly three years ago, but the number of businesses and houses had grown at an even more impressive rate.

He wasted no time in finding his crate and having the porters load it onto a carriage. His immediate plan was to find a hotel on the edge of town where he could get his bearings before investigating the newness of the city.

The carriage driver recommended the Queen Anne Hotel, which was located a few blocks from the downtown area. As they pulled up to the new hotel, Octavius felt underdressed in his chef's jacket. He was so used to wearing the uniform that he never thought to change out of it before arriving in the city.

The bellhop helped the driver unload the crate and other luggage, and Octavius entered the hotel and checked in. As he got to his room, he was surprised to see a private bathroom containing a toilet, wash basin, and small tub. Only the richest homes in London had such luxuries, and even the Langham Hotel didn't yet have private bathrooms in all its rooms.

After the bellhop brought him his luggage, he wasted no time unpacking his dress clothes. He hung his suit, overcoat, trousers, and dress shirts in the closet. He also hung up his nicest chef's jacket and packed the rest of his clothes away. He did not intend to work as a chef in the city, but he felt more comfortable seeing the familiar garment hanging in the closet.

He saved the hat carrier for last, placing it on a small desk and unbuckling the straps. He opened the lid, lifted out the top hat, and inspected every inch of it. He found a few scuff marks, so he took out his mercury dye and touched up the areas of discoloration.

He sat the hat on the top shelf of his closet and left the door open so he could keep a watchful eye on it. He then went back to the case and pulled out the copy of the *East End Observer* he had been saving for his arrival to America.

He sat on the bed and turned to the page containing Doctor Thomas Bond's report of Mary Jane Kelley's murder. His hands were trembling, so he closed his eyes to help him focus. Once his heart rate and breathing had normalized, he looked down at the paper.

He knew reading the report would change him, but change was the reason why he had made this journey.

The body was lying naked in the middle of the bed, the shoulders flat but the axis of the body inclined to the left side of the bed. The head was turned on the left cheek. The left arm was close to the body with the forearm flexed at a right angle and lying across the abdomen. The right arm was slightly abducted from the body and rested on the mattress. The elbow was bent, the forearm supine with the fingers clenched. The legs were wide apart, the left thigh at right angles to the trunk and the right forming an obtuse angle with the pubis.

The whole of the surface of the abdomen and thighs was removed and the abdominal cavity emptied of its viscera. The breasts were cut off, the arms mutilated by several jagged wounds and the face hacked beyond recognition of the features. The tissues of the neck were severed all round down to the bone.

The viscera were found in various parts. The uterus and kidneys with one breast under the head, the other breast by the right foot, the liver between the feet, the intestines by the right side and the spleen by the left side of the body. The flaps removed from the abdomen and thighs were on a table.

The bed clothing at the right corner was saturated with blood, and on the floor beneath was a pool of blood covering about two feet square. The wall by the right side of the bed and in a line with the neck was marked by blood which had struck it in several places.

The face was gashed in all directions, the nose, cheeks, eyebrows, and ears being partly removed. The lips were blanched and cut by several incisions running obliquely down to the chin. There were also numerous cuts extending irregularly across all the features.

The neck was cut through the skin and other tissues right down to the vertebrae, the fifth and sixth being deeply notched. The skin cuts in the front of the neck showed distinct ecchymosis. The air passage was cut at the lower part of the larynx through the cricoid cartilage.

Both breasts were more or less removed by circular incisions, the muscle down to the ribs being attached to the breasts.
The intercostals between the fourth, fifth, and sixth ribs were cut through and the contents of the thorax visible through the openings.

The skin and tissues of the abdomen from the costal arch to the pubes were removed in three large flaps. The right thigh was denuded in front to the bone, the flap of skin, including the external organs of generation, and part of the right buttock. The left thigh was stripped of skin fascia, and muscles as far as the knee.

The left calf showed a long gash through skin and tissues to the deep muscles and reaching from the knee to five inches above the ankle. Both arms and forearms had extensive jagged wounds.

The right thumb showed a small superficial incision about one inch long, with extravasation of blood in the skin, and there were several abrasions on the back of the hand moreover showing the same condition.

On opening the thorax it was found that the right lung was minimally adherent by old firm adhesions. The lower part of the lung was broken and torn away. The left lung was intact. It was adherent at the apex and there were a few adhesions over the side. In the substances of the lung there were several nodules of consolidation.

The pericardium was open below and the heart absent. In the abdominal cavity there was some partly digested food of fish and potatoes, and similar food was found in the remains of the stomach attached to the intestines.

Thaddeus sat in a large leather chair outside of Clarence Barron's office in New York City. He had met Clarence during his African safari, and the two men had created an immediate bond over their love of news and all manner of printed material. During their conversations Thaddeus shared his experiences in running a newspaper in London and his love of printing. This fascinated Clarence, an experienced journalist, who owned a news bureau in Boston. He had developed a broad network of reporters that supplied stories to publishers in Boston, Philadelphia, and New York. He had always been curious about the printing side of journalism and had convinced Thaddeus to travel to New York City to partner in a new business venture.

Clarence had recently started construction on a large building on the edge of Wall Street, which he now used as his headquarters. It was an ordinary brick and stone structure reaching seven stories high. Except for the headquarters offices on the top floor, the rest of the building was still being completed.

Half of the first floor would soon house a number of business fronts as well as a restaurant. The other half was a large open space with high ceilings that could be fitted for machinery. The other floors were being readied for more office space, with the fifth and sixth floors being reserved for apartments.

After about ten minutes, Thaddeus was sent back to Clarence's office, where he sat across from him in a plush leather chair. Clarence was in his mid-thirties and had a round face with a bushy beard. Even though his mouth naturally settled into a frown, he was an affable man with a booming laugh that would shake his round belly.

The two men spent several minutes recounting their adventures before getting down to more serious conversation. Clarence described his desire to start a new paper in the city that would focus on business and financial news.

His competition in the area was Dow Jones and Company, which was led by a man named Charles Dow. He knew that Charles was also looking to start a similar paper in the region soon, and he wanted to either beat him to the punch or join forces on the endeavor. Charles was already distributing daily small bulletins, called flimsies, that he sold to traders at the Stock Exchange.

The men spoke late into the night about what it would take to launch such a paper. Thaddeus' experience told him that one thing was certain, they would never succeed in the newspaper business unless they owned their own printing press. That was the only way to ensure that they would always have control of the process. The only question was, how big of a printer and how much money it would take.

Clarence told him to come back with a plan. He needed to know how many people they would have to hire and how big of a check he would have to write.

Octavius sat on the edge of the bed drenched in sweat. He had read the doctor's report over a dozen times, and each time it unlocked new memories. But even those memories were confusing to him.

The sharpest images he could recall were about dismembering her face. His mind's eye kept transposing Mary Jane's beautiful face with that of his mother's pursed lips and piercing hazel eyes. He could remember making every cut to that face, but the cuts were only meant for his mother's face and not the lovely Mary Jane.

In fact, every stab, cut, and slice had been to his mother and not Mary Jane. He knew this was all in his mind, but it felt real to him. That night he had not killed Mary Jane, he had killed his mother.

All the mutilation he had performed had been to his mother. The removal of her breasts, the emptying of her innards, even the slicing of the thighs and legs had all been done to his mother.

He wanted to cut his mother out of the beautiful Mary Jane. He needed to separate the two. He understood that none of this made sense logically, but that had not mattered in the moment.

He felt sorrow for Mary Jane. She did not deserve to die. She was not a whore like the others. She was young and beautiful and clean. She may not have been as proper as he would have liked, but she was certainly no whore. She was a reputable lady with proper papers and a tidy bed.

And she had that lovely singing voice. He could hear her singing that lovely Irish ballad she had sung that night. The words reverberated in his head like a symphony.

Scenes of my childhood arise before my gaze,
Bringing recollections of bygone happy days,
When down in the meadow in childhood I would roam;
No one's left to cheer me now within that good old home.
Father and mother they have passed away.
Sister and brother now lay beneath the clay;
But while life does remain, to cheer me I'll retain
This small violet I plucked from mother's grave

Only a violet I plucked when but a boy,
And oft' times when I'm sad at heart, this flow'r has given me joy,
But while life does remain, in memoriam I'll retain
This small violet I plucked from mother's grave.

Well I remember my dear old mother's smile,
As she used to greet me when I returned from toil;
Always knitting in the old arm chair,
Father used to sit and read for all us children there.
But now all is silent around the good old home,
They all have left me in sorrow here to roam;
White life does remain, in memoriam I'll retain

As he listened to the song, he imagined himself dancing with her as she wore that wonderful red dress. She had those pretty blue ribbons in her hair. She was smiling as she sang, and he was laughing.

Then his memory started to morph. He was now a boy, dancing with his mother to that same song. They were in the steerage section on the SS *Frisia*. Each time he twirled his partner she would switch between Mary Jane and his mother. The only thing that remained the same was the dark black hair fitted with lovely blue ribbons.

Thaddeus was standing on a stool barking out orders. He looked like the conductor of an orchestra, waving his arms in all directions.

"That steam engine needs to be pushed further back in the corner or we will never be able to fit the belt around the spindle."

"Yes, sir." Is the only response he ever received from the German machinists he had hired to build the massive printing press. It was going to be an impressive piece of equipment capable of printing and folding at least fifteen thousand newspapers an hour.

Clarence had found a couple of investors willing to put up some money for the new venture, but the lion's share had come from the man himself. He had also put up the real estate, allowing Thaddeus to use half of the first floor of his new building to house the printing press, along with five offices on the second floor, one being large enough to serve as the typesetting room.

It would take nearly a month to build the enormous printer. All the major parts had been constructed in Germany, but the final assembly had to take place on site. The builder had sent a crew of seven men along with the parts, and it took all seven men to move the large engine to the corner as Thaddeus had instructed.

He was excited about the new paper and the chance to build something from the ground up. His biggest problem was that he didn't know much about financial news and especially the New York Stock Exchange, which was now a driving force in world economics.

Thaddeus decided the best way to learn about the financial scene would be to start a bulletin to rival the one already being produced by Dow Jones and Company. What Thaddeus lacked in financial knowledge, he could make up for in printing and distribution experience.

He ran the concept by Clarence who wasn't so keen on the idea at first. He was afraid it would tip their hat as to what they had planned in the near future.

Thaddeus assured him that the hat had been tipped the moment they started construction on the huge printing press, which could now be seen by everyone on Wall Street through the large windows of his building.

Octavius had been holed up in his room for three days and the staff at the Queen Anne Hotel were starting to become alarmed. He had not left his room once since checking in. The maids hadn't been allowed in to service his room, and he had not ordered any food.

At noon on the fourth day, the hotel manager knocked on the door. It took him several knocks before Octavius answered, only opening the door about a foot.

"Is everything alright, sir? The maids said you have refused service for several days. Is there anything I can bring you?" He could tell that that his guest was in some sort of distress. He was unshaven and looked like he hadn't bathed in a while. He was also pale and looked almost sickly.

"No, thank you. I am fine. I just had a very long journey from Europe the past month and I am catching up on my rest." He went to close the door but the manager's foot was in the way.

"Can we at least bring you some food and some clean towels?"

"No, thank you." He had the feeling that was not going to suffice, so Octavius pulled the door open a bit more. "I could use some water and maybe a bit of bread."

The manager appeared relieved by the request. He nodded and pulled his foot away from the door. "Right away, sir."

"Just have them leave it in the hallway and I will grab it in a while. I was just about to take a bath."

Octavius turned around and looked at his disheveled room. The report from the doctor had taken its toll on him. Once he realized what he had truly done to Mary Jane, he could not stop the flood of emotions that emanated from him. At first, he rotated between guilt and anger. Then pity and self-loathing took over for a while.

It wasn't until he put on the top hat that a new emotion had started to creep in, resolve. This emotion was much more useful, and it would also allow him to regain his ability to show his face in public.

He was now resolved to confront his mother. He wasn't sure what that meant, but he was determined to find out. He doubted that even as Jack the Ripper he would be able to kill the vile woman. She was still his mother after all, but maybe he could finally tell her how she had hurt him. How she had shamed him. How she had ruined him.

But first he needed to get things together. Get himself together. He needed to get a better lay of the city in its new form. He wanted to establish himself in the city before confronting her. He wanted to meet his mother on equal footing, and not allow her influence to overpower him.

He took a bath and shaved. Then he put on his suit and overcoat, affixing his trusty chef's knife in the coat pocket. He pulled the door open and grabbed the pitcher of water and bread sitting in the hallway. The water was refreshing and helped to put color back in his face. The bread was bitter but edible.

He grabbed his knife roll and removed his personal chef knives storing them away in the closet. He filled the empty pockets with several fine blades that he had collected during his visit to the blade shops in Solingen.

He put on the top hat, tucked the roll under his arm, and headed out the door. It was time to visit an old friend.

Charles Dow was standing on the other side of the Stock Exchange fuming. The man had dark hair, an even darker beard, and wore a black suit. His beard was full and long enough to be bushy if it wasn't for the thick coat of Macassar oil that he used to keep it slicked down.

Thaddeus knew that Charles was not pleased to learn that another publishing company had moved in on his territory. Wall Street was the hub of American commerce, so the man must be used to seeing journalists in all corners of the exchange. He should have also realized that competition among publications was bound to happen sooner or later.

The experienced newspaper man had taken quickly to the financial sector. The stories were easy to write, and getting information out of subjects was a breeze. Every member of the

Stock Exchange was eager to tell the world about their business in hopes that they could sell more shares of stock. He thought it would take him weeks to gain the trust of the major players, but he had been welcomed with open arms by most in only a few days.

Thaddeus' warm outgoing disposition was a contrast to the more serious nature of Charles Dow, who always looked like he was interrogating subjects rather than soliciting quotes for a story.

Still, Charles was a stalwart of the Stock Exchange and everyone knew and respected him. He had access to even the staunchest of members. He also had a strong financial mind and could write the most eloquent stories about business, money, and all matters involving economics. He was known as a man of the highest journalistic ethics and never allowed advertisers to interfere with his company's reporting.

What had truly aggravated Charles was the fact that Thaddeus had developed a robust distribution network in the area after only a few days in the market. He had struck a deal with the cigar vendors throughout the area to sell his financial brochures in exchange for letting them keep half the revenues. Now he had dozens of distribution points on nearly every corner of Wall Street.

Thaddeus understood that a challenge had been laid down, and he was eager to see how Dow Jones and Company responded. Worst case, they would step up their game and try to push him out, but he was betting they would likely be more interested in partnering in the near future.

He just needed to make sure he kept the thorn stuck deep enough to keep his competitor's attention.

Octavius walked the few blocks to the downtown business district. Three years ago there had been less than forty small store fronts in the district, now there well over a hundred businesses and dozens of street vendors.

The streets were muddy and rutted caused by a combination of heavy traffic and recent flooding from a tidal surge. However, the bad roads and wet conditions did not appear to be affecting commerce in the area.

A few shop owners could be seen cursing and pushing broom loads of human waste out the front doors of their shops. Most respectable establishments in America now had toilets, and Seattle businesses were no different. However, the downtown business district had been built below sea level in many areas. This meant that a sudden storm surge could cause the plumbing to backup and create mini-volcanos of waste in the businesses located on the first floor of many buildings.

Octavius avoided the mess as much as he could as he walked through the district. He was surprised to see so many new seamstress companies had opened in such a public area. Most prostitutes were encouraged to claim seamstress as their occupation for the sake of decorum in the Methodist city. This did little to stave off tax collectors who still collected entertainment taxes from brothels and their "seamstresses," which made up a large percentage of the city's revenues.

He wondered what the influx of competition had done to his mother's brothel, especially since her house was located outside of the downtown area. That was something he planned to investigate later.

He reached the edge of the business district and turned south toward the Duwamish Waterway. He walked about fifteen minutes before arriving at the storefront for Green Isle Blades, owned by his old employer Seamus. He was pleased to see that the store had been expanded to include a small showroom. He also saw three pillars of smoke coming from the back, which meant that he had added a couple more forges.

Octavius walked into the store and looked around at the selection of knives, axes, straight razors, and other blades hanging from the walls. There were plenty of workman tools, but not many upscale items, as he had anticipated.

Seamus came walking out from the back of the shop wiping

his hands on a towel. "How can I help you young…"

He stopped short looking like he had seen a ghost. "Is that you, Octavius?"

"Yes, Seamus. It's me."

"By the gods, you look like a shiny penny in that fancy suit. And would you look at that hat. What have you been up to my friend?"

"I spent some time in France, then London, and finally Germany. Now, I'm back in Seattle for a spell."

"Goodness, you have been busy. I see you still have that fancy knife roll I gave you. I hope you have added some new knives to that thing after visiting the old world."

"Since you brought it up, I do have some things I would like to show you."

He unrolled the canvas and started removing the shiny German blades. Seamus' eyes widened at the sight of so many quality knives. The two men spoke for hours as Octavius described his travels through Solingen. The old shopkeeper was enthralled with the amazing craftsmanship. He had always wanted to sell higher end knives, but his blacksmiths were already overworked making and sharpening axes and other tools for the loggers, farmers, and trappers in the area.

The two men agreed on a business arrangement to sell the collection of German blades on consignment. Octavius also agreed to help Seamus build a water powered grinder and teach his assistants in how to properly hone the unique edges.

Octavius left the shop feeling energized. He knew this business endeavor would be short lived, but it would provide a needed distraction during the day, so that he was not overwhelmed by his nocturnal investigations. It might also prove to be a very profitable venture.

Thaddeus had been looking for an opportunity to run into Charles Dow outside the restraints of the loud and busy floor of the Stock Exchange when he saw the businessman enter a restaurant by himself. He wasn't sure if he was meeting someone or just grabbing a quick bite, but he figured it was worth the effort to follow him inside.

The two men had only seen each other in passing a couple of time in the few weeks that Thaddeus had started work on Wall Street. Today was the first time that they had been in the same room with each other, and it happened to be at a small café during lunchtime.

Thaddeus saw Charles sitting in a booth by himself and took the opportunity to introduce himself. "Good afternoon, Mister Dow. I'm Thaddeus Donleavy."

Charles waved for him to take a seat. "Call me Charles. I have seen you around the Exchange the past few weeks, peddling your little flyers."

"Just trying to get a lay of the land. You know, see what news is fit to print and all."

"You seem to have gotten things figured out pretty quickly, Mister Donleavy. At least when it comes to distribution and making money."

"Please, call me Thaddeus. And correct me if I am wrong, but isn't the idea of publishing to find a few readers and sell a couple of papers."

"Well, it would help if you could also provide meaningful news. You have sensational headlines, but the articles lack substance."

"I see, well you've got me there. I am a novice to the financial world. I cut my teeth running a paper in London that focused on murder, politics, and the royal family. But I needed a change, so I thought I would try my luck in your big American city."

Charles sat back in his chair. He wanted to hate the arrogant European sitting across from him, but he actually found himself enjoying the conversation. "Hell, what do I know? I've been at this for nearly a decade. There is enough financial news in this town to fill ten papers, but right now my company is grinding away on daily bulletins."

"You know Charles, there may just be a way we can work

together to change that situation. I have an idea that might help both of us to get what we want."

Seamus hung ten more blades in the display case that he had built to hold the German knives. It had been just over three months since he and Octavius struck their deal to sell the knives on consignment, and it had been a highly lucrative venture for both sides.

Octavius had removed twenty of his favorite specimens from the crate before Seamus had helped him haul the heavy wooden box to the store using a wagon.

The first month had gone fairly slow, but once people heard about the unique blades, customers started coming into the store looking for them. Sales had remained robust ever since.

Looking into the crate, Seamus was sad to see that there were now only eight knives, five straight razors, and two pairs of scissors left. He couldn't believe they had sold over three hundred blades in such a short amount of time.

Octavius came in from the back of the shop wearing a pair of coveralls that he had borrowed from the shop owner. His arms were wet up to his elbows and he was wiping black oil off his hands. "We fixed the water grinder. We just had to tighten the fitting and add some oil to make it run smoother. Leon should probably oil it and tighten everything once a week."

Seamus looked out the window at the large stone grinding wheel and watched as his assistant sat on the stool as he sharpened an ax head. The water grinder had been an excellent addition to the shop. His old peddle grinders took a lot of energy to get moving and were not smooth enough to work on more delicate blades.

The new water grinder was powered by water flowing down the Duwamish Waterway that turned a paddle wheel. The paddles on the wheel could be angled by pulling a rope, which would slow down or speed up the grinding stone as needed. The smooth turning grinding stone could also be lowered into the water when needed to turn it into a wet stone. His assistant could now sharpen three times as many edges in a day, and he could work on finer, more delicate blades with the wet stone.

"Here is your share from this week. We sold ten more blades yesterday, and there isn't much left. There are a dozen pieces in the crate and maybe twenty or so on the shelves. The skinners and straight razors sold fast, but we still have those fancy chef knives."

Octavius took the money and counted up one hundred and ten dollars. His total share so far was just over fourteen hundred dollars. "Did you have a chance to contact your brother about bringing you another shipment from Germany?"

"Yes, and it cost me a fortune to send the telegraph to Ireland. I hope he understood everything because the telegraph he sent back only said 'two months'. So either he will be here in two months or he will be sailing in two months. Either way, I will be ready for the shipment when he arrives."

"I hope it all works out. At least you won't have me to worry about on those sales."

"Are you kidding? I would gladly keep sharing the profits with you if you were willing to stick around. You are the only one who knows how to properly sharpen the damn things."

Octavius took off his coveralls and tossed them in a cupboard. It was getting late in the day and he needed to get back to the hotel so that he could clean up for his nightly routine.

"I will see you in the morning, Seamus. Try not to work too late."

Octavius had used the first month to get things setup at the store before venturing out to explore the city. He avoided his mother's side of town for the next month, and finally started moving further north by mid-May.

He knew his mother rarely left the brothel, so he wasn't too concerned about her spotting him. He also wasn't worried about the other prostitutes seeing him. Most of them had probably changed out by now, and it was doubtful any of them would recognize him wearing a suit.

He was most concerned about Tumas seeing him. He had avoided the nicer restaurants and markets in fear of running into his old mentor. He missed his friend and wanted to reach out, but he knew the meeting would create questions he was not ready to answer.

He had spent the past few weeks walking the northern part of the city circling the brothel. Now that it was early June the weather was consistently more pleasant. He could stay out later into the night during his walks without having to deal with the rain.

It was early in the evening on Tuesday, and he knew that his mother always left the brothel on Tuesdays to meet with Carl Coats as part of their business arrangement. He stood in a dark cutout of a large building diagonal to the brothel where he had a view of the front door. He was wearing his suit and top hat, so he would not be easily recognized even if his mother did look his way.

At seven he saw her step out of the doorway. She was wearing a red dress with blue ribbons in her hair. He let out a gasp and had to put his hands over his mouth so that he wasn't heard. He thought he was ready to see her, but the sight of her in that red dress was almost more than he could bear. He watched as she entered the carriage and pushed himself against the wall as she passed by his position.

Once the carriage was out of sight, he placed his hand on the wall to steady himself and noticed large beads of sweat were now pouring from his forehead.

Clarence sat in his chair eying Thaddeus with a doubtful look on his face. He was fairly certain that he had just been asked to give up on his dream of publishing his own newspaper.

"Run this by me again and speak slower. It might be your English accent that is affecting my understanding."

"I know this is different than what we originally talked

about, but I think it warrants consideration. Everyone agrees this city needs a newspaper dedicated to reporting financial news. Your bureau and the Dow Jones Company have built reputations as the foremost experts in American financial news. By joining forces, it would eliminate the competition and cement your combined influence on the world economic stage.

"But if he owns the newspaper, then how do I fit in."

"You now control the largest publishing operation on Wall Street, and his new paper will give you instant credibility and drive even more printing business. Your company would also manage the distribution network, which controls revues and provides an avenue for disseminating future projects. Also, your news bureau would receive distribution rights to the articles printed in the paper, and your network would be able to sell wire stories to the paper."

Clarence pushed back in his chair and stroked his beard. He knew that Charles Dow and his company had a huge head start in reporting the news on Wall Street. Dow Jones and Company had nearly fifty employees, a third of which were dedicated to financial news reporting. He wasn't sure about the equity of the partnership, but he also didn't like the idea of trying to compete head-to-head with fledgling newspapers.

"So he gets all the glory and name recognition, while I am relegated to making money off printing, distribution, and selling wire stories."

"I know it may not sound exciting, but I believe this is the right business decision. If you control the printing and distribution, you essentially control the paper. That means that Dow Jones would be taking all the risk, and you would get all the benefits. If the paper succeeds, then your influence and profits will continue to grow. If it fails, then you can still make money from outside print jobs and start another paper on top of the ashes."

Clarence let out a loud laugh and pounded his fist on his desk. "Thaddeus, you could sell hay to a farmer. I hate that Charles gets to put his pretty face on everything, but I do like to make money. And I like that he gets to take all the risk. So what the hell is he going to call his new paper anyway?"

"He just sent out the trademark paperwork for the *Wall Street Journal*."

Octavius was standing at the counter in the store watching Leon use a wet stone to sharpen a straight razor. He had to correct him a few times to make sure he wasn't thinning out the hollow ground edge, but the assistant picked up the technique fairly quickly.

The two men had their backs to the door when it opened and a customer walked in. Leon greeted the man who said he just wanted to look around for a minute. The hair on Octavius' neck stood on end when he heard the familiar voice of his mentor.

He turned around to see the man wearing his white chef's jacket and eying a fine German knife on the wall. He walked behind him and watched him in silence for a moment. "Hello, chef."

Tumas nearly dropped the knife at the sound. He spun around quickly and his eyes widened at the sight of the man standing in front of him wearing an expensive suit and top hat. "Octavius! What are you doing here? I thought you were in Europe."

"I was. I just got back to Seattle a while ago."

"I don't understand. Why have you not come to visit your mother? Why have you not been to the brothel?"

"I know. It is hard to explain."

"What happened in Paris? Did you see Henri? Did you give him my letter?"

"I did, Tumas, and he was wonderful. I learned to make all the foods you told me about. I was his sous chef for two years. Then I got my own restaurant in London."

"That is amazing. But then why are you here?"

"That is even harder to explain, but I promise I will tell you everything. Just not here and not right now. Can you meet me for lunch at that restaurant we both like? You know the one we ate at the morning after Augie died? I have business downtown at the cabinet shop tomorrow, but we should meet on Friday."

"Yes. I will be there." His confusion was clear, but he was comforted by the fact that he would get answers soon. He started backing toward the door.

"Chef, here take this." Octavius handed him the chef's knife he had been looking at.

"I can't afford such an expensive blade."

"Please, I want you to have it. I owe you far more than a simple knife my friend."

Octavius watched as the old chef walked out the door and down the street. He had hoped he would have had more time before being seen. He thought about asking him not to tell his mother that he had seen him, but that would have raised even more questions.

He would just have to wait until Friday to explain everything.

Thaddeus grabbed a bulletin off the printer and looked it over. He hated the title *Customers' Afternoon Letter*. He also hated that many of the words on the page were smudged to the point of being blurry. He had been working with the German press operators on tuning the printer to get the ink to print dark black without smudging.

They had tried several different calibrations, but it still was not perfect. They were running out of time before today's distribution deadline, so he would have to give up on perfection and settle for good enough.

This was the twentieth bulletin they had printed since inking the deal with Dow Jones and Company to print and distribute their new daily publication. The negotiations had gone fairly smoothly, especially given the shrewd business acumen of all the parties involved. Clarence was highly respected by both

Charles and his partner, Edward Jones, and at one point Charles even referred to Clarence as the father of modern financial journalism.

But that respect only went so far at the negotiating table. Clarence had pushed hard for an ownership stake in the newspaper, but Charles and Edward held a strong line on that point. They did, however, agree to give Clarence's news bureau exclusive rights to sell the articles written by the new paper's journalists. This would make his news network the most powerful financial news service in America.

Thaddeus was named Director of Operations for the joint venture, which meant his salary would be paid by both companies. He welcomed the idea of running the print operations and staying out of the journalistic side of the business. He was still atoning for the sins he had committed in London and believed he could make his strongest mark running the backend of the paper.

At the end of the negotiations they all agreed to run two full months of weekday bulletins before launching the full newspaper and announcing the new name.

Charles and Edward had settled on the name *Customer's Afternoon Letter* for the temporary bulletin, which was just a combination of eight, single page articles that they would assign their reporters to cover throughout the day. They would then send the pages over to Thaddeus to be typeset, printed, and distributed the next morning.

Thaddeus gave the signal to start printing the run, then he scrunched up the page he was holding and threw it in the trash. He knew they were going to have to get better quality out of the printer in the next few weeks or the whole deal might go up in smoke.

It was after two o'clock in the afternoon on Thursday when Octavius turned down Front Street toward Madison Avenue. He had traveled to the heart of the downtown business district to meet with Victor Clairmont, who owned a local woodworking shop.

He had recently commissioned the carpenter to build him a wooden case to carry his now smaller selection of knives. Once he was finished with his business in Seattle, he planned to travel back to New York and would no longer need the cumbersome crate.

It had been unseasonably mild and dry that week, so there was little mud in the streets. Octavius felt comfortable wearing his suit and top hat without worrying about getting them soiled.

He reached the corner and entered the Pontius Building. The shop on the first floor showed a sign for Jim McGough's Paint Shop. He passed by the entrance to the paint shop and descended the stairway to the basement.

He entered the Clairmont and Company Cabinetry Shop and asked the lady standing behind the counter if Mister Clairmont was available. She told him he was probably in the back office and asked him to wait while she went to fetch him.

He could see a man in the middle of the shop melting a pot of glue on the stove. He was adding more balls and shavings of glue to the pot, which was sitting on a gasoline stove. He could see glue splashing over the side of the pan and drip onto the dirty floor that was covered with wood scraps, saw dust, and pales of turpentine and stain.

He did not notice the woman sitting in a chair behind him. She stood up after the lady left the counter. "Otto, is that you?"

The hair on the back of his neck stood tall, his heart rate sped up, and he began to tremble. He did not immediately turn around. He was not ready to face her.

"Otto, turn and look your mother."

He wanted to comply, but his legs wouldn't move. Her grating voice reverberated in his head, and his eyes began to narrow.

"FACE ME BOY!"

Something snapped inside of him, and he stopped trembling. Then his heart rate slowed. He turned around to see that she was standing in front of him still wearing her red dress and her hair was fitted with those blue ribbons. He matched her icy stare, but did not speak.

"I had to hear from Tumas that you had returned to the city. You are smart enough not to come to me for money. So what is that you want from me?"

He realized that she was in this place not out of coincidence, but because she wanted to confront him. Tumas had told her that he had business in town today, and she felt compelled to ambush him in this public place. He wondered how long she had sat waiting in that chair.

"Did you just come to gloat about your success? You think that buying a fancy suit makes you better than me?"

He continued looking at her blankly not giving her the satisfaction of answers.

"And why are you wearing that stupid hat?"

Her words made the blood rush to his cheeks and his eyes flash with anger. He was about to respond when he saw her eyes widen in fear.

A loud shout rang out behind him. "Look at the glue!"

Octavius turned to see a man pour a bucket of water over the boiling pot of glue on the stove. The pot was shooting flames high into the air. The water hit the pot causing the glue to splash out in all directions, carrying flames with each small glob. Everywhere the globs landed immediately caught fire and the flames began spreading throughout the middle of the shop.

He was now ready to face his mother. He turned back to look at her with a face still devoid of emotion.

"Petulant child! We have to get out of here!"

He stepped in front of the door blocking her way. "No, Mother. You wanted answers, so I will give you answers."

The workers in the cabinet shop had given up all hope of extinguishing the flames and were now rushing out the back door. In a matter of moments, they were the only two left standing at the edge of the inferno.

"I am no longer the little boy you raised. I am no longer the young man you debased at Augie's funeral."

His mother looked around the shop trying to assess the situation. She was barely listening to her son's ranting.

"I traveled across an ocean to get away from you. From your cold looks. Your grating voice. Your cruelty. I did all I could to be rid of you, but you came after me all the same. You came to me in my dreams. In my memories. In my fantasies."

Victoria coughed as the smoke started to reach the area they were standing. The flames were quickly heading their way and she began to panic. She could not understand why Octavius was not being affected by the flames and smoke that surrounded them. "Will you shut up you spoiled brat! We have to get out of here!"

Octavius' expression did not change. "Your cruelty ruined me and caused me to change. Change into someone new, into something different, into a monster. And now I am here to introduce you to the monster that you created. The monster I have become. The monster named Jack the Ripper. That's right mother, I am Jack the Ripper. I am the Liberator, and I am here to liberate myself from you."

A glimmer of understanding showed in her eyes and she backed away from Octavius who suddenly looked ominous standing over her. As she stepped backwards, she could feel the heat of the fire on her legs. There was only one way out, and that was through the door behind her son.

She lunged forward using her long, polished nails as claws. She swiped at Octavius' face catching him with two sharp nails on the side of his cheek. Two lines of blood welled up on his face, but he did not react. Instead, he continued staring at her with cold, narrowed eyes.

She grabbed the lapel of his suit jacket with both hands and pushed hard trying to move him back. Octavius continued looking her in the eyes, then grabbed her around the throat with both hands. He lifted her off the ground and slowly walked forward as she thrashed and kicked wildly trying to get him to release his grasp.

Once he got to the edge of the flames he held her there squeezing tightly. He continued to stare into her eyes, but then something strange happened. She let out a wry smile and he could feel a sharp pain on his right side. He had forgotten about the knife she kept in her garter belt.

He looked down to see the small dagger sticking into his lower left rib cage. He dropped her to the ground and released his grip. The biting pain caused him to bend slightly.

Victoria grabbed the blade handle and twisted it, causing him to cry out in pain. "Do you think you are the only monster in this family? Whether you call yourself a boy, a monster, or even Jack the Ripper, I am still your mother. You want to be free of me? Very well then. I will leave you here to die like a rat in the flames."

She twisted the blade again and watched him bend over in pain. She released the handle and started to walk past him. He reached out with his arm and caught her around the waist. She grabbed his arm and tried to push it aside, but his grip tightened. He pulled hard, moving her back in front of him.

She could feel the flames lapping at her back now and she reached down grabbing the blade again. This time when she twisted, he did not react. Instead he stood up slightly and grabbed her shoulders. She sensed his intention and reached out with both hands trying to grab onto his shoulders.

Octavius fought back the pain and shoved her hard with all his strength. Victoria reached out desperately trying to grab onto him. She missed his shoulders and instead grabbed onto his top hat as she was launched backward into the roaring fire.

He watched as she became engulfed in the flames. Her red dress blending into the red and orange flames. As she continued to fall backwards, she landed in a large pan of turpentine which caused the flames to turn deep blue matching the ribbon in her hair. Finally, he watched as the top hat burst into flames and folded in on itself disappearing into the pan of fiery liquid.

Octavius watched for as long he could before the heat became unbearable. He pulled the dagger out of his side and rushed up the stairs and stumbled out into the street. He could see that the fire was raging in the liquor store next door and that the flames were already spreading to several other buildings.

He walked quickly down the street away from the fire as others rushed in trying to fight the flames with any sources of water they could find. He walked several blocks before finding a bench to sit on. He pulled out a handkerchief and wiped the blood off his face. Then he pushed the cloth into the wound in his side.

He sat on the bench for several minutes as his heart rate began to settle and his breathing returned to normal. Then he smiled broadly and began to laugh.

He was finally free. Free of his cruel mother. Free of the top hat. He was free of Jack the Ripper. He was finally free of all his demons.

Thaddeus pulled the latest edition of the *Customer's Afternoon Letter* off the printer and smiled at what he saw. They had finally found a way to calibrate the rollers and adjust the ink nozzles to just the right angle to produce clear black letters.

He gave the thumbs up for the print operator to turn up the speed and start printing the five thousand copies needed for their distribution network. He then waited the half hour it took to finish printing and binding the small booklets before grabbing the first stack and heading out the door.

He rushed to the floor of the Stock Exchange where he found Charles standing by the entrance waiting to go in to watch the ringing of the bell. He handed him a copy of the bulletin.

"This one looks very nice. I don't see any smudges on even the smallest of letters. If we can continue to replicate this every day, then we should be ready to launch next month."

"That is the plan. I still need to add more distribution points. We are selling out five thousand copies now, but I want to push that to seven by launch day. I just want to make sure that we run out by noon every day."

"Why do we want to run out? Don't we want to sell all the papers we can? Paper is cheap."

"We want demand to drive supply, not the other way around. People want what they can't have. We need to train the readers to get their copies early in the day so they aren't missing out on anything. That will let us know how quickly we can increase the print runs."

"That's why you are in charge of operations. I will worry about filling the pages, as long as you can get the blasted things printed and in the hands of readers."

The fire had spread from the cabinet shop to the upstairs paint store, then next door to the liquor store which had exploded sending balls of flame into the two saloons on the same block. Fueled by massive amounts of alcohol, the flames continued to devastate the tightly stacked wooden buildings packed into the downtown area. By the time the fire was extinguished it had devastated nearly twenty-nine blocks.

Officials were still sifting through the rubble, but they claimed that no one had been killed in the blaze. Octavius knew this was a lie, but he also knew that there was little chance they would find the one victim he knew was among the ashes. He had watched as his mother's body not only burn but nearly melt once she fell into the pan of turpentine. The entire building above the cabinet shop had collapsed into the basement, and he was certain no one would ever have a reason to dig through that pile of ash and rubble.

Octavius sat in the restaurant waiting for Tumas to arrive. He had to throw away his suit which had been badly burned and reeked of smoke. He was now wearing his chef's jacket, which felt more natural to him.

The whole world felt more natural to him now that he was rid of his mother and the Ripper. The fire had purged him of all those things, and he was now free to return to his one true love, the culinary arts.

Tumas entered the restaurant and sat at the table. He looked on edge.

"Octavius, can you believe this fire. The city was nearly destroyed. Thank goodness no one was killed, but so many people are scared. Have you seen your mother? No one can find her. She left the house yesterday before the fire and she has not returned."

"She is gone, Tumas."

"What do you mean gone?"

"She was killed in the fire."

"But the officials say no one was killed."

"I know, but I saw it myself. She reached for me, but it was too late. She died quickly."

"We must tell the authorities."

"I don't think it will do any good. I don't think the authorities want to find any dead bodies. I was at the center of the blaze. I do not believe she was the only person killed yesterday."

"But, what about your mother? We have to tell someone."

"If she is reported dead there will be an inquest. They will investigate the brothel and question all the girls. It would mean the end of the business."

Tumas sat back in his chair and sighed. He knew Octavius was right. City officials were fine with letting brothels conduct business as long as it was under the cloak of darkness and false pretenses. Even the tax collectors didn't mind the misclassification labor categories, as long as the city was paid properly. But an investigation would mean opening the ledger and interviewing the prostitutes and customers that were at the brothel last night. That would likely mean shutting down the business and confiscation of all valuables. It would also create quite a stir for many of the customers, many of whom undoubtedly had families.

"What are we to do then? Can you come and run the brothel?"

"I have left that life behind, Tumas. I have no need for brothels or prostitutes. Maybe you should take it."

"No, not me. I am a simple cook now and I am old. I have no love for money or women. I just want my kitchen and a warm bed at night. What about Carl Coats, your mother's business partner. He knows the most about the business and he is a man of ambition."

Octavius nodded his head. Carl Coats was the most likely benefactor. He agreed to speak with the man and see if an agreement could be made.

The two men continued talking for a several hours. Octavius told him about his training with Henri and the grumpy Marthe. He told him about starting the Café Langham and the wonderful Gustavo. He told him about his journey to Solingen to purchase knives and bringing them back to Seattle to sell.

In all his stories, he never lied to Tumas. He did leave out several details, but he felt it important to be honest with his old friend.

After their meal, Octavius took a carriage ride to Carl Coats' house and told him about his mother. Carl was saddened by the news but agreed that reporting Victoria's death to the authorities would be devastating to the business and harmful to everyone involved.

Carl agreed to take over the business and even offered to pay Octavius for the house, which he refused not wanting to deal with the legalities. His only demand was that he double Tumas' salary and make sure the old chef was well cared for in the future.

Later that day, Octavius returned to the brothel and told Tumas the news. He said that Carl would be by in the morning to speak with the girls. He then went into his mother's office and sat down at her desk. He flipped through the pages in his mother's ledger, but he had little interest in how the business had fared over the past several months.

He turned to the safe on the back wall and entered the combination, which he knew was her birthdate. He turned the handle and opened the door to reveal several stacks of cash, along with two large bags of coins. His mother had never been fond of banks, knowing that it was too easy to seize the accounts of madams. He found a leather satchel under the desk and stuffed it full of the money. He stood up and looked around the office one last time before heading for the door.

As he passed by the desk, he saw a spool of blue ribbon. He picked it up and stuffed it in his bag. It was the only memento he wanted from his dreaded past.

Over the next two days, Octavius said his goodbyes to Seamus and Tumas. He packed his bags, which now consisted of one suitcase full of chef's uniforms and clothes, a wooden box full of knives, and a satchel full of money. He headed to the train station and booked passage to New York City.

As the train pulled out of the station, he looked out the window of the Pullman car at the still smoldering city. The blackened rubble seemed a fitting metaphor for his past. He kept watching as the train rolled along. The further he got from the city, the greener and more beautiful the landscape became.

He breathed deep and closed his eyes rubbing the small piece of blue ribbon he had wrapped around his finger.

The presses were running and full blast as Thaddeus stood on the railing watching all the rollers turn in unison. He looked down to see Charles, Edward, and Clarence standing beside each other smiling broadly under their beards. Behind them stood a dozen other excited journalists eager to see what was about to come off the press.

Thaddeus gave the signal to release the catches and the web of paper started threading through the spindles. Charles moved in closer as he watched the line of paper reach the cutting and folding machine. Within seconds the machine started pushing out completed newspapers.

Charles reached out to grab one, but Thaddeus yelled down at him. "Not yet! It's bad luck to take one before the first hundred hit the ground. You have to let the ink settle into the rollers first. You don't want the first paper you see to be a smudged mess."

Charles stood back and did his best to count the folded

papers running off the conveyor belt and into a trash bin. Once he was certain a hundred had passed, he grabbed one of the papers and looked above the fold.

The Wall Street Journal stood out in large clear black letters. Clarence slapped him hard on the back, then shook his hand as he let out a hearty laugh. Charles held the paper up high so that everyone behind him could read the title. The journalists cheered wildly.

He waved for them to run up to the belt and start grabbing copies of their own.

Thaddeus ran down from the railing and grabbed a copy of his own. He checked it over to make sure the ink and folds looked good before pulling the lever to start the binder. Once the first few bundles were twined, he grabbed two and handed them to Charles. He grabbed two more and handed them to Edward. He continued the process until everyone in the room had two bundles.

In the future, this process would be handled by the distribution staff, but today was special. Everyone wanted to be part of disseminating the first edition. They waited until everyone was ready, and they let Charles and Edward lead the procession out of the building as they started the four block walk to the floor of the Stock Exchange.

Along the way, the journalists started handing out free papers to all the curious businessmen that started to gather around the unique parade.

Once the group reached the Stock Exchange, Charles and Edward were ushered inside where they rang the bell to open the trading session. The crowd of traders roared out in excitement. The cheers could be heard throughout the building and to the ends of Wall Street.

For people working on Wall Street, it was more than just a new newspaper. It was their newspaper and a representation of the growing influence of New York City as the soon to be financial capital of the world.

Epilogue

Thaddeus took a seat at a table in the new restaurant that had just opened up in Clarence's headquarters building. It was convenient to now have a nice little bistro located in the same building as the printing operation.

He waited impatiently for his guest to arrive. Sarah wrote to him letting him know that she felt ready to let Frank and the staff handle things on their own for a while, and she was coming to America on one of her famous sabbaticals.

It had now been more than a year since he left London, and he was excited to see her and share the stories about their mutual success.

After sitting for a few minutes, he saw her walk in the door. She looked as pretty as ever wearing her blue dress. He stood up as she approached not sure how best to properly greet her. Thankfully, she walked up and embraced him in a light hug.

They said brief hellos before a waitress walked up and handed them menus.

Sarah looked at the menu, which had a few unique items: a club sandwich, roasted chicken, sugar baked bean soup, and cassoulet. The last item caught her attention and she showed the menu to Thaddeus. "That is strange. What are the odds of finding a dish like that in New York City? I guess we should give it a try for old time's sake."

They ordered two bowls of the stew and started talking about work.

Sarah told Thaddeus about all the latest news in London and about the *East End Observer's* continued success. The paper had settled into a daily circulation of forty thousand copies keeping it firmly set as London's third largest paper.

She lamented the fact that Jack the Ripper still found a way to make it into the headlines at least once a week for one reason or another. But she was excited that Frank had added nearly a dozen reporters to the staff, three of which were women.

Thaddeus shared his experiences working with Dow Jones

and Company and his good friend Clarence. He told her about his work in setting up operations to print and distribute *The Wall Street Journal*, which had recently increased to fifteen thousand copies a day.

After their discussions about the papers, they started talking about their last week together. Thaddeus apologized again for the damage his ambition caused to both the paper and their relationship.

Sarah told him how much she missed him but was honest about how much she loved being the publisher of the paper. She had never realized how much it would mean to her until she had taken the reigns.

After the tab was paid, they decided to continue their talk during a stroll around Wall Street. Thaddeus was eager to show Sarah the city he now called home.

They walked out of the restaurant and looked up at the sign for the new establishment. It was the first time Thaddeus had seen it and he thought the name was unique for the upscale little bistro, THE BLUE RIBBON CAFÉ.

They started walking down the other end of the building when he noticed that a second new tenant had opened shop. He looked in the window to see a very nice looking stove pipe top hat sitting on a pedestal in the window of the *Wall Street Haberdashery*. The hat almost called to him it looked so sharp.

Sarah walked up beside him and looked in the widow. "You would look silly in such a tall hat. I prefer you in a bowler."

He smiled at her and offered her his arm. She took it and smiled back as they walked down Wall Street together.

Jason Mayer

Whitechapel Murders

The Whitechapel Murders were a series of murders committed in the impoverished Whitechapel District in the East End of London. The murders took place between April 3, 1888 and February 13, 1891, with the majority of the murders happening in the fall and winter of 1888. Most, if not all, the victims were believed to be prostitutes.

The Whitechapel District was considered to be a slum area that was a hotbed of criminal activity. Robbery, violence, illegal prostitution, and public drunkenness were especially common in the Spitalfields region of the district, which featured the notorious Flower and Dean Street.

In total, eleven victims were recorded by the authorities as part of the Whitechapel Murders. Authorities and historian differ on which, if any, of these women were murdered by the serial killer Jack the Ripper.

The consensus of many is that evidence heavily supports that five of the eleven victims were likely killed by the Ripper. These women are often referred to as the canonical victims of Jack the Ripper and include: Mary Ann Nichols, Annie Chapman, Elizabeth Stride, Catherine Eddowes, and Mary Jane Kelly. The first two victims, Emma Elizabeth Smith and Martha Tabram had unique deaths that did not fit the Ripper profile. Two other victims, Alice McKenzie and Francis Coles had their throats slit, but at much later dates and in different ways than the other five victims. Rose Mylett is believed to have possibly committed suicide or might have been strangled. Only a torso was found of one victim, so authorities had little evidence to go on regarding the identity of the victim or her murderer.

Emma Elizabeth Smith

Born: 1843
Died: April 4, 1888 (Age 45)

First Whitechapel Murder

Consensus: Not considered one of the canonical victims of Jack the Ripper. Most authorities believe Miss Smith was the victim of a criminal gang of young thugs. Little is known about her early life.

Martha Tabram

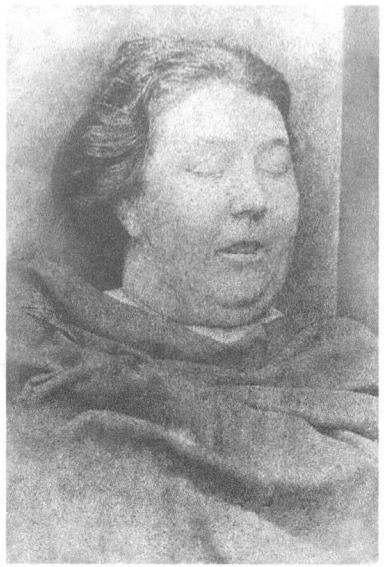

Born: May 10, 1849
Died: August 7, 1888 (Age 39)

Second Whitechapel Murder

Consensus: Not considered one of the canonical victims of Jack the Ripper. Due to the violent nature of Miss Tabram's murder, many believe she was killed by someone who knew her. She was born in Southwark, London. She married and had two sons. The marriage became troubled, due to her drinking, and her husband left her. She became a prostitute in the Whitechapel District sometime around the year 1876.

Mary Ann Nichols

Born: August 26, 1845
Died: August 31, 1888 (Age 43)

Third Whitechapel Murder
Consensus: Considered the first canonical victim of Jack the Ripper. She was born Mary Ann Walker in Soho, London. She later married a printer's machinist named William Nichols and had five children. The marriage ended when her husband ran away with a nurse. It is believed that she started working as a prostitute in 1881.

Annie Chapman

Born: September 25, 1840
Died: September 8, 1888 (Age 47)

Fourth Whitechapel Murder

Consensus: Considered the second canonical victim of Jack the Ripper. She was born Eliza Ann Smith in Paddington, on the East End of London. She later married her maternal relative John James Chapman, and had three children. The marriage ended by mutual consent in 1884. She started working as a prostitute in 1887 after her marital allowance stopped due to John Chapman's death of liver cirrhosis and edema.

Elizabeth Stride

Born: November 27, 1843
Died: September 30, 1888 (Age 44)

Fifth Whitechapel Murder

Consensus: Considered the fourth canonical victim of Jack the Ripper and the first part of the "Double Event." She was born Elisabeth Gustafsdotter in Stora Tumlehed, Sweden. She later married a ship's carpenter named John Thomas Stride. The couple had no children, and they had a rocky on-and-off marriage that ended in 1884 after John Stride died of tuberculosis. Soon after she started an on-and-off relationship with dock laborer named Michael Kidney, while she made a living working as a prostitute.

Catherine Eddowes

Born: April 14, 1842
Died: September 30, 1888 (Age 46)

Sixth Whitechapel Murder
Consensus: Considered the fourth canonical victim of Jack the Ripper and the second part of the "Double Event." She was born in Wolverhampton, England and was considered married by common-law to Thomas Conway with whom she had three children. She later became a heavy alcoholic and left her family in 1880 and started living with John Kelly whom she eventually became connected to by common-law marriage. While living with John Kelly she started working as a prostitute to earn an income.

Mary Jane Kelly

Born: Sometime in 1863
Died: November 9, 1888 (Age 25)

Seventh Whitechapel Murder

Consensus: Considered the fifth and final canonical victim of
Jack the Ripper. Little is known about her early life, but
according to her on-again, off-again boyfriend Joseph Barnett
she was born in Limerick, Ireland. She was rumored to have
come from a wealthy family, but had been disowned by her
parents. She was married for a short time at the age of sixteen
but her husband was killed a few years later in a coal mining
explosion. She then worked several jobs in Ireland and England
before settling in London East End as a prostitute in 1886 where
she rented a room for two years where she sometimes lived with
Joseph Barnett.

Catherine "Rose" Mylett

Born: December 8, 1859
Died: December 20, 1888 (Age 29)

Eight Whitechapel Murder
Consensus: Not considered one of the canonical victims of Jack the Ripper. Not much is known about her other than she was once married to an upholsterer with the last name of Davis. The two split up sometime in 1888, where she relocated to Baker's Row in Spitalfields. She was known by many as Drunken Lizzie Davis.

Alice McKenzie

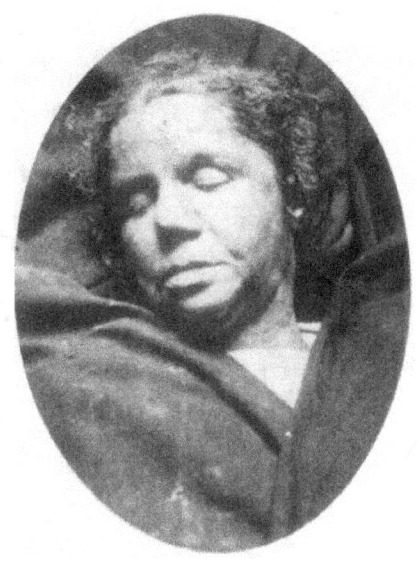

Born: Approximately 1849
Died: July 16, 1889 (Age Early 40s)

<u>Ninth Whitechapel Murder</u>
Consensus: Not considered one of the canonical victims of Jack the Ripper. Little is known about her early life. She moved to the East End of London around 1874. She later started living with an Irishman named John McCormack in 1883 and eventually became his common-law wife. She worked a variety of jobs, but the authorities considered her primary means of employment to be as a prostitute. She was also known to be a heavy smoker and drinker, and her frequent pipe smoking earned her the nickname "Clay Pipe" Alice. She was murdered by a slit throat, but the details of the murder were different than the five canonical victims.

Pinchin Street Torso

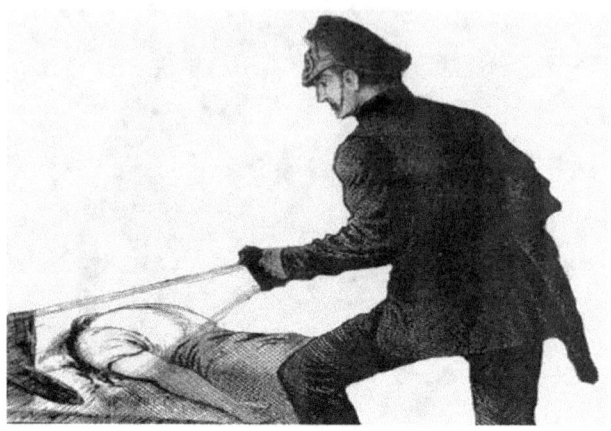

Found: September 10, 1889

<u>Eleventh Whitechapel Murder</u>
Consensus: Not considered one of the canonical victims of Jack
the Ripper. A female body with a missing head and legs was
found under a railway arch on Pinchin Street. The abdominal
region of the body had been heavily mutilated and the womb
was missing. It was estimated that the woman had been killed at
least twenty-four hours before the discovery. Some newspapers
and historians have theorized that the body belonged to Lydia
Hart, a prostitute from the region who had been reported
missing in the days leading up to the discovery. However, the
identity of the torso was never proven.

Francis Coles

Born: September 17, 1859
Died: February 13, 1891 (Age 25)

Tenth Whitechapel Murder

Consensus: Not considered one of the canonical victims of Jack the Ripper. She was born in the Bermondsey District of London. By 1880 she was living on her own, and worked a job stoppering bottles for a wholesale chemist shop. The work was painful for her, so she stopped after a couple of years and started working as a prostitute. She was killed by way of a cut throat, and the circumstances surrounding her murder were different than the canonical victims. She was violently thrown to the ground and her throat was sliced several times with crude uneven cuts.

Langham Hotel – Room 333

The Langham Hotel was built in 1865 and was London's first grand hotel. It is considered by many to be the most haunted hotels in the world.

Room 333 is the most haunted of all the rooms in the hotel, where many guests have reported seeing the ghost of a doctor, who murdered his wife then committed suicide while they were honeymooning at the hotel.

History does not provide a lot of details about the facts surrounding the doctor's murder and suicide, but it is believed to have happened between 1890-1900.

Mercury & Mad Hatter Disease

During the 1800s most English haberdashers would use mercury to stabilize animal pelts during the felting process to create high-fashion hats. They also used mercury dye on hats because it created a rich black color and worked well to hide blemishes and remove sweat stains.

Touching the element or even breathing in the toxic vapors caused a variety of ailments. Long-term exposure to the substance in any of its forms could cause people to drastically alter their personalities over time giving rise to the term "mad as a hatter."

Excessive exposure to mercury dye would often lead to erethism, also known as mad hatter disease, a neurological disorder that affected the central nervous system. Erethism would first present itself by a variety of behavioral changes such as irritability, depression, apathy, and shyness. With prolonged exposure more extreme symptoms could develop such as insomnia, loss of equilibrium, tremors, migraines, and diminished physical strength.

In extreme cases of erethism, victims could begin showing psychotic reactions such as delirium, hallucinations, and suicidal tendencies.

The use of mercury in textiles was finally phased out in 1941 when it was replaced by an alternative process using hydrogen peroxide.

Chef Octavius' Cassoulet (Non-Traditional)

Ingredients
3 Cans (15 oz each) Great Northern Beans, Drained
4 Slices of Bacon
4 Chicken Leg Quarters, Separated and Skin Removed
8 Ounces Boneless Pork Shoulder
12 Ounces Andouille Sausage, Cut into ½ Inch Pieces
2 Onions Chopped
2 Cloves of Garlic
1 ½ Cup Dry White Wine
1 ½ Cup Chicken Broth
1 Can (28 oz) Diced Tomatoes
1 Can (6 oz) Tomato Paste
1 Bay Leaf
1 Sprig of Thyme
¼ Teaspoon Ground Cloves
¼ Teaspoon Salt, Additional as Needed
¼ Teaspoon Black Pepper, Additional as Needed
1 Loaf Crusty French Bread

Cook bacon in pan until lightly crisp and set aside. Add pork shoulder to pan and cook for a minute on each side, then add chicken to the pan. Cook until chicken and pork are lightly browned. Set both aside. Add sausage to the pan and cook until brown, the set aside.

In a large pot, add 2 tablespoons of the drippings from pan, then add onions and cook until soft. Stir in garlic, tomato paste, and cloves. Cook for two minutes, then add wine, broth, diced tomatoes, thyme, and bay leaf. Bring to a simmer and continue stirring.

Add chicken and pork shoulder and bring to a boil. Reduce to medium-low heat, cover, and simmer for 30 minutes. Take off cover and discard thyme sprig and bay leaf. Stir in bacon, sausage, beans, salt, and Pepper.

Simmer for a minimum of 30 additional minutes or until the dish thickens into a hearty stew. Serve hot with crusty French bread.

Chef Octavius' Coq au Vin Soup

Ingredients
6 Slices Thick-Cut Bacon Cut into ½ Inch Pieces
2 Pounds Chicken Thighs, Bone-In and Skin-On
1 Pound Red-Skinned Potatoes, Cut in ½ Inch Cubes
8 Ounces Cremini Mushrooms, Sliced in Half
14 Ounces Pearl Onions (Fresh or Frozen)
3 Carrots, Peeled and Cut on the Diagonal into ½ Inch Pieces
2 Cloves of Garlic, Minced
1 Bottle Dry Red Wine (Burgundy works best)
1 Cup of Sherry
4 Cups Chicken Stock
3 Tablespoons Unsalted Butter
2 Tablespoons Chopped Fresh Parsley Leaves
½ Teaspoon Salt
¼ Teaspoon Pepper

Cook bacon in large pot over medium heat until crisp and set aside. Add chicken thighs to pan skin side down and cook until golden brown, about three minutes on each side, and set aside. This may need to be done in batches.

In same pot, cook potatoes, mushrooms, onions, carrots, and garlic over medium heat, stirring until mushrooms and onions are softened, about five minutes. Stir in broth, wine, salt, pepper, and bring to a boil.

Reduce heat, cover and simmer gently just until potatoes are tender, about 10 minutes. Stir in bacon and chicken. Cook, uncovered, until chicken is no longer pink inside, about five minutes. Stir in butter until melted. Stir in parsley and Sherry and serve hot with crusty French bread. A few dashes of Sherry can also be poured over filled bowls for added kick.

Modified Cullen Skink

Ingredients
2 Quarts Milk
8 Ounces Heavy Cream
1 Pound Smoked Haddock
2 Ounces of Butter
1 Onion, Finely Chopped
8 Ounces Mashed Potatoes (Can Be Leftovers)
3 Parsley Sprigs (Separate Stalks and Leaves)
1 Bay Leaf
Salt
Black Pepper

In a large pot, add milk, heavy cream, parsley stalks, bay leaf, and haddock. Finely chop the parsley leaves and keep to the side. Bring the milk mixture to a gentle boil, then reduce heat and simmer for three minutes. Remove the pan from the heat and let stand for five minutes.

Remove haddock from milk mixture and set aside. Remove parsley stalks and bay leaf from milk mixture (strain if necessary).

In a separate saucepan, melt butter and add chopped onions. Cook until translucent, about five minutes. Add cooked onions to milk mixture and stir, then add mashed potatoes and continue stirring until the soup has a thick, creamy consistency. More mashed potatoes can be added to increase thickness.

Flake the smoked haddock into chunks, removing any bones or skin you may find. Add haddock to the soup. Add the chopped parsley and bring to a simmer. Cook for an additional five minutes. Stir the soup gently as to not break down the fish too much. Add salt and pepper to taste. Garnish with more chopped parsley and serve with crusty French Bread.

Simple Manhattan

Ingredients
2 Ounces Rye Whiskey
1 Ounces Sweet Vermouth
2 Dashes of Angostura Bitters
1 Dash Orange Bitters
Garnish: Brandied (or Maraschino) Cherry and Orange Peel

Add whiskey, sweet vermouth and bitters to a mixing glass with ice.
Stir until well-chilled. Strain into a chilled class. Garnish with a cherry
and Orange Peel.

Gin and Tonic

Ingredients
2 Ounces London Dry Gin
5 Ounces Tonic Water
Garnish: Lime Wedge

Fill a highball glass with ice and pour in gin. Then pour tonic on top.
Gently stir to combine and garnish with a lime wedge.

The Langham (Sherry Cobbler)

Ingredients
3 Ounces Sherry
1/4 Ounce Simple Syrup
1 Halved Orange Wheel
1 Sprig of Fresh Mint
Garnish: Second Half of Orange Wheel

Add all ingredients to a cocktail shaker and fill with ice. Shake hard to
muddle the orange and mint and strain into a highball class filled with
ice. Garnish with orange wheel.

Tom Collins

Ingredients
2 Ounces London Dry Gin
1 Ounce Lemon Juice
1/2 Ounce Simple Syrup
Club Soda To Top
Garnish: Brandied (or Maraschino) Cherry and Lemon Wheel

Add gin, lemon juice, and simple syrup to a Collins glass. Fill with ice, top with club soda, and stir. Garnish with lemon wheel and cherry.

Mulled Wine with Brandy

Ingredients
1 Medium Orange (Peeled and Juiced; Keep the Peel)
8 Cloves
3 Sticks Cinnamon
2 Teaspoons Ginger
1/3 Cup Honey
1/2 Cup Brandy
1 Bottle Dry Red Wine

Add orange juice, orange peel, one cup of the wine, honey, cinnamon, and cloves to a large pot. Bring mixture to a rolling boil. Reduce heat to low, cover, and simmer for twenty minutes. Add remaining wine and brandy. Reduce heat to low and let the mixture steep for another twenty minutes. Serve at 170 degrees in coffee cups. Optional: garnish with piece of cinnamon stick.

About the Author

 Jason Mayer spent the first part of his adult life as a Marine Corps Combat Correspondent covering stories on five continents and more than 50 countries. After leaving the Marine Corps, he spent eight years working with government contractors supervising the development of more than 200 annual publishing projects.

Today, Jason is the partner in a construction company that designs, builds, and manages playgrounds and recreational construction projects.

Jason holds bachelor's degrees in Communications and Business Management as well as an MBA from the University of Maryland. He also has a PhD in Public Policy and Administration from the University of Maryland, Baltimore County. Jason lives in Columbia, Missouri with his wife, Angela, and two boys, Noah and Caleb.

Other Works by Jason Mayer include:

Parables of Lucas Fosterman
Parables of Sarah Blackstone
Fuzzy Dragons & Wild Yetis – Second Edition: A Kid-Friendly Introduction to the Wonderful World of Poetry
Reported for Duty: Poems and Stories from the War Zone, Home Front, and Beyond